It's girls nig

"So I guess having a man is as u...
as her gaze tracked the passing c...

"*Pero* you can always use th...
joined in, a strong flush of color ...
cuss sex. Ever.

Tori laughed. "I'm not sure I can call Gil my little Latin sexbot."

"Puleez, Tor. Admit that Gil makes the earth quake," Sylvia said.

Tori put her hand up. "Too much information being requested."

Sylvia shook her head. "After your big adventure, I thought you were done repressing your sexuality."

"*Vamos*, Syvita. It's almost genetic, the repression," Adriana replied in her defense.

"There's nothing wrong with being free about sex," Sylvia shot back as she took a pen and paper out of her purse, wrote down her number, and had the waiter deliver it to the handsome man she had noticed earlier, who sat at a table set for one.

"How about with being free *with* sex?" Adriana teased.

Juli hesitated for a moment before blurting out, "*Chicas*, if we worry about sex all the time, we won't ever be *liberadas, verdad?*"

"A zesty, sexy read about real single women today—dealing with love, family, careers—struggling to balance all the things that matter to them and yet be true to themselves. I couldn't put it down. *Sex and the South Beach Chicas* is fun, sassy, sexy, and honest."

—Jennifer Greene, *USA Today* bestselling author of *Blame It on Chocolate*

"Caridad Piñeiro presents us with several delicious slices of life bonded together in strong female friendships. I found myself in one of the chicas. Read it, love it. You'll find yourself there, too."

—Shirley Hailstock, bestselling author of *The Secret*

Sex and the South Beach Chicas

Caridad Piñeiro

doWn tOwn press

New York London Toronto Sydney

An *Original* Publication of POCKET BOOKS

 DOWNTOWN PRESS, published by Pocket Books
1230 Avenue of the Americas
New York, NY 10020

Library of Congress Cataloging-in-Publication Data

Scordato, Caridad, 1958–
    Sex and the South Beach chicas / Caridad Piñeiro.
        p. cm.
    ISBN-13: 978-1-4165-1488-6
    ISBN-10:   1-4165-1488-0
    1. Hispanic American women—Fiction. 2. Female friendship—Fiction.
3. Miami (Fla.)—Fiction. I. Title.
PR9240.9S36S49 2006
813'.6—DC22   2006046055

This Downtown Press trade paperback edition September 2006

10 9 8 7 6 5 4 3 2 1

DOWNTOWN PRESS and colophon are trademarks of
Simon & Schuster, Inc.

Manufactured in the United States of America

For information regarding special discounts for bulk purchases,
please contact Simon & Schuster Special Sales at 1-800-456-6798
or business@simonandschuster.com.

Acknowledgments

To my fellow Encantadoras—Berta, Sylvia, Liliana, Anna, Lynda, Tracy, Leticia, and all the rest—thank you for always being there when the dream seemed so far out of reach. Last but not least, to my agent Caren Johnson, for believing in that dream, and to my editor, Selena James, for helping that dream come true!

To my mother, Carmen Piñeiro, who taught me
to follow my dreams.

To my daughter, Samantha, a fellow dreamer who
I know will never stop reaching for the stars.

Sex and the South Beach Chicas

1

Las Amigas

Tori got lucky.

She was sure that was what her friends had wanted to happen six months earlier on the night of her thirtieth birthday, only they hadn't really expected that it would.

Boring and predictable Victoria Rodriguez had thrown caution aside and indulged in a night of incredible—she wanted to say sex, only it had been more than that—with Gil. He totally lived up to her and her *amigas'* requirements for the title of Extreme Boy Toy, or as he had playfully become known, Mr. Perfect *Papi Chulo*. His moves on the dance floor were nothing like Ricky Martin's, but his moves in bed . . . Not to mention eyes as blue as the waters in Biscayne Bay and a lean sculpted body. But what really did her in was Gil's scrumptious little boy grin that just made her want to eat him up when he used it and exposed the cutest damn dimple she'd ever seen.

So now, six months later, she was not only living in

sin with Gil—albeit lusciously rewarding sin—she was considering spending the rest of her life with him.

And Gil, her Perfect *Papi Chulo*, appeared to feel the same way.

This usually meant a ring and an engagement and a shower and a rehearsal, complete with dinner, followed by a wedding with lots and lots of friends and family, only . . .

The Tori that had emerged after that big birthday night didn't want to deal with all those conventions and the problems they usually wrought. She also had concerns about her family's reaction to the news, since nothing she did ever seemed to please them. More than anything, she wanted to get her *amigas'* impressions on what to do.

But she worried that her *amigas,* having just handled the defection of one of their high school friends to the bonds of holy matrimony, might not be ready for her revelation that she and Gil were thinking about making the big leap into marriage.

Lost in thought, Tori slowed her pace as she walked from Gil's oceanfront condo on Collins, where she now lived, toward her friends' restaurant on Ocean Drive. Since the condo lay just beyond the end of Lummus Park, the first block was relatively free of the tourists and party animals that crowded the central portion of the Art Deco district.

A strong ocean breeze blew across Lummus Park. A block away, he colorful pennants atop the Cardozo snapped with the breeze. A bit farther up, the oversized umbrellas protecting the alfresco dining area of another restaurant fluttered ominously. The breeze made it a little chilly for Tori. She slipped on her suit jacket as she passed by the mansion where Gianni Versace had once lived and died infamously. Before the black gates with the fanciful golden Versace emblems, fans and curiosity seekers posed for photos.

She stayed her course along the opposite sidewalk, where there was less activity. Normally she would have turned up Thirteenth Street to meet her friends at the Washington Avenue gym where they worked out on Monday nights. But tonight Adriana and Juliana had a meeting at their restaurant, which forced them to pass on the workout, but not their usual Monday night dinner afterward.

A dinner they were having at her friends' restaurant because of their prior engagement. Not that she minded. A goddess of the kitchen, Juli could make day-old bread tasty. Her skills, combined with Adriana's business savvy, had earned the nearly three-year-old restaurant its share of both local and national awards.

As she strolled to their building, one of the Mediterranean Revival structures along Ocean Drive, the breeze shifted direction and blew at her back as if to hurry her along, but she took her time, enjoying the view of South Beach's sizzle. Bronzed gods in muscle shirts and tourists in black socks and sandals. On the road beside her, car after car cruised along, from the latest luxury models to lovingly restored vehicles from the fifties and sixties. Their polished paints and gleaming chrome reflected the dazzling colors of the neon signs identifying the businesses along the street.

She ambled past the Clevelander Bar, Edison Hotel, and Larios to the heart of the Ocean Drive strip and her friends' restaurant. As she crossed the street, she noticed they had lowered the vinyl windshields to protect the patrons on the outdoor dining veranda from the breeze.

When she neared the hostess's podium, the young woman smiled in recognition and invited her to a table close to the windows along the veranda. "Juli and Adriana are almost done," she advised.

Tori could see her friends at the back of the restaurant, seated at a table with a bunch of business suit types. Suits much like hers, she thought as she glanced down at her conservative Brooks Brothers ensemble. She'd had time to drop off her car, but not to change before coming over to the restaurant. A complicated case had gotten even more complicated at the last minute, so the later time on this Monday night had proved helpful.

She had just taken a seat when the group at the back of the room broke up. The suits headed out of the restaurant while Juli and Adriana came her way.

Adriana wore an absolutely gorgeous dark green suit that perfectly accented her curvaceous but slender physique. Her precisely trimmed auburn hair framed the clean oval of her face, emphasizing her hazel green eyes. As always, Adriana's public face flawlessly represented the class and elegance of the restaurant and hotel.

Adriana was the brains of the business, while Juli's amazing culinary creations were the heart of it. A heart that rarely ventured into public, and when it did, like tonight, often seemed drab and tasteless. Totally unlike the food Juli prepared.

They embraced and were about to sit when Sylvia arrived.

Sylvia made heads turn, in an eye-catching golden gown that delineated her every asset. Long blonde hair swung in a curtain to the middle of her back, its silky texture reflecting a hue of gold and paler blonde highlights. She appeared ready for a bigger adventure than tonight's dinner—probably because she needed to cover a story at one of South Beach's hot spots for the monthly magazine for which she worked as the After Dark and Gossip reporter.

Tori couldn't help but glance at her own five-four, size six body, trying not to feel intimidated by her less than ample—but still perky—breasts and curves, which were . . .

She stopped herself right there. Gil seemed to have no problems with her body. On the contrary, he couldn't keep his hands off her.

"Tori. Mother ship to Tori," Adriana said and waved a hand in front of her face, ripping her from thoughts of Gil.

Tori shook her head. *"Perdoname.* Just thinking about—"

"Not work. Not with that googly-eyed look you just had on your face," Sylvia teased as she air-kissed all three of them and then slinked into the chair between Tori and Adriana.

Tori nodded but said nothing else, still a little anxious about giving her *amigas* the news that things between her and Gil were getting serious.

A waiter came by, sparing her from thinking about it further. He handed them menus and asked if they cared for drinks. As always, they ordered a round of ice cold mojitos and, after, deferred to Adriana and Juli's choices about what to order.

When the mojitos arrived, Tori held up the glass. "To life, love, and always being *amigas,"* she said, much as she had said at every Monday night gathering for as long as she could remember.

As they toasted, a raucous crowd from the street distracted them.

In front of the restaurant, a large group of people clustered around a hot hip-hop artist who had recently opened a store on Washington for his new fashion line. If she hadn't recognized him, the billboard bling would have tipped her off. His name glittered in silver and diamonds on a large chain around his neck.

"Another typical crazy night," Adriana teased and shook her head.

"I'm surprised he hit this part of the Beach so early. I expect him at the party I'm covering later tonight," Sylvia replied just as the waiter came by with appetizers.

"Speaking of expecting, didn't Josie look nice yesterday?" Adriana said.

Josefina Maria de las Nieves Gonzalez—now Mrs. Josie Johnson—was the most recent of their high school friends to be wed.

"Expecting?" Tori blurted out as Adriana's comment finally registered. "As in—"

"She had to marry the guy," Sylvia confirmed. "Josie's been living with him *for what?*"

"Three years. You'd think she'd be beyond the guilt factor by now," Juliana mused out loud, seemingly embarrassed by the discussion.

Adriana spooned up some garlicky shrimp and continued the conversation. "It must have been a massive dose of guilt for her to give in. Josie was always the most stubborn of us."

"And one of the most independent," Sylvia acknowledged as she finally helped herself to some of the appetizers.

Tori perused her friends as she took a sip from her mojito. She had never been one for bucking the status quo—her relationship with Gil was the biggest risk of her entire life. Before the night she had become Sinfully Sexy Tori with Gil, she had been Toe the Line Tori, always ready to do what everyone asked of her. But not anymore. Well, at least not as often.

Since she wanted to share her news, she decided to take another risk. "Maybe she wanted to. Maybe it was time."

Both Sylvia and Adriana dropped their forks, which

clattered against their plates. Aghast silence followed as all of her friends looked at her. They all knew that once a friend got married, things changed, and usually not for the better. But Tori couldn't imagine not being friends with these women. They were as close as sisters.

"You know, the odds are that eventually we're all going to end up married," she said, but glanced at her drink and played with the condensation on its surface to avoid her friends' inquisitive gazes.

"Are you trying to tell us something?" Tori heard a hint of anxiety in Adriana's voice.

She avoided the question for the moment. "What do you think Josie's parents said when she told them she was pregnant?"

Sylvia immediately launched into an Oscar-worthy interpretation of her Anglo mother, complete with a slow Southern drawl. "Dear Lawd. What were you thinking, honey pie? It'll be Kmart Blue Light specials for you for the rest of your life." Then she picked her fork back up and attacked her food with gusto.

Adriana wagged her finger at Sylvia. "Girl, you can't even begin to imagine the guilt levels possible in a Cuban household. *Mi abuelita* Ofelia would grab her rosary beads, clutch them to her chest, and make sure she thumped loud enough to wake most of Calle Ocho," she said, and then spooned food onto Juli's plate, since up until now, her friend hadn't taken a thing.

Even quiet Juliana had something to add. "And don't forget that since our *mamis* somehow became clones of their *mamis,* they'd be sure to join in, wailing and complaining." She clapped her hands together as if in prayer and rolled her eyes upward. *"Dios mio. Que desgracia! Mi'jita, que estabas pensando?"*

It struck a little too close to home, since Tori had barely survived such a scene during a family dinner, where she had been unable to give her family the news that she and Gil were getting serious. Her family had been too busy picking apart her life, and Toe the Line Tori—who hated confrontation—had decided not to create an even bigger problem.

As the waiter brought out the main courses, Tori gently eased into the discussion once more. "Marriage isn't necessarily bad, you know."

"Right. It's more about making wiser choices and avoiding men like our *papis,*" Adriana confirmed, although Tori detected even more apprehension in her friend's voice.

Sylvia dismissively waved her hand. "Darlin' Adriana. Not that I'm all that keen on dads, but your poor *papi* is not so bad. He's just been henpecked by your mama into trying to run your life."

Adriana couldn't deny it, so she playfully went along. "*Mami* needs some hobbies to take her mind off *Papi* and me. It's worse now that she's retired from helping *Papi* run the family business. Any suggestions, *chicas?*"

Sylvia threw her hands up with frustration, nearly knocking over one of the plates the waiter had been trying to serve. "If we knew, don't you think we'd get our mothers off our backs?"

Tori nodded and as she looked around, realized all were in agreement with Sylvia's observation. "We haven't made much progress in dealing with our *mamis,* have we, *amigas?*"

Shrugging, Juliana pointed to the meals she and Adriana had chosen, encouraging them all to begin eating. "*Por favor. Disfruten* before it gets cold. As for our *mamis,* old habits are hard to change, *sabes.* But your *mami* hasn't been so *loca* lately, has she, Tori?"

She thought about it as she ate the deliciously creamy

and flavorful tamales. By most standards, her *mami* wasn't so bad. Just exceptionally demanding. It hadn't occurred to her just how demanding until her first year of college, when she had brought home a 3.96 GPA and her mother had muttered, "Well, if this is the best you can do . . ."

"She hasn't been awful, but she also hasn't let up about Saint Angelica and how I have no life," she confessed, raising just some of the complaints her *mami* had noted during dinner the other day.

"So li'l sis is still golden for popping the first puppy?" Sylvia inquired, but Tori could see her friend's mind was only partially on the conversation as her gaze tracked the passing of a rather handsome man toward a table at the side of the restaurant.

"Which makes zero sense," Tori snapped. "All my life my family has pushed for me to make them proud, and here I am—successful and happy—and what do they say?"

"Be like your *telenovela*-watching, stay-at-home, making-babies *hermanita*," Adriana responded, but shot an apologetic look at Juli and added, "No offense meant on the *telenovela* part, Juli."

With a weak shrug that barely moved her oversized tunic top, Juli said, "*Bueno*. No offense taken."

"You'd think bringing home a prospective Mr. Right would silence the *mami* inquisition," Adriana wondered aloud and forked up a bit of roast pork from her plate.

Sylvia, often the cynic, said, "So I guess having a man is as useless as I thought."

"*Pero* you can always use them for sex toys, *verdad*?" Juliana joined in, a strong flush of color on her cheeks because she didn't discuss sex. Ever.

"Check you out, Juli! You're finally chillin'." Sylvia playfully nudged Tori in the ribs with her elbow.

"I'm not sure I can call Gil my little Latin sexbot," Tori playfully responded.

"Puleez, Tor. Admit that Gil makes the earth quake," Sylvia said, not about to let up. Sylvia never let up, Tori realized, and wondered if it was a leftover from her friend's job or if it was because she needed the attention. Everything about Sylvia screamed, "Look at me!"

Even though Sylvia's teasing had managed to bring a flush to her face, Tori would not spill about Gil. At least not right at that minute. She put her hand up and, with a small wave, tried to shut down her friend. "Too much information being requested."

Sylvia shook her head. "After your big adventure, I thought you were done repressing your sexuality."

"*Vamos,* Sylvita. It's almost genetic, the repression," Adriana replied in Tori's defense.

"There's nothing wrong with being free about sex," Sylvia shot back as she took a pen and piece of paper out of her purse and wrote something down. She handed the paper to the waiter and had him deliver it to the handsome man she had noticed earlier, who sat alone at a table set for one.

"How about being free *with* sex?" Adriana teased as she noted Sylvia's actions.

Juliana hesitated for a moment, rubbing her hands almost nervously along the edge of the table before she said, "*Chicas,* if we worry about sex all the time, we won't ever be *liberadas, verdad*?"

That eased the tension that had crept into the conversation and brought chuckles from everyone.

"That's right," Tori admitted. She slipped an arm around Juliana's shoulders and playfully shook her. "We don't want any restraints in our lives."

"But some restraints can be fun," Sylvia advised and

mimicked being bound, prompting raucous laughter before the conversation turned serious once again.

"We all agreed we were going to avoid controlling husbands," Adriana reminded.

"And unreasonable demands from our *mamis,*" Juliana shyly piped in.

All three women turned to look at Tori, waiting. "And we all agreed to have fun doing whatever we're doing. So what if I'm having fun with Gil? What if Gil is . . ." She hesitated, studied all her friends' faces as she finished. "Mr. Right."

No shock. Or surprise. Or anger. Or any of the emotions she had worried she might see. There was, however, concern.

Sylvia finally spoke, shaking her head sadly as she did so. "I just hope it won't turn into the Happily-Ever-After syndrome."

"It won't. I would never desert you," Tori answered vehemently, hands raised in defense as she brushed off the suggestion.

Adriana laid her fork down as if her appetite had suddenly disappeared. "I guess we just never expected that your one night of fun would lead to something permanent."

"I thought that's what you wanted that night. For me to get lucky."

"So, you're really serious about Gil?" Juliana asked hesitantly and laid a hand on Adriana's shoulder, almost as if she thought her friend needed comforting. Adriana possibly did. Of all of them, Tori and Adriana were the closest and this admission might worry her more.

"As in getting married serious?" Juli added for emphasis.

Instead of answering, Tori said, "I'm not sure how the family will handle it. Or how I will handle their reaction to Gil and me," she admitted, needing her friends' support more than anything.

Adriana nodded and perked up, seeming to throw off her earlier concern when she realized Tori was requesting her counsel. "You can't worry about them."

"They'll probably want babies right away and—"

"It's your life. Girl, don't let anyone force you to do something you don't want," Sylvia jumped in, emphasizing her point with a fork laden with a piece of fried ripe plantain.

Their reaction brought Tori a bit of calm, which gave her the strength to say, "I'm thinking of marrying Gil."

Time seemed to spin in slow motion after her pronouncement. One by one, each friend reacted to the news.

A hesitant smile unfolded on Juliana's face. Sylvia had a ghost of a frown on hers. Adriana was the hardest to read until she said uneasily, "That's . . . wonderful, Tori. We couldn't be happier. Right, *chicas?*"

Juliana and Sylvia stumbled over each other in their eagerness to reply.

"Girl, of *course. Sí, como no.*"

Despite their words, worry colored her friends' voices. "I can see that you all think that if I marry Gil, I'll escape to the suburbs of Kendall, bear a brood of kids, and forget that I was ever your friend."

Reluctantly, Juliana admitted, "It's happened to almost everyone."

Adriana shrugged. "Except for Sarita. But who knew she would fall for a Ms. Right?"

Sylvia raised her hand. "I did. She made a play for me after a volleyball game one night."

Tori grew astonished at that one. Sarita had been one of her best friends and she had never suspected. Sarita had come out of the closet and run away to Los Angeles after high school. "Why you?"

"She liked blondes," Sylvia responded. She resumed eating and encouraged the others to do so as well.

For a moment it seemed as if things might just get back to normal. Especially when Adriana said, "Well, marriage isn't a bad thing if it's with the right man."

Juliana nodded with some bravado. "*Cierto*. It just takes a lot of *ranas* before you get a prince like Tori did."

Adriana forced a smile and motioned to Tori. "You're nothing like Margarita and Esperanza. They married major mistakes, not like Gil at all. Now they're back with *Mami*, along with their kids, and hearing on a daily basis how they screwed up."

"*Pobrecitas*. Living with *Mami* the first time was hard enough," Juliana commiserated.

Relief slowly blossomed within Tori. She had sensed they liked Gil, based on their reactions whenever she had brought him around. It seemed they could handle the relationship becoming more. "I really like Gil. *Really like*, as in I love Gil."

"Ah, so he does make the earth quake," Sylvia teased, and something made Tori want to shock Sylvia. She leaned close to Sylvia as if to share a secret, but spoke loud enough for all of them to hear. "We've really put that blindfold from my birthday night to good use. Just thinking about it makes my toes curl."

Laughter erupted and Sylvia nudged her playfully. "Girl, should I be shocked that you're really a vixen under that boring and uptight exterior? It's kind of nice that you're thinking this might be more than just living with him. Just living with guys . . . Call me old-fashioned, but that kind of arrangement only benefits them. When they're done with you, *hasta la vista*, baby."

Sylvia's comment added to Tori's relief, as she was usually the most difficult of the group when it came to men. With reason, considering her dysfunctional family life. But when her friends settled back to finish their meals, Tori still kept the knowledge to herself about her upcoming engagement.

First she had to survive breaking the news to her family.

And maybe her friends would handle her upcoming marriage just fine. Maybe they would even be able to trust that the Happily-Ever-After syndrome would not happen to her. After all, they had been best friends forever.

She was not about to let anything interfere with that.

2

Sylvia

Her job.

    Her mother's latest man friend.

    Her own lack of a man friend.

Her job.

Tori.

Her job again. Shit.

Sylvia hated that her job had become a repeated thing to worry about in her life. Being a journalist had been her dream since the third grade, when she wrote an article for the school newspaper. Landing a spot at the brand-new monthly magazine that everyone who was anyone was talking about had been quite a coup. After all, for the last three years she'd had an all access pass to every major event in Miami.

From movie premieres to the openings of the latest hot spots on Ocean Drive to every celebrity party thrown in the city, Sylvia Amenabar was there. If ever there was an It Girl with Miami's hip crowd, she was it.

And she hated it. For the most part there were the

same old people, worried about either who they would screw or how to score some blow or whether they had made a fashion statement that would look good in the photos when the magazine came out.

Shallow is as shallow does. Sylvia worried she was somehow becoming as superficial and callous as the people she covered on a daily basis.

How had she drifted so far from her original journalism roots? she wondered while driving to her mother's condo for her customary monthly visit. *And why, after this past Monday night's gathering, did Tori suddenly rank so high on the list of things to worry about?*

Her friend Tori—responsible, practical, dependable Tori—had somehow succumbed to the power of the penis like her mother and so many other sensible women. Tori, who everyone knew was level-headed and capable, had decided living with Gil was a good idea.

Definitely a bad idea, Sylvia thought. At least now Tori was thinking about something more respectable, but maybe it was still not good.

Sylvia wheeled her BMW 325i convertible off Brickell Avenue and up to the guard gate for the Atlantis, her mama's condo complex. The guard waved her through and Sylvia parked beneath a long row of palm trees in a spot that faced Biscayne Bay.

She didn't get out right away. She needed time to fortify herself for the visit.

Not that her mama was all that bad. Just eccentric. Kind of like the unique building in which her mother lived.

The Atlantis was probably one of Miami's more well-known structures, thanks to the opening scenes of *Miami Vice.* Today, blinding sun and bright skies reflected off the building's south-facing wall. At the center of the building was a large square courtyard with a very visible palm tree and red corkscrew stairs. The area served as a pool and sky court for the residents of the condo.

Sylvia used to live at the Atlantis with her mama. That was years before she had snagged the job of her dreams.

The job that now arguably sucked.

Like her mother's latest man friend.

And her own lack of a man friend.

And Tori. Not to mention the horse's ass she called her boss.

Last night over dinner, Sylvia had sensed that Tori had been on the verge of bubbling over with all kinds of things. Only she hadn't. Her friend had held back on telling all of them what was really on her mind.

Yet another new development with her friend, who had always been as easy to read as *People* magazine. Ever since Gil had come into the picture on the night of Tori's surprise birthday cruise, Tori had changed.

Guiltily, Sylvia acknowledged that she'd had a major part in bringing about that change. It had been mostly she and Adriana who had planned Tori's birthday celebration. Mostly she and Adriana who had been pushing for Tori to find someone that night and just get lucky.

And Tori had done just that.

It was supposed to have been a let's-enjoy-ourselves-for-the-night kind of luck. Not let's-live-together-and-fuck kind of luck. As for the love-and-honor kind of luck . . . the true-love-and-honor kind of thing rarely happened. Women who somehow deluded themselves into believing in such impossible dreams invariably found themselves miserable and lonely.

Like her mama.

Sylvia prayed Tori's choice would be wiser. From what she had seen of Gil over the past six months, he seemed to be a good choice. Only one could never tell with men.

Men were dogs, after all.

Perspiration rolled down Sylvia's brow as she sat there in the humid midday heat of a Miami September. She swiped at a trickle of sweat and realized that worrying about Tori accomplished a big fat nothing. On the next Monday they got together, maybe she would find out what was actually going on in Tori's life.

Sylvia finally stepped out of her BMW, grabbed her bag, and headed to meet her mother.

She easily spotted her mama as she walked through the lobby of the building and out toward the pool nestled by the waters of the bay. At the far end of the courtyard, a trio of older men surrounded a chaise lounge. Sylvia had no doubt who regally reclined on that lounge.

She didn't think her mama intentionally attracted men. Virginia, named after the state of her birth, was just one of those women who had built-in magnetism, a pull those of the opposite sex found hard to refuse. Blonde and voluptuous, Virginia was an older Marilyn clone, which accounted for the men she generally now attracted—the late-fifty-plus crowd. In actuality, they were a bit far removed from her mother's forty-six years of age. She was fairly young to be the mother of an almost thirtysomething, but then Virginia had birthed Sylvia when she had been barely seventeen. And in those close to thirty years, Virginia had been a good, if somewhat unusual, kind of mother.

As Sylvia neared, her mother peeked at her from behind Chanel sunglasses before waving to her. The men turned to observe what had captured Virginia's attention and popped up out of their chairs as they beheld her. Amusement settled within Sylvia as the would-be lotharios excused themselves and rushed to other chairs around the perimeter of the pool.

"Boy, talk about clearing out the house," Sylvia said as

she bent and kissed her mother on her perfectly made up and moisturized cheek.

Virginia eased her sunglasses down with a perfectly manicured finger and peered up at her daughter. "My friends sense a little . . . *chill* would be an understatement, darlin'. It's more like frostbite when you're around."

Not that she cared what her mother's male friends thought. Sylvia shook her head and mumbled under her breath, "Men." Easing off her beach wrap, she exposed a dark blue crochet string bikini and draped the wrap over the top of the chaise lounge next to her mother, who had already laid out a towel for her.

After she was settled, her mother said, "Men. Can't live with them—"

"Can't live with them," Sylvia finished and Virginia laughed huskily.

"Sweetie, you just haven't met the right man," her mother said and patted Sylvia's thigh.

Slipping down her own Escada sunglasses, Sylvia exhaled sharply. "And you have, Mama?"

The flush that came to Virginia's cheeks wasn't from the sun. Her mother put enough SPF45 on her to guarantee that no rays would dare etch a line into her still flawless face or bring but the most faint stain of color to her creamy white skin. Nope, that flush came from chagrin, Sylvia thought. And possibly guilt.

"Your father—"

"You mean the man who impregnated you, don't you? It takes more than sperm to be a father." Sylvia instantly regretted her harsh comment when pain flashed across her mother's face. She was surprised, therefore, when her mother calmly replied, "Yes, it does, baby. But it's not a one-way street. He's been here and you haven't gone to see him. He's here now. At a tournament in Palm Beach."

"Ah, yes. With his horses, I guess." Not a guess on

her part, however. During yesterday's meeting to choose the articles for next month's issue, her editor had suggested a joint assignment with the sports reporter to cover the polo matches in Palm Beach. Uneasily, Sylvia had hedged about how the horsey crowd wasn't really her thing, and another reporter had literally jumped at the chance to cover the big event.

"You should go see him," her mother pressed, but Sylvia shook her head.

"This is an old story, Mama. All he did was send checks for support and birthdays. Not even a card."

Virginia grabbed a glass from the small table between both lounges—an umbrella drink sans the alcohol. Virginia blamed excess libations for the poor judgment she had shown in going off with Pablo Amenabar, the handsome Argentine polo player who had fathered Sylvia. Now, she was strictly a virgin drink kind of woman. After taking a sip, she said, "Some men wouldn't even have done that. They would have left poor white trailer trash like me with a belly and empty promises."

An age-old debate and one Sylvia didn't want to get into . . . again. "Let's just agree to disagree."

Virginia nodded and took another sip of the icy fruit drink. "Someday you'll have to deal with it."

"I *have* dealt with it, Mama," she said brusquely.

"Hmm. I suppose that's why you come here, Sunday after Sunday, and glumly tell me about all the parties and events you've been to, and not once mention a man." Virginia slammed her drink down on the table and swiveled on the chaise lounge to face her daughter.

Sylvia was taken aback by the vehemence of her mother's response, but didn't have a chance to reply. Virginia leaned forward and spoke in tones low enough that only Sylvia could hear. "I've spent nearly thirty years alone, but so have you. And while I'm in no rush to have a passel of little rug rats calling me Grandma, I would like to think that you're not going to spend the next thirty years alone as well."

Gripping her hands tightly in her lap, Sylvia glanced down at them in major avoidance mode. A moment later, her mother placed a bejeweled hand over hers. The rings and bracelet had been gifts from some of the men her mother "kept company with," as she liked to call it.

Sylvia needed no similar company. And certainly no men like the Latino Bad Boy who had sired her and then split. Finally facing her mother, she said, "I'm not alone, Mama. I have my job and my friends."

Virginia sat back and rolled her eyes. "Ah, yes. I forgot. Your little psycho pep squad." Her mother hesitated and suddenly jerked upright in her chair. "You're not gay, are you? I mean, because it would be all right—"

"I'm not gay, Mama."

"Are you sure, baby? I mean, how do you—"

Sylvia's withering gaze silenced her mother. "Mama, I have had sex. I like men—physically. That's it. That's all." She slashed her hand in the air to drive the point home.

Virginia shrugged, leaned back in her chair, and grabbed her drink. She sipped it, but remained silent, which drove Sylvia crazier than if her mother had said something. When she glanced at her mother, she noticed a self-satisfied little smirk.

"Okay, what's up?"

Virginia took a long draw on the straw and then paused dramatically, inching her sunglasses down again to meet Sylvia's gaze. "One of these days, one of those men will start an itch that just sex can't scratch. When that happens, don't run from it, Sylvia Lourdes."

Sweet Jesus, Mama had used her whole name, a name reserved for serious discussions and trouble. "Sylvia, Mama. The name's just Sylvia."

Sylvia leaned back in her chair, choosing to ignore her mother's comment. There wasn't a man she had met who could make her itch that badly. If she ever met one who did, she'd run as fast as her four-inch-heeled Jimmy Choos would let her. After all, poison ivy made you itch like crazy, but it wasn't a good thing.

3

Tori

Sunday inquisitions with the families.

Despite being single, independent, and success-ful, that monthly ritual somehow persisted. Tori wondered what she'd have to tell her friends after this particular visit. She hoped that for the most part it would be good news.

Or at least that's what she told herself as she and Gil headed for her parents' house.

The early afternoon sun still had some bite in it and the air hung heavily thanks to the humidity. That didn't stop Gil from putting down the top on her Sebring for the short ride from South Beach to Little Havana.

Tori shot a quick glance at Gil as he drove her car up and over the MacArthur Causeway. Most people would probably be enjoying the sights of Star Island with its multimillion-dollar homes, or the other neighboring islands, possibly hoping to catch a glimpse of one of the many celebrities who lived there.

But Tori would rather stare at Gil's silhouette against

the backdrop of Government Cut and the assorted cruise ships waiting to pull out to sea. It was somehow appropriate since she and Gil had met on that fateful overnight cruise months earlier. In those months her life had substantially changed. If she and Gil could somehow survive today's dinner with her family, her life was sure to change even more in the months to come.

A scary thought. Almost as scary as facing her family, who were aware of the announcement they intended to make. Gil, *Dios lo bendiga,* had invited her father to a midweek lunch at Versailles to ask his permission and assure her father that he had nothing but good intentions toward his daughter. Notwithstanding the living in sin, that was.

She told herself she just had to stay firm no matter what happened. Since the day of her big three-oh, she'd become Take Charge Tori and would not regress to Toe the Line Tori if her family made a fuss.

Armed with that conviction, she whispered her mantra. "Take Charge Tori. Good-bye to toeing the line. Take Charge Tor—"

"Worried?" Gil asked, as if picking up on her vibes across the small space in the car.

She shrugged. "Why do you ask?"

"You were mumbling something under your breath, *amorcito.*"

He didn't say more as he turned his attention to exiting onto Le Jeune and making a few quick turns off Calle Ocho to bring them to a modest sized one-story home on one of Little Havana's side streets.

Many years earlier, Adriana's family had lived a few houses down and had also owned a small *bodega* on the corner of Calle Ocho. That was before Adriana's father and a local beat cop had risked all they had to go into the import/export business together. Once the business had taken off, Adriana and her family had moved miles away to Coral Gables and a more upscale home near the famed Venetian Pool.

Gil parked the car in the driveway, took off his sunglasses, and faced her. The wind during the ride had ruffled the sun-streaked strands of his caramel-colored hair. She smoothed some errant locks back into place, unable to keep from touching him.

But then she dropped her hands into her lap, nervously clasped and unclasped them, mentally repeating her mantra.

Take Charge Tori. Take Charge! Damn it.

She shot an anxious glance at the house and noticed the curtains at one picture window part slightly before dropping back into place.

"They know we're here," she said, but Gil made no motion to leave the car and neither did she.

"You're scared? Big tough lawyer can face the world's worst judge or opponent—"

"But can't face her family?" She sighed, chagrined by his comment.

"It's what I love about you." He cupped her chin and applied gentle pressure so that she would look at him.

"You love my lack of—"

"The yin and yang of you. The way one part of you is strong and dependable, but the other part is uncertain and kind of wild."

His blue eyes glittered with an icy fire that left no doubt about how much he liked her wild side. She did as well. It had been Sinfully Sexy Tori that had risked a night with him. That gamble had paid off better than she ever could have expected.

His comment dragged a chuckle from her, but the uncertain part of her rebounded speedily. "They make me *loca* about everything. But especially their crazy-ass need-to-be-better-than-the-Joneses hang-up. I've done what they've asked, but they still make me feel like . . ."

"A failure?"

A long silence filled the air, and once again she caught a glimpse of the curtain shifting at the window. "They're going to wonder what we're doing out here."

"So let's give them something to talk about." He leaned over to kiss her, moving his lips against hers slowly at first, but then increasing his demand.

Tori lost herself in the moment of it, let herself be sexy and in command. She took charge and opened her mouth, deepening the kiss until they were straining toward each other and she wished she could slip into his lap. Regretfully, she came up for air and whispered against his lips, "Do you think they'd notice if we just turned around and went back home?"

Gil chuckled and whispered in her ear, "*Amorcito.* I think there's now at least two faces peering out of that window, which means we have no choice but to go in."

She groaned, but knew he was right. After putting the car top up to safeguard against one of Miami's unpredictable changes in weather, Gil circled the car, took her hand, and escorted her to the door.

As Tori neared the entrance, she reminded herself she was Take Charge Tori and would not cave to whatever her family carried on about.

Her mother waited for them at the door with a bit of a scowl on her face. "*Niña!* What will the neighbors say?" she hissed while shaking a head of hair dyed a too deep brown and held immobile by hair spray.

"It's nice to see you too, *Mami,*" Tori replied sweetly, then hugged her mother and stepped inside. For a second, as her mother embraced her, comfort suffused her. She wished it could be like that always. It vanished as quickly as a soap bubble in the wind when her mother pulled away and said, "You're late."

She wouldn't apologize. "Gil and I were busy this morning."

The look her mother shot her told her just what she thought she and Gil had been busy doing. Since it was the truth, she didn't attempt to deny it.

But she did pick her chin up a notch, daring her mother to call her on it. Her mother backed down, however, and led them into the living room. *Score one for me*, Tori thought.

Her home hadn't changed in forever, except for the new forty-two-inch LCD television she had gotten her parents for Christmas last year. In fact, it felt much like Christmas since the dining room table sported her *mami*'s best white linen tablecloth as well as the holiday china. The smell of roast pork, redolent of garlic and citrus, permeated the air. Beneath that aroma was the earthier scent of slowly simmering black beans.

Touched that her mother had gone to such trouble, Tori experienced a second of guilt for her earlier defiance.

"It smells wonderful, *Mami. Gracias* for making my favorite," she said, which only earned an annoyed kind of huff.

"*Sí*, thank you, Nieves," Gil added as her mother motioned for her and Gil to seat themselves on the flowered chintz sofa in front of the television.

A Sunday in September meant that her *papi* would soon have a baseball game on, even with company present. Even despite the fact that on this Sunday, she and Gil were going to make the most important announcement of their lives.

Gil had barely seated himself when Tori's *abuelita* shuffled out of her room at the back of the house. She was nearing ninety, and Tori felt blessed to still have her and wasted no time going to greet her grandmother.

Gil did the same, stooping from his six-foot height to hug her petite and fragile frame. Tori's *abuelita* embraced him, then straightened the light pink sweater she wore over her shoulders, even with the heat. The gaiety of the pink clashed with the somber black of the simple dress she wore in mourning for a husband dead nearly twenty years now.

Abuelita shuffled to a *sillon* at one side of the room, pulled out her rosary beads, and while smiling at the two of them, fingered the long string of black beads and prayed. Tori always wondered for what.

A moment later, her father entered and welcomed them. "It's good to see you again, Antonio," Gil said and shook her father's hand, but as Tori anticipated, her father plopped himself in a well-worn recliner that groaned under his bulk. He spoke to Gil about the standings and surfed the channels until he located a game.

Excusing herself, Tori tracked down her mother in the kitchen. Her mother seemed ready to serve the meal, which surprised her. "So early? Aren't we going to wait for Angelica?" Saint Angelica. Her perfect sister who had the perfect little baby and husband, but as always was terribly late to arrive.

"Angelica can't make it today."

Tori shook her head in disbelief. "Angie can't make it? Today? You spoke to *Papi* so I can't believe you didn't tell Angie—"

"I did tell her, but she said she couldn't make it today."

So much for sisterly support and affection. But then again, Angie and she had taken different paths as adults and it seemed unlikely those roads would intersect anytime soon. The closeness of their youth had vanished long ago.

Tori said nothing else as she helped her mother finish up in the kitchen. Gil came in a bit later and helped take everything out. As they were sitting down, a knock came at the door.

Tori knew without opening it who it would be—her *tia* Carmencita, who lived up the block. Her *mami* clearly felt in need of reinforcements and had called in the cavalry to come for dinner.

Tori smiled at her *tia* and sat at the table, enjoying the marvelous food her mother had prepared and the conversation that flowed between her father and Gil, and her mother and aunt. Occasionally she interjected her opinion, but for the most part, she built the courage to deal with the announcement that she and Gil wanted to make that day.

After her *mami* served a delicious flan and the espresso had been poured, Tori shot a hesitant glance at Gil, who nodded in understanding.

Time for Take Charge Tori to break the big news.

"*Mami. Papi. Tia* and *Abuelita.* Gil and I wanted to let you know that we're getting married."

"*Mi'jita que bueno,*" her grandmother said, and leaned over and embraced her.

"It's about time," her *mami* replied, which prompted her father to issue a curt rebuke and a stony stare at his wife.

"But it's true, *marido.* They've been living in sin now—"

"*Dios mio, hija,*" her grandmother complained. She whipped out her rosary beads and murmured a short prayer beneath her breath.

With but a quick glance at Gil, Tori began the carefully worded wedding statement she'd practiced time and time again in her head. "*Mami,* Gil and I really would like . . ."

She stopped, suddenly sure that it was boring and dependable Tori—Toe the Line Tori—adopting that needy tone. Take Charge Tori knew what to do—divert her mother's mind from the expected response so that she could follow her own game plan.

"*Mami.* Gil and I totally enjoyed that lingerie I purchased with the gift certificate you and Angelica gave me for my thirtieth birthday. Gil particularly liked—"

"*Basta,*" her mother said with a sharp snap of her hand, seeming unfazed by her comments. "Have you and Gil thought this through, *niña?* It's only been a few months and—"

"We're very sure that we love one another, Nieves. I'm sure Antonio told you about my intentions toward your daughter."

Beneath the table, Tori grabbed hold of Gil's hand, thankful for his intercession.

Her mother picked up her chin a notch and examined Gil carefully down the length of her patrician nose. With a sigh bordering on annoyed, she said, "*Bueno,* I can see you *think* you are serious. So, I guess we should discuss planning the wedding. That will take some time."

"*Sí,* at least a year," Tia Carmencita offered, but Tori couldn't imagine a wedding like that of her cousin. The bridal party alone had been nearly two dozen people, who had paraded around in a rainbow of colors garish enough for the circus.

Fortifying herself with a deep breath, she jumped into the conversation. "Gil and I want a small wedding. No more than fifty and—"

"*Mi'ja,* that'll barely cover the neighbors . . ."

"*Mami, por favor.* Let me finish. We plan on getting married in six months."

From beside her came the now nervous and rapid click-clack of her grandmother's rosary beads, accompanied by the louder murmur of an even more urgent prayer. Across the table, her father sat silently, until *Mami* leaned over and whispered in his ear.

At that, a flush raced across his cheeks. Clearing his throat, he said, *"Mi'ja.* Is there some reason why we must rush this event? Are you—"

"I'm not pregnant, *Papi.* I wouldn't be that irresponsible. I thought you would know that about me, but you obviously don't know much about me," she shot back, undeterred.

Gil squeezed her hand, offering his support. When she met his gaze, he smiled with sympathy.

It would have been funny if it was someone else's life or a *novela* on television. But it was neither. Her family bemoaned the plans she and Gil had proposed for their upcoming wedding, their voices escalating until she thought her head would burst from the noise. And this wasn't even the start of the ordeal. Gil and she still had to pick out the engagement ring, and Tori had vowed to tell her friends before anyone beyond immediate family knew of her engagement.

It would only get worse once the rest of the family and the neighbors became aware.

Gil leaned near to her and whispered, "They're not happy, are they?"

Tori laughed harshly and glanced at her erstwhile husband-to-be. *"Mi amor.* Nothing that I do will ever make them happy."

"But I know what will make you happy," he whispered.

She flicked him a glance from beneath lowered lids and let Sinfully Sexy Tori emerge. *"De verdad?* And that would be?" she said suggestively.

Gil gazed around the table and grinned, displaying that delicious dimple in one cheek. He shifted his chair

closer and no one noticed. They were all too busy argu-
ing about who had to be invited, as if they hadn't even
heard that Gil and she wanted to keep the wedding small.

He placed his hand on her thigh beneath the table.
Her pulse accelerated a notch from just that. "Gil—"

He ignored her warning, brought his face near to
hers. The warmth of his breath spilled against the side of
her face as he whispered in her ear, "I want to be home.
In bed. Inside you."

Heat and desire rocketed through her. "Gil, *por favor.
Mi familia—*"

"Is going to make us crazy, Tori. Tell them again. *Por
favor.* Then let's go home," he urged and moved away.

She glanced around the table, where the conversation
continued spiritedly, and coughed to get their attention.
Nothing happened. She coughed a little louder, which
finally drew her mother's attention.

"*Mi'jita,* are you getting sick?"

"*Sí, mami.* I'm sick of all this talk when Gil and I
have made ourselves clear."

Her *mami* immediately protested. "But *mi'jita—*"

"No buts, *Mami.* The wedding will be in six months—"

"But people will think—"

Tori cut her mother off with a slash of her hand. "I
don't care what people will think."

Stunned silence followed that pronouncement. Flushed
with success, Tori inched her chin up rebelliously, and
slowly and carefully made their announcement once more.
"*We* will be married within the next six months. *We* will
make a list of who we would like to invite, but will keep
your wishes in mind."

She raised her index finger into the air to emphasize
her last point. "*We*—as in me and Gil—will decide what
to do." When she finished, she motioned to Gil with her
free hand, for Gil still gripped her other hand tightly.

The silence continued, uninterrupted except for the rattle of Tia Carmencita's espresso cup as she set it down and the clack-clack of her *abuelita*'s rosary beads. Her father finally broke the hush by addressing Gil.

"*Hijo.* You are going to allow Tori to speak to us like this? To tell us, her *familia,* that we have no say in this marriage?" With each word his voice escalated in volume.

Gil looked her way and beneath her breath, Tori began a little prayer of her own, hoping that he wouldn't say the wrong thing or, worse, give in to her family's demands. That would only set a dangerous precedent for the future.

Straightening his shoulders, Gil glanced at her father, and then at her mother. He inclined his head respectfully and said, "Nieves. Antonio. I don't tell Tori what to do, just as Tori doesn't tell me what to do. This is a partnership. Together, Tori and I have made a decision about what *we* want. I know that what *you* want most is to see her happy."

"*Sí, como no.*"

"Of course that's what we want."

Her parents tripped over each other with their replies, belying their haste to set things right. Her *abuelita* and *tia* mumbled similar agreements beneath their breaths. *Score one for Gil,* Tori thought, battling the smile that wanted to emerge.

"Then I assure you that I will make her happy and that whatever plans Tori and I make together will make her happy," Gil finished.

Silence reigned again and Tori breathed a sigh of relief. This was but the first skirmish, and she didn't want to linger for the start of another argument. "*Vamanos,* Gil." She rose and tugged on Gil's hand. "I have to be in court early tomorrow and I have some papers to finish tonight."

Gil looked at her oddly for a moment, then quickly jumped up from his chair. "*Sí. Perdoname.* I forgot you had that . . . case in the morning."

"*Ay, mi'jita.* You're always working so hard. I hope that when you and Gil are married, you'll find more time—"

"*Mami,* I really have to go," she reminded and rushed around the table, planting perfunctory kisses on the cheeks of each family member and hurrying Gil out to the car.

As they drove home, Tori envisioned the nightmare that would follow if her family continued to meddle with the plans she and Gil had for their wedding. She thought about her discussion with her friends earlier in the week, and their admonishment that she should not let anyone force her into doing what she didn't want to do.

She didn't want the whole big traditional wedding thing. The only thing she did want was to have Gil as her husband, as quickly and as painlessly as possible.

"We should elope. Avoid all this craziness and just do it," she said.

"Just get married? And your family—"

"Will deal with it. Just like they've dealt with us living together."

Gil gave a strangled chuckle. "*Mi amor,* they didn't speak to either of us for a couple of weeks."

"And that was bad because?" She arched one eyebrow to emphasize her point.

As if realizing she was truly serious, Gil pulled off the road just before the start of the causeway and into a parking lot for a copter service. He killed the engine, turned in his seat, and looked at her, concern etched into his features. "You really mean that, don't you?"

Tori looked down at her hands, nervously clasped and unclasped her fingers. Softly she said, "My whole life

I've done what everyone's expected of me. Measured up to whatever stick they used."

She raised her head and turned to face him. "I'm tired of doing what everyone else wants. I'm tired of conform-ing, of being the boring and predictable Tori everyone expects."

Sadness and a hint of hurt flickered across Gil's face. "Doesn't seem like a very good reason for rushing into a long-lasting relationship."

Tori cradled his cheek. "Then how's this—you make me laugh and smile and even cry sometimes. But the one thing I want more than anything is to have you in my life forever. Starting as quickly as possible, so I can have my wicked way with you." She paused for a breath and finally said, "Guillermo Gonzalez. I'm asking you to just do it—just marry me."

A broad grin spread across his face. "Well, when you put it that way . . ."

4

Juliana

"Comprendo, Mami. Sí, entiendo," Juli assured her mother, although she didn't completely understand and probably never would.

She stared at the phone for a moment, tempted to beat it into the cradle and vent her anger much as Sylvia would have. But she wasn't Sylvia—*gracias a Dios*—and so she gently replaced the receiver in its cradle. She took a calming breath and went to the kitchen and fired up the stove, intent on making the French toast for the Sunday breakfast with her *mami* that would not be.

Disappointment and anger warred within, but she wouldn't say a thing to her *mami* about the cancelation. Her mother had taught her well the advantage of avoiding confrontation.

Be like a quiet little mouse, *Mami* had admonished Juli time and time again while her *mami* worked in the fine kitchens of Miami's elite. Her *mami* had followed that adage and more than once, while tucked away in the corner of the kitchen, Juli had seen a more bothersome servant get the boot.

Being in that kitchen had also taught Juli something else—she loved food. The texture of it between her fingers. On her tongue. The smell of it—comforting or enticing. Sensual. The power of food when prepared properly.

She'd known for some time that she wanted to be a chef, but since she wasn't into confrontation, she'd gone to college and earned her degree. After, with the strength of Adriana's brains and money, she had finally reached for her *sueño*.

The years since then had confirmed that stirring a fine sauce was infinitely more rewarding than stirring up trouble.

But maybe she had been that quiet little mouse for too long, she considered. She was nothing like her glamorous *amigas*, and sometimes wondered what they saw in her. Why they stayed her friend.

Did they see the real her? The one who inside had so much passion?

She grabbed a bowl, a whisk, and the challah she'd made the day before. As she sliced the challah, she thought about her *mami*'s defection and wished her *mami* would get some backbone and stop kowtowing to her former employers.

And maybe you could develop a similar backbone and show your mami *that you don't just work in the kitchen, you own it!* the little voice inside her head chastised.

Juli beat the cream and eggs in a bowl, added a little Amaretto, and soaked the homemade challah in the mixture. After, she cooked herself a few slices in rich clarified butter.

When the French toast was perfectly browned, she removed it from the pan and doled her version of bananas

Foster over the slices. For the heck of it, she treated herself by flambéing it. No sense wasting the effort behind the meal just because her *mami* had deserted her . . . again.

After the flaming finished, she topped off the plate with a healthy dollop of freshly whipped cream, grabbed a fork, and went back to her living room, intent on finishing the *telenovelas* she had taped during the week. Her schedule didn't permit real-time viewing, but come the weekend, she fit in all the melodrama and excitement she had missed.

In the current *telenovela,* two characters reminded her of Tori and Gil and how they had looked on the night they first met. The heated glances. The elegant way Gil carried himself, and Tori, in an incredible gown unlike any her friend had ever worn before . . . Taking another bite of the French toast, Juli wished to be that glamorous. That sexy, only . . . On the outside, she was as drab as a kitchen mouse, but unfortunately not as sleek.

Glancing at the suddenly empty plate, she decided she would have to exercise extra hard tomorrow when she did the workout with her friends. And dinner afterward . . . it would be *solamente ensalada* for her. Just salad.

But for now, she licked the last little smidgen of cream off the fork and stopped the tape since she had reached the end of one *telenovela* and had to head to the restaurant.

Sundays were a late start, but still a workday. Adriana had probably completed her errands and checked the schedule for the upcoming week since she had to head to her parents this week with Riley for her Sunday meal.

Riley.

Another little sigh escaped her as she thought about Adriana's longtime friend. Again, not coveting, but what a shame that her friend could not see the very sexy surfer dude who had been sitting right in front of her face for nearly the last twenty years.

If Juli had a man like that in front of her, she would know what to do. First, she would make him a meal he couldn't resist. Once he was replete and satisfied, she'd offer him the perfect dessert—her—and satisfy him in other ways.

A rush of heat blasted through her at the thought of what could happen if she had a *papi chulo* in her life. But life was just too busy and demanding.

Juli cleaned up the remains of breakfast and went out to her Jeep Cherokee for the ride to work. Turning up the CD player, she hummed to Gloria's latest and sped along the nearly empty streets until she reached the municipal lot just a few blocks from the restaurant. Using one of the electronic passes assigned to their hotel, she parked the Jeep and quickly walked across Collins and up to Ocean.

The sanitation crews were out early, removing the refuse and debris from a night of South Beach partying. She hated the mess and the smells left behind by the crowds. Plastic cups, the remnants of food, and the aftermath of too much alcohol littered the gutter and sidewalks. A street sweeper inched by her, brushes swooshing against the concrete and misting water onto the ground as it cleaned. She stepped closer to the building to avoid the spray and hurried along, eager to make sure everything was in order.

Much as Juli suspected, when she unlocked the front door Adriana busily flitted from the kitchen to her office. When she noticed her, Adriana shot her a smile and waved.

"Didn't expect you so early," her partner replied as she walked over and hugged her.

"*Mami* canceled—"

"Again? Why this time?" Adriana asked as she strolled beside her to the kitchen. Juli went to the espresso machine to prep a fresh batch of coffee, knowing that there was no end to Adriana's caffeine addiction.

"Same as last time. When the Hendersons call for Consuelo, *Dios mio,* she can't say no." She worked as she spoke, filling the machine with fresh-ground coffee, tamping it down, and inserting it into the unit for brewing.

Adriana arched one perfectly waxed brow. "Hmm. But she can say no to you?"

She shrugged. "*No soy importante, amiga.*"

"I beg to differ, *chica.* You are very *importante* to all of us," Adriana said and accepted the first cup of coffee that came out of the machine.

"*Gracias* for saying so, but—"

"You let what your *mami* thinks bother you too much."

"She thinks I'm *nada.* A servant in the *cocina.*"

Adriana leaned on the table for the espresso machine. "You *let* her think that, but worse, it's almost as if you believe her."

"*No lo creo.* I know who I am. What I am." Juli shook her head for emphasis.

Adriana hugged her again, playfully rocking her as she did so. "You are a genius, but one who lets what her mother thinks bother her too much."

Juli chuckled while she waited for her own cup to fill. "You do *tambien, chica. No lo puedes negar.*"

"No, I can't deny it, so let's just ignore them for now. Do you need help with anything?" Adriana asked.

Juli heard a little excitement in Adriana's voice and she suspected just what had put that tone there—besides the coffee. "No, *gracias.* I can handle things on my own. In a rush? Hot date?"

"*Chica*, it's just Riley," Adriana replied. With a flick of her hand, she walked back to her office to finish her Sunday morning chores, and what was probably her fourth or fifth cup of coffee.

Dios mio. Pobrecito Riley. Luckily he hadn't been there to hear Adriana dismissing him so matter-of-factly.

Sipping her coffee, Juli walked to the prep table and paused, taking time to admire the empty kitchen that in less than two hours would become a beehive of activity. Her sous chefs and their assistants would be prepping the regular selections on the Sunday brunch menu while she experimented with something new for the daily special. Hoping to use the wonderful divers scallops she'd picked up late yesterday, she went to the fridge to see if they'd held up well overnight.

The large wall-to-wall refrigerators at one end of the kitchen were stocked with the essentials—*her* essentials. *Her* selections. Inside, the scallops looked as fresh as they had the day before. As she examined the remaining ingredients, she was satisfied that her kitchen would be ready for later.

Her kitchen, Juli thought with pride as she walked past the gleaming stainless steel tables and shelves and ran her hands over the pots and pans hanging above the work areas. The stoves and ovens were state of the art and had been put in new when she and Adriana had purchased the restaurant and building from the former owners nearly three years ago.

Turning to the pantry area, she grabbed the clipboard by the door so she could take a quick inventory of anything they might need for the remainder of the week. After, she slipped on a clean apron from one of the shelves and envisioned the daily special—those gorgeous scallops resting on a bed of saffron risotto and drenched with a delicately seasoned beurre blanc sauce. Add a garnish of finely julienned and fried vegetables—carrots, zuc-chini, and onions—and *voila!*

A perfect meal for the day, she thought, imagining herself serving it up to Señor Right. Watching him appreciate the textures and flavors. Seeing him smack his lips as he beheld her, much as the handsome *telenovela* hero had done that morning while the nubile and desirable servant girl had offered up the meal and, eventually, herself.

Servant girl! Juli thought with disgust.

The fantasy painfully reminded her that her *mami* still viewed her as little more than a highly paid domestic in the kitchen. Suddenly the joy was gone from that sensuous daydream.

As she assembled the ingredients for the daily special, Juli vowed that one day her mother's perception would change.

Sin duda. She'd show her *mami,* and anyone else who had any doubts, that she was the Chief Chef. Master of the Mixer. Ruler of the Roaster. Keeper of the . . .

She stopped, realizing how silly she was being.

She had *nada* to prove to anyone. *Nada.*

With that, she returned to the prep table to create her perfect meal.

5

Adriana

She scooped her beeping PDA off the night-stand while slipping into her sweats.

7:00 a.m.: Text message from ChefJuli—No dessert delivery. Again. What do you want to do?

Fingers flying on the keys, Adriana text messaged back: "Call Tom. Can he help us out? Be there in 20 minutes."

She quickly perused the remaining items on her calendar while she finished getting dressed.

7:30 a.m.: Discuss daily specials with Juli
8:30 a.m.: Hotel briefing with Gloria

The PDA was programmed to enter the last two events daily, although why she had done that she could only begin to guess. She could no more forget to check on the restaurant and the newly opened hotel above it than she could forget to breathe. They were her life.

She might kid her best friend, Tori, about being anal and always in control, but Adriana suspected she was much worse. Shaking her head in self-chastisement, she continued.

8:00 a.m.: Get books ready for afternoon meeting with accountant

She had prepared everything days ago since she hated to leave anything until the last minute. This was a chance for her to conduct a last-minute check to make sure things were in order. Which they were—again, because she wouldn't tolerate things not being the way she wanted them to be. Order and control were what made life run smoothly.

10:00 a.m.: Volleyball with Riley
3:00 p.m.: Meet travel agent about hotel bookings
4:30 p.m.: Drop off papers at accountant

Volleyball with Riley, she thought with a sigh. Every Thursday and Sunday. Religiously entered into the PDA and again, Adriana had to bite back a laugh. Forgetting Riley—a definite impossibility. She only wished she could forget, then maybe . . .

What? She could find someone else? Someone who wouldn't be as overprotective? Not that Riley intentionally tried to do so. She ascribed it to Riley's inability to stop being a hero, even years after he had stopped being a cop.

But since it had taken her a long time to break free of her mother and father's overzealous protectiveness, she wasn't ready to let a man—even a gorgeous and incredibly amazing one like Riley—put her in bondage again.

Well, maybe some kind of bondage would be fun.

A psychologist would probably have a field day with her relationship with Riley. Or rather, her lack of a relationship with Riley. She was somehow certain that anything more involved than the current friendship status would prove problematic in many ways and mentally listed them just to remind herself.

1. Their fathers were business partners.
2. Their mothers were longtime friends who had probably hoped for years that Riley and she would unite the two families on a personal level.
3. Getting personal would make life with Riley virtually impossible.

The last was drawn from Sylvia's somewhat extreme theory about how the power of the penis led to foolish choices. While penises had their place in life—and elsewhere—Adriana had no doubt that if she and Riley ever just did it . . .

Only she and Riley wouldn't just do it, for all the reasons that had just occurred to her.

Plus, in all the years they had known each other, Riley had never made any romantic overtures to her, nor let on that he wanted to change the nature of their very long and abiding friendship. That was fine with her.

Riley was almost like her big brother and yet ignoring him physically when he was near always proved difficult. It was even harder to deny that she liked his sense of humor and honor. In some ways, the day that Riley had walked into her father's *bodega* at the age of nine was as memorable as the days she had met Tori, Juliana, and Sylvia.

Her attraction to him made Riley not so safe to her carefully ordered world. Above all, order had to be the rule in her world.

As she drove thoughts of Riley away and selected an olive green double-breasted Versace suit from her closet for later that day, the PDA beeped again, signaling an incoming message.

7:15 a.m.: Text message from ChefJuli—Tom came through. Desserts will be here by 11.

One crisis averted, she thought with satisfaction, and finished gathering her clothes and gym bag. She'd be late if she didn't get moving. That wasn't good. She had too many things to do today.

Looking a bit like a Tasmanian devil on speed, she flew out the door of her South Pointe condo, the suit in its dry cleaning bag hanging from one finger and her gym bag with some casual clothes draped over her shoulder. She wore a tankini bathing suit beneath a loose-fitting Miami Heat jersey and Fila sweatpants in anticipation of her beach volleyball date with Riley. Once they were done with the game, she would shower and get dressed for the rest of the day.

She hurried down Ocean Drive, passing older apartments and small cinder block homes that had escaped the development boom along the beachfront, until she hit Fifth Street and the start of Lummus Park.

When she jogged with Tori early in the morning, they would take the wide and winding path close to the small ocean wall that separated the park from the beach. Now, however, she crossed the street and hurried along the strip of hotels and businesses, which were still quiet at such an early hour.

The only people out were those cleaning or readying the tourist areas in anticipation of another sunny and profitable day in South Beach. As she passed by the Park

Central Hotel, her PDA buzzed to announce another message.

Expecting to see one from Juli, she stopped in surprise. Pleasant surprise.

7:25 a.m.: Text message from Riley.Evans—Lunch after the game?

Lunch? Riley wanted to do lunch? It wasn't like they had never done lunch before, only . . .

She cautiously gazed at the PDA, wondering what was up. She could count the times Riley had wanted to do lunch. All usually revolved around something of importance. Breakups with his latest girlfriends—because somehow he thought Adriana could give him a clue about what to do to appease the soon-to-be ex-*novia*. The latest toy of interest—from Windsurfers to his brand-new candy apple red Viper. And most important—and probably the hardest discussion she had ever had with anyone in her life—Riley's decision to leave the police force after being shot during an undercover sting that had gone wrong.

To this day, she found it hard to accept that Riley placed so much importance on what she thought. They were, after all, just friends. Granted, the best of friends. Almost as good friends as Tori, Sylvia, and Juliana.

She had heard it said that it was impossible for men and women to be just friends. So far she and Riley had managed to prove that adage wrong.

An annoying little voice in her head suddenly chimed in, *And if you believe that, I've got a piece of swamp land to sell you.*

She marked his email for follow-up and started walking again, the heat of the Miami sun working up a light sweat as she hurried along.

* * *

"So you were able to get the desserts from Tom?" Adriana asked.

"He had a last-minute cancelation." Juli labored at the prep table, chopping vegetables. Her movements were precise and almost balletic as she worked with the knife.

"Tell me again why we don't use Tom for the desserts?"

"You said he was too expensive, and besides, he's got a full load. He couldn't fit us in even if we wanted to pay the price." Juli paused and glanced uneasily in her direction. "We should do our own, *sabes.*"

They had talked about it in the past. Juli had been itching to do the restaurant's desserts for some time. When they had first started up the place, Juli had been overworked and it had been impossible. They had opted for buying their desserts to give Juli more freedom to create the main dishes. Things had changed in the last year or so, but Juli still carried a fairly full load. "I'm not sure you have the time—," Adriana started.

"But it might be cheaper. Certainly more reliable, since it would give us control," Juli said as she resumed her chopping, seeming to avoid hearing what Adriana had just said.

Adriana was about to answer when Juli's sous chef came over to stand by them, obviously needing instruction.

"Let's talk about it when things are a little quieter," Adriana said, aware that the dessert snafu had eaten into her partner's precious morning prep time.

With an almost anguished sigh, Juli nodded and turned her attention to the sous chef's questions. Adriana headed to the large industrial espresso machine and coffee mills located on a side counter. A pitcher of steamed milk already waited there. The aroma of freshly milled coffee lingered in the area. Juliana had probably had a cup before heading out to the markets that morning.

While Adriana banged used coffee grounds off the filter mechanism of the espresso machine, she glanced over her shoulder at her partner. Juli had finished with the sous chef.

"Were you happy with what you got today?" she called out.

"Produce was exceptional, as were some amazing prawns," Juli answered while Adriana made a fresh batch of coffee. Soon the aromatic brew dripped into the mugs she had slipped beneath the spouts. She prepared the coffees and with one mug in each hand, walked to join her partner and review the daily specials.

Her stomach rumbled as she and Juli discussed the meals. Mentally calculating what to charge for each item, she suggested some pricing to her partner.

Juli shrugged and replied, "You're the numbers whiz. It sounds fine."

A momentary twinge of annoyance raced through her at Juli's indifference. Sometimes she wished . . . But then again, these were the roles they had agreed upon. Juli was the creative end of the business, and she was the brains. Being the brains of the operation meant she had a mess of things to do before she could head out for her game with Riley.

No, she had forgotten to answer Riley's email.

With their discussion completed, Adriana excused herself to take care of her morning demands.

At eight, her PDA beeped to remind her that she had not responded to Riley, but the phone rang and the caller ID showed her mother's number. Adriana hadn't had enough coffee yet to deal with her mother, although for a moment she wondered why her mother was calling so early in the morning.

Sipping on her coffee while stuffing the papers for the accountant into her briefcase, Adriana glanced at her PDA to see if she had forgotten something relating to her mother. She scrolled up and down for the remainder of the week.

An assortment of meetings filled her days. Ones with the bank loan officers about the additional funds for the hotel renovations. Lunch dates to woo a variety of travel agents to steer clients to the new hotel. A preinterview with an executive from a well-known food network that wanted to include them in a show featuring restaurants in Miami. Finally, a dinner meeting with an advertising agency for a small ad campaign for the restaurant and hotel.

But nothing, absolutely nothing, having a thing to do with her mother.

Which made her wonder what bug her mother had up her butt? Her *mamacita* must have had a major issue with something to be phoning so early in the day. Repeatedly, she realized as her cell phone now beeped to say she had three missed calls and a voice mail message.

Feeling a bit guilty that it might actually be important, she checked her voice mail, only to hear a rather ambiguous message from her mother.

"*Mi'ja.* It's not an emergency, but I have to speak with you as soon as possible."

She'd call later, Adriana thought. *Mucho mucho mucho* later. Like in tomorrow later.

She dealt with a few other essential items, including a linen delivery problem. By the time she finished speaking with the driver and his boss about a missing order of tablecloths, and had given careful instructions to the lunchtime hostess about the insertion of the daily specials into the dinner menus, nearly half an hour had passed.

Back at her desk, she sat down with a fresh cup of

coffee. The message light blinked on her office phone. She scrolled through the caller ID log. Three out of the four calls had been from her mother. *No.*

The other one had been from Riley.

She glanced at her watch. She had to leave to meet him at their game in just over an hour and had yet to get back to him about lunch. She reached for her PDA, but the office phone rang—it was Riley from his cell phone.

"Riley," she answered, slightly breathless, and heard his amused chuckle.

"So busy that you forgot I existed?" he teased, and in her mind she pictured the grin that had likely accompanied his statement. A spurt of unwelcome warmth flared up at the image. She tamped it down. Just friends, her and Riley. Just friends.

"*Amorcito,* how could I forget you?" she joked in response and cradled the phone to her ear while shuffling papers. She quickly glanced at the PDA on her desk and noticed she was late for her daily briefing with Gloria in the hotel.

She ignored that entry for the moment, giving Riley her full attention. "What's up?"

She reached for her cup of coffee and sipped it as she awaited Riley's answer.

"Too busy for lunch today?"

"Of course not," she quickly answered. "So what's the momentous occasion?"

A long pause followed before Riley said, "I'm thinking of asking Becca to marry me."

Adriana's coffee mug slipped from nerveless fingers and landed on the PDA, which sputtered for a moment before going dead.

It seemed apropos somehow.

She mumbled a reply to Riley and agreed to lunch

before hanging up the phone. She glanced at the soaked and totally defunct PDA.

Not about to let that stop her—at least not until she bought a new one—Adriana picked up a pad and pen and began a new list.

1. Meet Riley for volleyball.
2. Have lunch with Riley.
3. Ask Riley if he's crazy.
4. Tell Riley . . .

She paused, unable to complete the last entry. Thinking better of it, she crossed it off, tearing through the paper with the pen as she did so. Frustrated, she ripped the sheet off the pad, crumpled it into a tight ball, and stuffed it into the garbage.

Again, somehow totally apropos.

6

Tori

Tori and Adriana had been playing a wicked game of telephone tag since Thursday afternoon. Tori wondered what had been so important to her friend that she would call . . . repeatedly.

But she had been too busy with something important. Although guilt had threatened to rise up every time she had missed her friend's calls this new Tori had resolved that no one and no thing would make her guilty about following her own heart.

Liar, the voice inside her head challenged. A voice that sounded surprisingly like her mother's voice. Not that her mother or any of the rest of her family had had much to say yesterday. Even her sister, Angelica, hadn't really said anything. She had just sat there with a Mona Lisa–like smile on her face as all hell had broken loose, and Tori and Gil had decided to make their exit. It was their second time fleeing dinner to avoid her family.

She wondered how she would fare tonight with her friends. Tori searched the street before the veranda of the Cardozo, where she anxiously waited for them at a table.

She repeated her mantra. *Take Charge Tori.* Even with her *amigas,* she realized for the first time. She had never felt she had to be strong with them before, but now . . .

She had canceled their workout and asked her *amigas* to meet for dinner. The Cardozo was close enough to her condo that she could make a quick exit if things got too . . . heated.

Tori craned her head and looked past the people and cars along Ocean Drive, expecting to see her friends walking up from Thirteenth. She caught a glimpse of Adriana and Juli, and within a few minutes, they were on the corner.

When they reached the steps to the hotel, Sylvia bounded up to them with her long-legged stride. She had just entrusted her late-model BMW convertible to the restaurant valet at the curb. She was dressed casually in a black cargo skirt that Tori had seen in that month's *Ocean Drive* magazine and an off-the-shoulder white blouse that showed off her buff yet naturally curvy body.

Like Sylvia, Tori was dressed casually in clothes that screamed conservative—sharply pleated khaki pants and a pale yellow Ralph Lauren dress shirt—rather than trendy. Adriana matched Sylvia in a casually chic outfit, while Juli, as always, looked like a fashion victim.

When the three reached the table, Tori motioned to the mojitos she had ordered just moments before. She grabbed one, raised her glass, and repeated the words she had uttered for years at almost every Monday gathering, birthday, or other special event. But even as she said them, a bit of sadness entered her voice. A slight tremor shook her glass as she took a sip.

Tori put down her mojito and cleared her throat. It

was time. "I have something to tell you." Only she suddenly had trouble finding the words, so instead, she raised her left hand and held it out for all of them to see. No telling. Just showing. A big diamond engagement ring. And something beside the engagement ring.

Even in the dim light, it gleamed and demanded attention. A wedding band—thick, golden, and shiny. On her finger.

Juli reached for her hand, paused, then pulled her own hand back as if unsure if she could touch Tori.

Adriana, apparently, had no such hesitation. She jerked hold of Tori's hand and moved it close for inspection. Adriana's actions brought the ring into better light, making the wedding band look bigger and even more golden than before.

"You got married. That's wonderful," Juli said, seeming truly happy.

"This is for real, isn't it? Not some prank?" Sylvia's words were loud and harsh.

Tori slipped her hand off the table and down beneath its surface, almost as if to hide the evidence of what she had done. "You should know by now that I'm not a prank kind of girl, Syl."

Adriana had yet to utter a word. She was clearly in shock, her green eyes wide and slightly unfocused.

Tori could understand the shock part of it. She was the foundation of their group. Always calm. Always the mediator. Always constant. And always closest to Adriana. Guilt reared up again, but she tamped it down.

Adriana's mouth opened and closed like a fish freshly pulled from the tank and plopped on the fishmonger's counter. Then she bolted from the veranda into the restaurant and escaped via a side door into the Cardozo.

Tori and Sylvia barely missed a beat before chasing after their friend.

When they arrived in the bathroom, Juli trailing behind them, Adriana had already locked herself in a stall.

Tori and Sylvia waited by either side of the stall door, urging Adriana to come out and talk.

"*Amiga, perdoname.* I know I should have said something before," Tori said and laid her hand on the door of the stall.

"Tori, no. This has nothing to do with you," Juli advised and gently squeezed her shoulder.

Sylvia put her hands on her hips and glared at Juli as if she had two heads. "What *are* you talking about?"

"Adriana, *por favor.* Please come out and talk to us," Juli pleaded and lightly rapped on the metal of the door with her knuckles.

From behind the door they heard hiccups, toilet paper rolling, and nose blowing. The latch on the door squeaked a second before it opened to reveal Adriana, her face blotchy and tear-stained.

"I'm sorry, Tori. I'm really happy for you. I truly am." She wrung a wad of toilet paper between her hands.

Sylvia slung her arm over Adriana's shoulder and playfully shook her. "Girl, you have a weird way of showing it."

Adriana looked down and mangled the paper in her hands. "It's just . . . I'm a little . . ."

Confused about why her best friend did this? Tori thought, then she remembered the missed calls all weekend. The slightly dazed sound in Adriana's voice in the messages, saying she needed to talk.

"When you called this weekend, Gil and I—"

"Were getting married. I get it. I didn't mean to interrupt, only . . ."

A long tortured inhalation followed Adriana's interruption, along with more tears and one single word. "Riley."

"Oh, no, Adriana. What's up with Riley?" She also slipped her arm around Adriana's shoulders and led her to a small lounge area in the bathroom.

Adriana leaned against a glass and wrought iron table that was close to one garishly painted purple and red wall. Juli and Sylvia took up spots on either side of her, while Tori stood in front, trying to understand what had happened with her friend and Riley.

Adriana swiped at the trails of tears on her face and shook her head. "It was just another Thursday. We were supposed to play volleyball just like we always do. Only Riley called to ask if I could do lunch."

"A sure sign of trouble, the whole doing lunch thing," Sylvia interjected.

Tori glared at Sylvia, who raised her hands in surrender and said, "Sorry. So you had lunch with Riley."

"Eventually. After he called to say he was thinking of asking Becca to marry him."

The tears came more furiously after that, as did all their questions. In between hiccups and nose blows, Adriana relayed the story about Riley's call, what had happened at their game and then at lunch that past Thursday. How hard it had been to see him and Rebecca together on Saturday morning when she was on her way to the restaurant. She had canceled Sunday's volleyball date because she couldn't bear to be with Riley, knowing he planned to propose to Rebecca.

Tori listened silently until Adriana tossed her hands up in the air and said, "And that's it. Riley's going to ask Becca to marry him."

"That's it? You're going to let the love of your life marry someone else?" Juli said with more vehemence than her friends had ever heard from her.

Everyone looked at her, clearly shocked she had finally had the courage to speak up. "What? We all know how Adriana feels about him. We've just been avoiding it because she's been avoiding it."

"So what am I supposed to do?" Adriana asked.

"Take charge. Tell Riley what he means to you," Tori said.

"*Sí.* Go after what you want. Like you did when you told your *papi* you didn't want to work in the family business," Juli seconded.

"And when you decided to open the hotel," Sylvia added with a smile and a nod in Juli's direction.

Tori jumped in again. "March right up to him and plant one on him. Tell him how you feel."

"You'd think he'd know. After all these years . . . " Adriana couldn't finish. Shaking her head, she walked away from them and to one of the sinks in the bathroom.

They all followed and stood behind Adriana as she splashed water on her face, then grabbed some paper towels and dried off. While she did so, Tori gazed up at the wall, a mosaic of tiles of varying colors and pieces of mirror.

An odd little picture. Definitely jarring to see the splintered bits of all of them scattered across the wall. Almost prophetic, she thought, since in the course of just a few days, their lives were slowly fragmenting and spreading apart as some of them went in different directions.

She was now married.

Adriana appeared at a loss.

Only Sylvia had arguably remained the same. And Juli had finally shown some spirit.

With an approving nod at Juli, Tori slipped her arm around Adriana's shoulders and urged her back to the table. After dinner and a few rounds of mojitos, they finally called it a night.

At the steps to the Cardozo, Adriana swayed a bit.

Tori immediately wrapped her arm around Adriana's waist to steady her.

"Come on, *amiga*. You and I are going to take a nice long walk home."

"Are you sure, Tori? I can drive the two of you," Sylvia offered. Juli also piped in with an offer of assistance.

"Not to worry. I think the fresh air will do her good."

Adriana nodded and her head kept on bobbing up and down, like one of those little dogs people kept in the back windows of their cars.

"*Estas cierta, amiga?* She looks a little . . . Well, not a little. Really really *boracha*," Juli noted.

"We'll be fine," Tori said, thinking that the walk would be good and not just on account of the fresh air.

Adriana had needed her and she hadn't been there. Worse, she hadn't told her best friend that she was eloping. Having to lug Adriana's butt for twenty blocks seemed like just punishment for those two things.

With her arm securely wrapped around Adriana's waist and her friend holding on to her just as tightly, they crossed the street to the path in the park, where there were less people to avoid. They strolled along, silent for the first few blocks, but then the walk and the fresh breeze coming off the ocean seemed to have worked a bit on Adriana.

"You got married."

"*Sí*, I did. I'm sorry I didn't tell you beforehand."

A noise, more like a snort than anything else, erupted from her friend. "*Verdad*. You didn't tell me. You're besht-est *amiga* in the whole entire world."

"I know, only . . . I was scared," Tori confessed, and as Adriana started to slip, Tori steadied her and opted for walking her to the beach wall and sitting for just a moment.

Adriana plopped down on the low cement and seashell wall and stared up at Tori. Pointing at her with one shaky finger, she said, "You, *amiga*, are never ever sh-scared. *Nunca.*"

She appreciated Adriana's faith in her. "*Gracias*. But you're also hardly ever scared. So why haven't you been able to tell Riley—"

"That I love him."

The admission came so suddenly that it shocked both of them. Adriana clapped her hands over her mouth and shook her head. "That was the alcohol talking," she mumbled from behind her hands while continuing to shake her head.

"*In vino veritas?*" Tori wondered aloud.

"I don't want to talk about this anymore," Adriana said. She rose from the wall and teetered for a moment before Tori slipped beside her and they started walking again.

As before, they were silent for long blocks, appreciating the beautiful night and the relative quiet along the beach path. Quite different from the activity that continued across the way in the restaurants and bars along the street.

The path ended on Fifth Street, where a group of teens had set up an impromptu skating course with bright orange cones. As they passed the gathering, Adriana said, "I like Gil. I think he'll be good for you."

Tori smiled. "I like Gil, too."

Adriana chuckled and jostled her in jest. "I hope it's more than like, *amiga*. I hope it's lust. Lots and lots of lust."

She shook her head and laughed as well. "Possibly."

"I'm glad," Adriana replied, then fell silent again as they walked side by side for the last few blocks to her condo. At the door to the building, Adriana stopped. "I think I can make it up on my own."

Tori examined her, and although it seemed she could manage, she wanted to be certain. "Are you sure?"

When Adriana nodded, she embraced her and whis-pered, "See you in the morning for our jog?"

Adriana groaned loudly. "I'll try, *amiga.*"

"Try, Adriana. Things don't have to change." She hoped her friend would understand.

As Adriana tightened her hold, she knew she had. Pulling away, Tori said, *"Hasta mañana,"* and walked away, eager to get home to Gil.

Gil was sound asleep when she got home. No wonder. By the time she had walked back from Adriana's, it was nearly two in the morning.

He lay on his side, his arm slung over her pillow. His skin was golden against the vanilla color of the sheets. Muscles firm. Sleep warm, she thought as she caressed his shoulder.

Tori undressed quietly and sat on the edge of the bed beside her husband. Her newlywed and very sexy hus-band, she thought with a smile and some interesting ideas on how to wake him. But despite those wickedly naughty ideas, she let him sleep on. They both had hectic work schedules for later that day.

She had no doubt it would be a difficult one, between the late night and dealing with the emotional upheaval today had caused on so many levels.

So many levels except one, she thought with a smile as she replaced the pillow beneath Gil's arm with her naked body.

He reacted immediately, hugging her tight and mum-bling a sleepy "How did they deal?"

"Surprisingly, we hardly spoke about it."

Gil propped his head up with one elbow and gazed down at her. "You didn't talk about it? Why? Did the restaurant burn down?"

"Close to it."

"Being tight-lipped are we?" he asked and laid his hand on her stomach before slowly trailing it up to cup her breast.

"Think you can pry it out of me with . . . *Dios*, that feels good," she murmured as he replaced his hand with his mouth. She clasped his head to her and he said, "Can I?"

"Can you what?" she asked, having lost all train of thought.

"Pry it out of you? With something like this?" Gil asked with a lick.

"Definitely." She exerted gentle pressure to urge him onto his back and slipped her body over his.

"Still want to talk?" she questioned as she moved her hips.

"No," was his quick reply.

7

Adriana

The shiny new Tungsten PDA, complete with cell phone, Bluetooth, and all the latest bells and whistles, beeped loudly and repeatedly. Colorful animated messages flashed across the crisp new screen to remind Adriana of past due dates. Past due because the computer geek to whom she had taken her coffee-soaked PDA hadn't been able to revive her old one, but had been able to save the data.

She had been lucky. At least she thought she had been until the reminder for Sunday popped up.

9:00 a.m.: Volleyball with Riley

Riley, she thought and groaned, cradling her head in her hands as she peered at the PDA. She snared it off her desktop, and deleted the past due dates, and scrolled up and down the entries for the remainder of the week just to confirm the data seemed accurate.

With the PDA in order, she opened the notepad and typed in her list of to-dos for the day.

1. Call Tori and apologize. Again.
2. Get Tori a wedding present.
3. Get Riley a new volleyball partner.

After the last entry, she raked back her hair and plopped against the thick cushioning of her leather executive chair. Scrubbing her face with her hands, she leaned forward and buried her head in her hands once again, before examining the PDA. Again.

The screen got hazy, looking like a blurry watercolor. No technical malfunction, just an emotional meltdown.

"You okay?"

She jerked her head up and swiped at a tear. Juli stood at the door to her office, dressed in her chef's whites, a concerned look on her expressive face.

"I feel like a shit."

Her partner came in and laid a cup of cafe con leche on the desk along with two aspirin. "It's no wonder. How many mojitos did you have last night?"

"No, not shitty. 'A shit,' as in I acted like a total idiot last night," she snapped and reached for the coffee. But Juli snared her hand. Adriana followed the line of Juli's white-jacketed arm up to meet her friend's clear, brown-eyed gaze, so different from the bloodshot one that had greeted her in the mirror that morning right after she had called Tori to beg off on their morning jog.

"Stop being a bitch." Juli's voice was soft and calm as always, but surprisingly there was steel in her tone as well.

"I'm sorry. I don't know why—"

"You're upset. We all understand why. The question is—what are you going to do about it now?"

Juli released her hand, and she scooped up the two aspirin and grabbed the cup of coffee. She swallowed the aspirin and coffee, which tasted as bitter as all get-out.

Bitter. A state that could be used to describe the emotion of the moment.

She couldn't help but be bitter about Riley and his upcoming engagement to Rebecca.

And still slightly bitter about the fact that her very best friend in all the world had chosen to elope and not say a word about it.

"Adriana? What are you going to do?" Juli prompted again after her prolonged silence.

"I'm sorry. I was just thinking about . . . I need to do something special for Tori. To congratulate her on—"

"I wasn't talking about Tori," Juli clarified as she placed the list of the daily specials before her and handed her the receipts for that morning's purchases just as she did every morning.

Only, this morning nothing was quite the same, Adriana thought.

"I was talking about Riley," Juli finished.

Riley. Just thinking about him brought a fresh round of pain, but not only in her head. Inside, there was an ache so strong she had to put down her cup of coffee and rub at a spot above her heart. "I can't do anything about Riley."

Juli once again stopped her as she reached for her coffee. *"Que? Estas loca?* Of course you can do something about Riley."

Adriana didn't want a repeat of last night's discussion. She glared at her friend and partner, who withdrew her hand from the much-needed coffee. "You know the rules. You know I can't do anything."

"Rules? What frickin' rules?" Juli almost shouted, shocking her not only with her vehemence, but by questioning her. It was something Sylvia would do. Or Tori . . . Well, not the old Tori. Who knew what the new Tori would do? But Juli? Never ever Juli.

Adriana eyed her partner. "What's up with you?"

"Nada." Again said with a little bit of backbone, but Juli avoided her gaze.

Determined to put an end to the Riley discussion, Adriana explained. "I don't poach on someone else's property. 'Thou shalt not covet,' remember? He's Becca's—"

"He's not *her* property. They're not engaged yet, *verdad*? So for now—'All's fair in love and war,'" Juli shot back and finally met her gaze directly.

Love? As Tori had walked her home and even after, as she had poured herself into bed, the one thing she remembered was thinking over and over and over again that she wasn't sure if she loved Riley. But she couldn't imagine not having Riley in her life.

However, if a Happily-Ever-After syndrome existed for men, Riley would soon be out of her life. What normal wife would want her hunky husband spending inordinate amounts of time with another woman?

The ache in her heart tightened considerably. The pain in her head made her grimace. She'd had enough talk of Riley. Time to get to the business she had to run and the life she had to live that had nothing to do with Riley. Not to mention Tori, who had hurt her with her actions, but whom she had also hurt with her reaction last night.

"I'd like to do something for Tori," she repeated again, grabbing her coffee cup in both hands and taking a bracing gulp of the drink.

Juli remained silent and she looked up to examine her. Her friend had something to say, but seemed to recognize that it would only lead to an argument. Eventually, almost hesitantly, Juli placed a folder on the large mahogany surface of her desk. She pulled out a sheath of papers from the folder, placed them in the middle of her desk, and started explaining the Lovers' Special dinner she had been developing.

"You knew?" Adriana interrupted, surprised and annoyed.

"Not about the marriage. But Tori pretty much said an engagement was imminent. I thought Gil might want to propose to her here at the restaurant with a special dinner. But I guess that isn't going to happen now, is it?"

Adriana shook her head and placed her hand on top of Juli's papers. "No, I guess not. But we can give them a celebration meal. Maybe even a special night in one of the rooms in the hotel."

Juli shrugged, and Adriana couldn't get an accurate read on her. "Something wrong?"

"*Nada.* I guess there's no reason we couldn't plan *una noche especial.* A really special one to congratulate them."

Trying to positively acknowledge Juliana's idea, Adriana rose, stepped around the large desk, and slipped an arm around Juli's shoulders. "So let's see what this culinary marvel has planned."

Beneath her arm, Juli's muscles relaxed. After shuffling around the papers, Juli went through each dish, noting the aphrodisiacal powers of some of the ingredients.

"A Lovers' Special, huh? Maybe we should add this to the regular menu. Get all of South Beach clamoring for their own little dose of sexual sizzle," Adriana teased, and rolled her eyes, too practical to put much stock in the supposed powers of love concoctions.

Juliana playfully elbowed her. "*Vamos, amiga. Esto es confidencial.* Just a little bit for Tori, not that she needs any more *suerte* in the man department. *Mucho, mucho mas* for the man Sylvia should find, if she should find one—"

"Because he'll need all the luck and energy in the world to handle Sylvia." Sylvia was a difficult bird when it came to matters of the heart, Adriana thought. At times she wondered if Sylvia even had a heart.

Juli continued with, *"Y un poquito* for you—"

Adriana raised her hand to stop her friend. "I know where you're going, so let me just say, let's save it for you instead. You deserve someone wonderful like Gil."

Juli snorted indignantly. "As if anyone would look at me with the three of you around," she muttered under her breath and nervously shuffled the papers for the Lovers' Special menu.

She had suspected how Juli felt, but hoped that she'd been wrong. She faced her friend, cupped her cheek, and gently applied pressure until Juli met her gaze. "You're a beautiful woman. I just always thought you weren't interested—"

"In men?" Juli jumped in, her gorgeous brown eyes flashing wide.

"In fashion and all the latest things," she corrected.

"How can I be interested when half of those models in the magazines you read look like they haven't eaten in months? When all those women in the gym disappear when they turn sideways?"

So many emotions warred in Juli's tone that Adriana didn't know where to start. "If you want, we can go shopping together. I saw some things the other day that would look great on you."

Juli hesitated and began moving the papers around again. Adriana laid a hand on Juli's. "You can make a change that will make you happy—"

"Y tu tambien. You can talk to Riley."

Adriana eyed her partner. Juli had no intention of doing anything for herself unless she agreed to do something about Riley.

"Deal."

"*De verdad?*" Juli asked in surprise, her jaw dropping from the shock of Adriana's acquiescence.

"Until I find Riley a new volleyball partner, I have no choice but to see Riley when we make up Sunday's game later today."

"You will talk to him, *verdad*? That was the deal," Juli reminded, wagging a finger in her face.

"I promise to try. I think Sylvia will be down there covering a Volleypalooza tournament with some models. If you come with me to the beach for your break, the three of us can talk about Tori's special night. Maybe go shopping later?"

Juli couldn't stifle her amusement. "Sports, bikinis, and me are like oil and vinegar—"

"Unmixy things, huh?"

Nodding as she gathered all her notes for the Lovers' Special, Juli mimicked her and said, "Major unmixy." She paused as she stuffed the papers back into her file and asked, "But if you can face Riley—which is a major step for now—I can brave the beach and shopping."

"Don't forget Sylvia," Adriana reminded as she walked back around the desk and picked up the materials for the daily specials.

"As if anyone could forget Sylvia," Juli added with a roll of her eyes as the two of them finally got down to planning the day's menu.

Getting back to everyday things helped, Adriana thought. It made it easier to forget that Riley planned on marrying another woman. But in the back of her mind, she wondered how she would handle seeing Riley at the game, knowing as she did that her tomorrows with Riley were possibly finite in number.

8

Sylvia

He had forgotten about her.

How could that be?

How could her editor have handed out all the assignments of any journalistic weight and forgotten about her when they had only just discussed it?

With their Wednesday morning editorial meeting concluded, she had, as always, been left with nothing but her typical night-on-the-town stories. It stung, especially since two of the assignments he had handed out to others were ones she had suggested to him earlier in the week.

"This sucks, Harry," she said as she chased down the hall after him, her three-inch stiletto heels tapping noisily on the tile floor. Harry might be short, balding, and nearing sixty, but fast like the rat that he was.

"Maybe next time, Sylvia," he said, not even looking at her as he waved his hand in dismissal.

She grabbed hold of his arm to stop his flight.

He turned and looked at where she held his arm, then allowed his gaze to travel up her body in a manner that was anything but professional. His gaze skimmed from her high heels to the long bit of thigh exposed by the short dark blue Dolce & Gabbana skirt to the wraparound silk knit Cavalli blouse. Once at her cleavage, Harry lingered for an even longer look-see.

Great. He was a lecher in addition to everything else, she thought.

Sylvia ignored his untoward perusal and said, "That's what you said last month. And two of those stories were mine, Harry. Mine." She stressed the point by tapping her chest with one hand.

"You work for us, Sylvia. Your stories are ours." As he licked his thick lips, it occurred to her he believed she was his to drool over as well.

A red fog clouded her gaze, and in her mind she heard Tori's and Adriana's voices urging her to count down from ten to control her temper.

Ten, nine, eight . . .

This job might suck for the moment, but it was a job, and journalism jobs were hard to come by.

Seven, six, five . . .

Sucking up to this chauvinist cretin was the right thing to do.

Four, three, two, one . . .

"I quit."

The words came out of her mouth with dead calm and control. Release washed over her at the realization she had uttered those words.

A stunned look sprung across Harry's face, followed by a scarlet flush to his normally pasty cheeks. Beads of sweat erupted on his upper lip. Harry swiped at them, then ran his hand up over the few remaining gray hairs at the top of his shiny head.

Sylvia allowed herself only a second to savor his discomfort. Smiling, she turned and walked away from him.

"Sylvia," Harry called out, but she kept moving toward her cubicle, heels tapping a happy beat on the tiled floor of the main office space.

The magazine's offices were located in a multistory building on Española Way. Rumor had it that the building had been everything from a warehouse to a whorehouse, but the space had been renovated for the magazine. The magazine's staff was crammed into cubicles covered with beige fabric and trimmed with mahogany-stained wood. Only guests and management types like Harry rated an area with windows, but even then, the views were only of the other Mediterranean-style buildings along the streets of the historic Spanish Village.

"Sylvia!" he yelled, more loudly than before, possibly bordering on a bellow.

As she continued, almost joyfully skipping down the center row of the office, heads turned their way. Some even peeked over the edges of the cubicles, searching out the source of the problem.

From behind her came the sound of Harry's gum-soled Thom McCanns squeaking on the terra-cotta tile as he finally scurried after her. He snatched her arm as she rounded the corner to her cubicle.

She glared at him, the menace in her gaze enough to make him instantly drop her arm and step away. The red staining his cheeks spread to his ears. "Sylvia, you cannot quit. We have a contract."

"But I have a very good lawyer. I'm sure if you check, you'll see not only that I can quit, but that there's nothing to stop me from walking through the doors of the *Miami Herald* in, let's say . . . " She paused, raised her arm, and dramatically pushed back the sleeve of her silk knit shirt to reveal her solid gold TAG watch. "The time it takes me to pack."

Harry rubbed at his disappearing hair with a hand

that still held papers from the earlier meeting. "Don't be hasty. I'm sure we can work this out."

Sylvia looked around. Virtually everyone in the magazine's workroom watched the confrontation with interest. Conscious of that, she adopted a casual stance. Crossing her arms, she leaned against the edge of her cubicle and lowered her voice so that only her editor could hear. "The designer drug story you gave to Phil. It was mine. I want it back."

Harry's gaze anxiously skittered around the room before settling on her once again. After a phlegmy cough to clear his throat, he said in a loud voice, "I've been thinking you should try something different."

"Well, thanks, Harry." Knowing that she might incur future wrath over her actions, she threw him a bone to hopefully lessen the repercussions. "That designer drug story you thought up is a great idea. There's this man I can talk to about—"

"How do you know he'll want to talk to you?" Harry asked, apparently unappeased by her giving him the credit for her story.

She raised an eyebrow in challenge, and from various cubicles came restrained laughter and snickers of disbelief. Spreading her arms and motioning to herself, she said, "Harry. What straight man wouldn't?"

Crimson now stained all of Harry's face. Sylvia hoped he wouldn't stroke out right in front of her. He motioned with the papers he held and warned, "Just have a report for me by Monday morning. Then we'll decide if there's enough of a story for a future issue."

She mock saluted, grinning as he waddled away. With a quick wave to those who had been watching, some of whom silently applauded, Sylvia slipped into her cubicle. Barely four by four, her space provided little comfort, but then again, she rarely spent time there.

Her stories took her all over Miami, both during the day and night. Thanks to the demands of being the It Girl, her odd hours dictated she work whenever she could. Generally, that meant scrunching over her laptop in the nearest coffeehouse or her condo, which was only blocks away from the magazine's offices.

Her cubicle space, therefore, had only basic work essentials and a small plaque posted to the outside fabric to identify it as hers. There were few knickknacks and even fewer photos. Just a double frame with a picture of her mama on one side and her friends on the other. Her friends. Her best friends.

Which reminded her that she needed to make a call.

She picked up the phone, dialed, and when Tori answered, she said, "I need you to take a look at a contract for me."

Lincoln Road had once been an outdoor mall. A collection of retail shops had lined the broad pedestrian walkways and a trolley had run from one end to the other to help shoppers lessen their load. Like many sections of South Beach, it had fallen into disrepair before being rediscovered and recycled into something new and different.

Now, upscale stores, restaurants, and clubs lined the broad roadway, and the walkways along the former mall section were jammed with people.

The magazine's offices and her condo were both just blocks away from Lincoln Road. With a gorgeous September night unfolding, Sylvia walked the short distance from her condo to the nightclub where she hoped to begin her investigation. There were crowds of people strolling along the walk, and a line had already formed in front of the nightclub.

She strolled up to the bouncer, who smiled as she

approached and motioned her to the front of the line. With an elegant bow, he lifted the velvet rope to let her pass.

"*Gracias*, Roberto." She air kissed his cheek as she skirted by him and into the club.

She added some extra sway to her walk, wanting to be noticed. The dress she'd chosen—a teal Michael Kors design slit down the front nearly to her navel—advertised her real estate quite well. As she walked through the crowd, more than a few men seemed ready for a closer inspection, but she passed them by, interested in finding one man in particular.

Kismet was with her.

He stood by the bar, elegant in a light gray Helmut Lang suit and dark maroon silk shirt open to midchest, exposing muscles sculpted by . . .

Not just a gym, Sylvia thought to herself as she examined him carefully. Something a little rough lurked beneath his understated refinement. She had thought that the first night she'd seen him a couple of months ago. He had caught her eye, and that of about a dozen other women, as he walked into the club.

She would have had to be dead not to notice him. Tall, dark, handsome, and dangerous, he was a Latino Bad Boy who made heads turn at every event at which she'd seen him since that first night. Initially, her interest had been purely physical.

She had been wondering about the possibility that he would be as hot between the sheets as he was in the latest designer clothes. Then had come the realization that he wasn't at the social gatherings just for a good time. The way he moved between crowds signaled the very real possibility that he dealt drugs, as did the little exchanges she had noted. And if not a dealer, he was well-connected enough to those with the drugs to be a person who could provide her the kind of information she needed for her investigative report. He always seemed to be in the party crowd.

Her investigative report. Finally.

She had been waiting for an opportunity like this for a long time and was pleased she had finally been able to make it happen.

Which was so totally a positive thing, considering all the negatives that had piled up during the past week. First, Tori's totally aberrant behavior and unexpected marriage. Not that Sylvia wasn't happy for her, because she was. Then, Adriana's total loss of control, from her reaction about Riley to her current frenzied planning to provide Tori a very special night. Which had somehow inspired a normally repressed Juli to create some super-sexy sustenance.

With all that upheaval with her friends to worry about, it was nice to know work had taken a turn for the better. It made for one less thing to worry about. And possibly one enjoyable thing to look forward to, she thought while she sashayed toward the bar where her Latino Bad Boy nursed a martini.

No reason why she couldn't mix business and plea-sure, was there?

She smiled, pleased when the man next to her target stepped away, leaving an empty stool with her name on it.

Slipping onto the seat, she motioned to the bartender, who beamed her a smile and removed the dirty glass from before her. "Evening, Sylvia. The usual?"

"Cosmopolitan," she answered and glanced at her target out of the corner of her eye. "What about you? Can I get you a refill?"

"No," her Bad Boy replied, and in one gulp, downed the remains of his martini.

"What?" She faced him, incredulous at his refusal.

He eyed her directly. Definitely a dangerous thing. His eyes were a dark blue flecked with bits of teal and green. Not what she had expected with his darker coloring. Nor did she expect what he did next. He leaned close to her, his big body barely inches from hers. The rasp of his evening beard teased the side of her face as he whispered into her ear, "You strike me as the kind of woman interested in one of two things."

Sweet Jesus but his voice enticed. His tones were rich and warm and slightly husky. "And what would they be, Mr. . . ."

"Carlos," he filled in for her. Reaching up with his hand, he laid his fingers in the vee of skin exposed by the nonexistent neckline of her dress. The pads of his fingers were rough on her skin as he slowly trailed them up and down her body.

Definitely the hands of a man who worked hard for his money.

Carlos continued with his assessment of her interests. "Women like you want either a fast fuck out in the alley or something pharmaceutical to make their pleasure just a bit more intense."

She chuckled and mimicked his actions, slipping her hand beneath the fabric of his shirt and onto his chest. Smooth, hard, and oh so warm, but she didn't let that distract her. She raised her head until her mouth nestled close to his ear. "Carlos, let me clue you in on something. I have no need for the latter, and as for the former . . ."

Pausing, she lowered the tone of her voice just one sexy notch and said, "When I fuck you, it will be so painfully and delectably slow that you will beg for the pleasure to end, and when it does, you'll beg for more."

Carlos gave a strangled cough before yanking his hand away from her.

She eased from the stool and met his stunned gaze. *"Buenas noches,* Carlito."

Tossing some bills on the bar to cover her drink, she walked away quickly, navigating through the crowded club and out into the hot Miami night, where she paused and leaned against the outside wall of the club and took a few deep breaths to steady herself. She was certain Carlos wouldn't say no the next time they met.

She was also certain that she'd definitely require help to battle her attraction to the very dangerous Bad Boy. She blamed her mother for the apparent genetic weakness that had her needing to scratch this particular itch so badly that she was almost shaking.

Sylvia laughed as she recalled what her mother had said to her a few Sundays ago. She knew just how to take care of the itch.

Good thing the Energizer Bunny could keep going and going and going . . .

9

Juliana

Everything was going just right, Juli thought as she rushed around the kitchen, putting all the finishing touches on her Lovers' Special dinner while making sure that the remainder of the dinner orders were under control. Fridays were always one of the busiest nights of the week.

Her two sous chefs and assorted assistants busily prepped meals for their patrons while another assistant helped with Tori's sexy meal. Another half dozen or so busboys and helpers not only kept the kitchen clean, washed the pots, pans, and dishes, but also made sure staples such as bread and salad were available for the wait staff. Relieved that the kitchen appeared in order, she hoped things were similarly fine with her friends' preparations.

Sylvia and Adriana were up in the room, spicing it up with the little extras they hoped would make Tori's night one to remember. Rose petals strewn in various key locations. Vanilla scented candles throughout the space, to be lit when appropriate. Flavored oils and enticing lingerie to complete the mood Juli planned to create with her unique meal. Each course was filled with foods sure to add to whatever magic already existed between Tori and her newlywed husband, Gil.

Tori's newlywed husband of only one week, she thought with a smile as she finished preparing the asparagus and quickly dropped them into boiling water to blanche. She already had a citrus and ginger vinaigrette prepared to accompany the tender vegetables.

Wiping her hands on a towel tucked into the waistband of her apron, she rushed over to check on the risotto. Her assistant stirred away and she peered over her shoulder. The risotto was gorgeously creamy. With its finishing truffle oil touches, it would create an explosion of earthy flavor on the tongue. "Perfect. When you're ready to plate it, let me know."

Everything was almost ready, she thought, pleased with how all the dishes had come together. Granted, it will probably be a little disconcerting for the newlyweds to have the entire meal ready and waiting up in the room. But then again, for the night to be romantic, they needed no interruptions.

Tonight would be perfect. Or at least the food would be. Juli had given all of her attention, time, and love to each dish. In a little while, Tori and Gil could enjoy them.

She hoped the passion in her heart had infused each molecule of the meal she had prepared for her friends. Passion, like salt, being a necessary ingredient to avoid a tasteless and bland existence.

Like your life? the voice in her head rebuked.

She ignored it, knowing that her life was about finding the right ingredients to create a perfect mix. Like her friendship with Adriana, Tori, and Sylvia, which had turned out so well.

That relationship sustained her on so many levels, like bread sustained life. In retrospect, Adriana was like the flour in the bread, since she had been the one essential to all of them finding one another. Tori was the water, binding them together despite their differences. And the yeast? Without a doubt—Sylvia, always bubbling and churning up the mix.

And you? the voice asked with some amusement.

I'm the salt, she thought. Adding taste and keeping all the other ingredients in line. Giving the mix flavor and balance.

As for Gil, the latest ingredient to the mix, she had to figure out where he went and how he changed things.

For the better, she thought optimistically and remembered that Tori and Gil would be arriving shortly. Adriana had given the key to Tori earlier in the day, wishing for their present to be as unobtrusive as possible.

At least that had been the original plan, she thought, a bit worried about whether whatever Adriana and Sylvia were doing had altered that grand design.

She quickly checked out the beverages on the serving cart. Dom Pérignon champagne, perfectly chilled, for that little perk at dessert time, and a little known cabernet sauvignon she had recently discovered that would set the perfect tone for the meal.

Juli was smiling, satisfied with everything, when Adriana and Sylvia burst into the kitchen, giggling and jostling each other playfully. Juli pointed a finger from one friend to the other and said, "You *chicas* seem a little too happy. *Por favor.* Tell me you didn't do anything—"

"Erotic," Adriana jumped in and giggled once again.

"Outrageous," Sylvia added with a roll of her eyes.

Juli thought of the elegant but sensual meal now being wheeled out the door and up to the room and cringed at the thought of what her two friends had possibly concocted for Tori's night. *"Que hicieron?"*

"Everything we agreed to do, plus a little something extra," Adriana explained, glancing at Sylvia out of the corner of her eye. When Sylvia met her gaze, they both started laughing again.

Juli plopped down on a stool by her prep table and truly began to worry. Sylvia was sexually outrageous—the blindfold on Tori's birthday being a prime example. What would it be now? she wondered. Handcuffs?

As for Adriana, she might be all giggly girlie-girl tonight, but her *amiga* was not over the whole Tori-didn't-bother-to-tell-her-best-friend thing, not to mention the even worse Riley's-getting-married fiasco. Which had her wondering whether Adriana was thinking clearly about whatever she and Sylvia had dreamed up.

"Chicas, I'm getting a little worried."

Sylvia waved off her concerns. "Don't get all twisted, Juli. It was a good thing."

Juli glanced at Adriana, who nodded and said, *"Sí.* It was just a little . . . encouragement, *sabes."*

Rising, she crossed her arms. "Encouragement? As in—"

"Think of it as a rainy day sex kit," Sylvia clarified.

Dios mio, she thought and bit her lip. Poor Tori had enough to handle already. Her family wasn't talking to her. Adriana had freaked out, and now this—Sylvia's idea of helpful sexual suggestions.

"I hope you know what you're doing, *amigas."*

Sylvia stepped over to her and wrapped an arm around her shoulders. "Girl, I think what we need to worry about is whether Tori and Gil know what *they're* doing."

As she met Sylvia's gaze, Juli realized that her friend wasn't talking about tonight, but the whole let's-run-off-and-get-married thing.

"*Ojala* they do," Juli said with a nod, a bit surprised that she and Sylvia seemed to be in agreement, since like salt and yeast together alone was not a good mix.

Adriana leaned on the edge of the prep table and smiled. "You worry too much. It'll all work out."

Juli looked from one friend to the other. She hoped Adriana was right, because you couldn't make bread without water.

10
Tori

Tori paused for a moment before the hotel and gazed up at the lights shining from virtually every window.

Did her friends consider that her rather precipitous marriage required celebration, or a wake on her behalf?

Tonight would tell, she thought. Considering how poorly her family had dealt with her marriage, her friends' attempts to provide her with a special night to remember were appreciated. And since her friends' last surprise, a birthday cruise, had resulted in her finding Gil, she hoped tonight would provide her with something as pleasant to remember.

Tugging Gil's hand, she led him to the entrance of the hotel. The narrow lobby was occupied by a security guard, who nodded his head in greeting and motioned them to one side of the room. To the right of him, the hotel receptionist behind the front desk smiled at their entry.

Dark hand-carved wooden doors disguised the elevators, and if not for the buttons between the two elevator banks, they might have missed them. When the doors slid open, they stepped inside and Tori handed Gil the key to the room.

On their floor, he walked her to the door, but paused after he stuck the magnetic card into the lock. "Is it safe, you think? No surprises?"

She smirked wryly when the green light on the door popped on without incident. Opening the door, she peered inside.

The room glowed invitingly with the golden light from a few small lamps and some strategically placed candles. The faint scent of vanilla teased her nose. She grabbed hold of Gil's hand and urged him to follow her inside.

Her friends had wanted the hotel to be the height of luxury after their renovations, and from the design of the suite, Tori was sure they had succeeded. As they entered the central part of a larger suite, Gil walked to a bistro-sized table by the windows while she strolled to a door at the far side of the room and opened it. The bedroom was beautiful. Inside was a king-sized bed with a rose-petal-strewn surface, and on the nightstand and dresser, vases held dozens of roses. Something clenched deep within her at the thought of Gil and her on that bed later, soft petals beneath her back. Gil, hard above her. Even harder within her.

She fanned her face with her hand, which prompted Gil to ask from across the room, "You okay?"

Nodding, she didn't press her luck by opening the next door—probably the bathroom. If her friends had continued their rose theme in there . . .

"There's a note on the table. For you." Gil picked up a peach-colored envelope and held it out to her.

She hurried over. The thick parchment envelope felt

rich and lush against her fingertips. The note inside read:

Here's wishing you a Night to Remember in celebration of your marriage. There are five other notes to wish you even more joy. Open one before dinner; one after each course; and the last . . . You'll know by then.

Love,
Adriana, Juliana, and Sylvia

She looked up at Gil, who scrutinized her intently, and handed him the note.

He read it and grinned, the dimple in his cheek prominent. "You and your friends are all . . . would 'demanding' be the right word?"

Still sexually charged from her glimpse of the bed that awaited them, Tori leaned close to her husband . . . *Whoa, her husband,* an idea she was not yet used to. As she brushed herself against him, she inched up on tiptoe and nuzzled the side of his face. "I think modern women prefer the word 'empowered.' "

Gil brought his hand down to her waist and applied gentle pressure until she was closer. It was impossible for her to ignore that he was ready for the night. "I'm all for power. Right now, I'm a little energized myself."

She shot him a provocative half glance. "Let's hope your batteries are fully charged."

Gil laughed and urged her closer. "I promise there won't be any power failures tonight, *querida.* Only we wouldn't want to ruin your friends' surprise by starting too soon. Would we?"

Tori let out a little chuckle, whirled away from him. Swaying her hips suggestively, she purred, "You're a tease. Get a girl all worked up and then . . ."

Gil followed her the short distance to the wall of windows. The windows faced Ocean Drive and the beach, providing glimpses of the activity below on the street, and the palm trees and ocean across the way. Because of their position on one of the uppermost floors of the hotel, seven stories up, they were nothing more than a silhouette to those on the street or across on the beach.

Beside them, two place settings graced the table, laid adjacent to each other. A covered plate rested at each place, along with a glass of red wine. Next to the plates sat a petite peach-colored gift bag and some small boxes. A few feet away was a serving cart loaded with an assortment of plates, some on a warming tray, and a bottle of Dom Pérignon champagne on ice.

Removing the envelope numbered one from the bag, Tori said, "I guess we should get to this before the food gets cold."

Gil came up behind her as she stood at the window, pressed himself against her back while wrapping his arms around her waist. Shifting his hips back and forth, he said, "Are you only worried about the food getting cold?"

Before she could reply, he kissed the side of her neck, diverting her attention from the note in her hand.

"*Por favor*, Gil. You're distracting me."

A satisfied, male chuckle escaped him as he put space between them.

Tori eased the note from the envelope and read aloud. "Slip into something comfortable before dinner. In the bedroom for Tori, and the bathroom for Gil."

Turning, she glanced up at her new husband. "Well?"

He raised his hands in surrender and hurried into the bathroom. "Far be it from me to ruin the plan."

She wondered what awaited him. She had trepidation about entering the very enticing flower-filled bedroom, but if Gil could brave the unknown, she could also.

Returning to the bedroom, she noticed the box on top of the dresser—a dresser with a large mirror over it that was sure to reflect whatever went on *in* the bed. Flustered, she grabbed the box and ripped off the peach-colored wrap. Peach was clearly a recurring theme. Flipping the top off the box, she gazed at the contents— an amazing confection of pale peach-colored silk with a coral lace trim. She pulled out the camisole, noted the matching panties, and wondered how she'd ever feel "comfortable" in this outfit.

When she held up the lingerie, the mirror beamed back her reflection: Toe the Line Tori in her stylish but preppy clothes. Boring and Predictable Tori who wore small and lacy—but sensible—underthings even when she had known tonight was intended to be a night for . . .

So maybe her friends knew her too well, she thought, and speedily changed into the lingerie. Then she stood before the mirror and stared at herself again. Or maybe it was better to say at the exotic and sexy creature gazing back at her. The panties were cut high, making her legs look longer than they really were. And the camisole made her breasts look lush, like juicy ripe peaches just waiting to be eaten.

She tousled her hair until it hung fuller around her face, took a deep breath, and headed for the door.

Behind the door, however, hung a large white terry cloth robe. A last blast of uncertainty and modesty hit her. She slipped on the robe and headed out to meet Gil.

Her husband came out of the bathroom wearing nothing but a pair of black silk boxers. He stopped short when he noticed her and placed his hands on his hips.

She gulped. He looked good enough to eat. Much as he had looked the first night they had shared.

She strode over quickly and brought her hand up to rest on his chest.

Gil covered her hand with his and grumbled, "Not fair. I get to be a boy toy—"

Rediscovering Sinfully Sexy Tori, she eased her hand from beneath his and replied, "And you get to see this." She eased the robe off her shoulders and into a puddle of terry cloth on the floor.

His swift inhale and groan were reward in and of themselves. "Like?" she asked, although the telltale movement beneath the black boxers clearly proved it. "I guess the answer is yes," she finished with a low, sexy chuckle.

"Come on, Gil. Time for the appetizer."

From the look in his eyes, she knew there was only one appetizer he wanted. That knowledge created a spark inside her. A powerful one. She felt naughty at the recognition of her control over him right now and realized the restraint he was showing in an effort to please her. She took a steadying breath and held out her hand, inviting him to join her by the table.

A flush spread to Gil's cheeks as he sat next to her. She motioned to the plate sitting before him. "Time to eat. Before it gets cold."

Gil just nodded and dug into the appetizer—asparagus with a citrus vinaigrette. Tori wondered if his haste came from hunger or a desire to see the contents of envelope number two.

Before she knew it, she had also devoured the appetizer and awaited the main course.

"Hungry?" he asked and she met his amused gaze.

"Famished," she replied while licking her lips. He watched as she did so, his gaze intense. With a sexy grin, he leaned over the narrow width of the table and licked the edges of her lips.

"Hmm, delicious." A needy edge made the tones of his voice vibrate as he settled back and picked up his wineglass. "A toast?"

She grabbed her own glass, a little surprised that her hand trembled. "To our new life together," she said, clinking her glass with his.

Gil's gaze never left her face, and after she had taken a sip, he whispered, "Ready for envelope number two?"

She was ready to skip to dessert, but wouldn't confess it. She snagged the second envelope from the bag, tore it open, and quickly read the note aloud. "Your wedding bands mark your bond to each other to the world. The box on the table contains signs for just the two of you to see. The bonds of eternity and integrity."

With a puzzled look, Gil picked up the box, impatiently ripped off the paper, and opened the box to reveal a small tongue depressor and two rub-on tattoos. He raised his eyebrows and held up the tattoos—the Chinese symbols for Eternity and Integrity. "Which for you? And where?"

Two simple words. Such a hard choice. And the where. "Why do I have to go first?" she groused, pressured by the moment and his too intense gaze. For a second she wondered if there were things she'd failed to consider during the course of their impetuous relationship and equally speedy wedding. Which prompted her inner voice to begin a silent mantra. *You're Sinfully Sexy Tori. Sinfully Sexy Tori.*

Gil shrugged, but didn't seem to have the same hesitation. "Okay. I choose integrity because I want you to know you never have to doubt anything about me." He handed her the tattoo along with the tongue depressor. He inched his chair close and tapped a spot on his chest. "Here. By my heart."

She laid the piece of paper with the tattoo on his chest and gently rubbed, slowly transferring the mark to his skin. She finished and drew the paper away to view her handiwork.

The tattoo was black against his tan. Smooth, she thought as she ran her thumb across his skin. When he was dressed, only she would know the mark existed. But when he went to the beach or elsewhere, her mark on him would be visible to the world. A tiny possessive thrill ran through her at the thought.

"Your turn," he said, his voice dark and dangerous. She met his gaze when he held out the second tattoo to her. His pupils were wide, dilated with desire, his eyes a blue bordering on indigo. "Where?"

She had been spared the *which* by his choice. But the *where* . . . She wanted her *where* to be a trifle more private. A *where* that only he would know.

She stood before him and urged him to spread his legs so she could step between them. Raising the hem of the camisole but a tad, she eased down the edge of the tiny panty to expose the side of her hip. She pointed to the flare just above her buttock. "Here."

Much as she had done before, Gil placed the paper on her hip and applied pressure. The way he gripped the sensitive flesh along her buttock and just above her hip bone with his hands branded her his. When he finished, Gil blew a warm breath across the tattoo even though it wasn't wet. The heat of it made her shiver. He glanced upward.

"Gil?" she questioned at the look in his eyes.

"Sshh." He moved one hand beneath the line of the panties, parted her with his fingers, and applied gentle pressure. When she moaned at his actions, he urged her forward so he could kiss the tattoo on her hip.

She murmured a protest, but he silenced her by deepening his caress and asking, "Will you love me forever?"

The intensity of the moment forced her eyes shut. She leaned on the edge of the table, pushing away the plate and cutlery as Gil stroked her and then brought his mouth to the skin just below her navel.

"Forever, Gil. Forever." After the last few months with him she couldn't imagine him not being in her life.

At those words, Gil slipped off her panties.

She almost protested, what with the windows and everything, only . . . No one could see them this far up. No one could tell that he was doing all kinds of wicked things to her. Sinfully sexy things.

Eventually Gil moved his mouth upward to her navel, pausing to lick that indentation before he said, "It's time for the main course."

She experienced shock that he could leave her wanting, but he was as aroused and had yet to have any kind of pleasure. But not for long.

Grabbing just one of the plates from the warming tray, she placed it in the corner of the table between the two place settings, forcing Gil to sit close. They were nearly shoulder to shoulder, their bare legs entwined.

She removed the cover from the plate. "Hmm. Ginger. Asparagus. Scallops. Saffron. Truffles," she noted as she forked up one of the scallops and held it up to Gil's lips. Beneath the table, she placed her free hand on his thigh. The muscles of his leg jumped and clenched beneath her fingers.

His face, however, didn't betray a thing as he accepted the forkful. "Delicious. But what about ginger and truffles and all those other things?"

She moved her hand up higher until she reached the edge of the silk boxers. Fingering the hem, she ate the risotto he had forked up for her. The rich, earthy taste from the truffles exploded in her mouth. "They're supposedly aphrodisiacs. Like the vanilla we're smelling."

"Really? And why do you suppose—"

He couldn't finish, as she'd moved the final distance

and stroked him through the silk. "Do you think they thought we needed the help, *mi amor*?"

He forced a tight smile. "Two lawyers. Boring, right?"

He groaned as she increased the pressure of her stroke.

"Right? So, let's finish the main course, Gil." She fed him again and he returned the favor. The whole time she kept touching him, the movement of her hand timed to keep him on the brink. Delicious payback for his appetizing actions of before.

The plate was finished almost before they knew it and Gil eagerly reached for the third envelope, slipped out the note, and read it aloud. "The night is young. No rush for dessert. Take a bath to relax and get ready for sweets later."

They both nearly knocked over their chairs in their haste to reach the bathroom.

Gil stood, water sluicing down his body and an errant rose petal glued to his midsection. As her gaze trailed over his body, Tori realized he was rising to the occasion again. Gil shook his head. "This night may ruin me."

Smiling, she said, "But will it have been worth it?"

Gil surprised her. "I won't know until after dessert."

He stepped from the bath, and left the room while toweling down. She grabbed a towel and chased after him. Gil stood at the table opening the bottle of Dom Pérignon champagne with only the towel wrapped around him. As she approached, he asked, "Can you lay out the dessert?"

His words prompted a picture of her spread across the table. His dessert. She shook her head to clear the thought, quickly made a makeshift sarong with the towel, and then tackled Gil's request to bring on the dessert.

She stared at the covered dishes remaining on the table.

Tapping her mouth with her index finger, she guessed at what could be dessert.

"Peaches," she said aloud even as she removed the cover from the plate.

They both chuckled as her prediction proved true. Succulent slices of peach surrounded a smaller bowl filled with a glistening cream-colored sauce.

"What do you think—"

Gil didn't get to finish as she stuck her index finger in the bowl and brought a bit of it up to his lips. Her gaze locked on his face as he licked the sauce off the tip of her finger. "Mmm. It's creamy. Sweet. Cold. A little hint of vanilla and of Tori."

His stomach growled and she teased, "Still hungry?"

As his gaze settled on her, no doubt existed in her mind about the meaning behind his answer. "I still want more. Feed me."

Tori picked up a piece of peach with her fingers, dipped it in the cream, and brought it to his mouth. As she did so, he grabbed hold of her hand, steadied it for his first bite. He slowly chewed and swallowed, took the second bite, and then licked her fingers before sucking each one into his mouth. Tori shivered in excitement and gently pulled her hand away.

"You know what turns me on?" As she said that, she prepared another peach slice and offered it up to him, much as she would soon offer all of herself to him. Her heart. Her body. That little piece of her that up until now she had been keeping private. She knew now that she could trust him with even that.

"I hope I do." He gently took hold of her hand and held it as she spoke, telling her more than he ever had before.

Eventually she realized the lateness of the hour and

motioned to the last envelope on the table. "Do you think it's time?"

Gil nodded and removed the note from the envelope, only it was blank. He held it out to her. "Do you think they forgot?"

She smiled and shook her head. "I think they realized that by now we both know what we want. Don't we?"

Gil smiled broadly, which displayed the one dimple in his cheek. His eyes glinted with amusement and desire as he said, "I've known since the first moment I saw you."

11

Adriana

Adriana slipped her PDA from the little black Prada purse she had just tucked into the metal gym locker.

7:10 p.m.: No text messages. No voice messages. No missed calls.

No Tori.

Just to make sure, she checked the battery and signal strength. Full bars on both. *Ño.* She juggled the PDA and thought back to her conversation that morning with Tori. Her friend had confirmed she would be here tonight, but so far she was a no-show.

She glanced at her watch, then at Sylvia and Juli, who stared back at her, looking for direction. Direction she didn't want to give, what with the knot of pain that had been sitting behind her eyes for hours and steadily growing, making it almost impossible to think clearly. She averted her gaze and looked all around the locker room, where women prepped for workouts.

Lots of women. Lots of activity, but no Tori.

She glared at the PDA: 7:12 p.m. Still nothing.

The PDA's screen sat as blank as the faces of her two friends. Unlike its predecessor, this PDA barely had any new entries. Somehow keeping track of all the banalities of her life no longer seemed so important during the last several weeks.

Weeks during which she'd gone through hell waiting for Riley to take action on his surprise announcement and ask Becca to marry him.

Nearly a month since Tori had eloped with Gil without telling her. Without offering any kind of explanation on why she hadn't said a word to her best friend. Tori not showing up tonight signaled that things were possibly changing with her friend.

With a hint of disappointment, she said, "I guess Tori isn't going to show."

"It's not like Tori not to call," Juli said, as she stepped up onto the low bench before the row of lockers and anxiously scanned the room, disbelieving that their friend was not coming.

Sylvia shrugged and stuffed her bag into a locker. A chill filled her voice when she spoke. "Let's face it. The Happily-Ever-After syndrome just started."

Adriana wanted to believe otherwise. After all, in the nearly three weeks since Tori's Night to Remember, their friend had yet to miss their usual Monday night gatherings. Granted, she had detected something different in her friend. A hard to pinpoint difference, and yet a disturbing one. Or maybe unsettling might be a better word. Unsettling enough to be the reason for the headache brewing in her skull.

And now this, she thought, scoping the area again, but seeing no sign of her friend. Tori was missing in action. "Maybe something came up."

Sylvia snorted loudly. "Yep, something's *up* all right. Tori's been cock-tamed."

Juli raised her hands and waved them in denial as she blustered her response. "She's not like that. She's sensible and responsible and so . . . sensible."

"What's sensible?" Tori asked as she breezed over to the lockers.

Tori had her lawyer duds on. Her shoulder-length chocolate brown hair was scraped back from her face and held in place with sedate silver combs. As Tori sat on the bench before the lockers, she pulled out the combs and ran her fingers through her hair to set it free. "Sorry. I had a problem at work and things ran really late. I didn't have time to call."

Adriana laid her hand on Tori's arm. "That's okay, Tori. We know you—"

It finally occurred to Tori that they had been discussing her before her arrival. "You didn't think I was coming."

"Not exactly," she lied and shot half glances at Juli and Sylvia. Juli ducked her head, clearly in avoidance mode. Sylvia's arms were crossed, her chin stuck out in an I'm-ready kind of stance.

Tori quickly parried with, "Exactly what part am I not getting, Adriana?"

The pain behind her eyes increased and her head throbbed from the tension. The last thing she wanted was a fight with Tori, but she, like Sylvia, seemed to be spoiling for one. "We were just saying—"

"That the Happily-Ever-After syndrome finally kicked in," Sylvia finished for her, although Adriana didn't want to dredge up that whole discussion.

"Sylvia, that's not—"

"What we were talking about?" Sylvia paused and pretended that she was trying to remember. Then she snapped her fingers and with challenge in her voice said, "Oh, yeah. That's right. *I* was the one who mentioned it. Right after you said, 'Tori's not going to show.' "

An unlikely mediator stepped into the fray as Juli pleaded with them. "*Vamos, chicas. Por favor.* There's no reason to—"

"But there is, Juli. Just because I'm a little late, you all assume I'm not coming. You assume that things are different and not in a good way," Tori snapped, surprising her. Tori always treated Juli with kid gloves, as if she thought Juli couldn't deal with confrontation.

Trying to get control back over the situation, Adriana offered an apology. "Tori, I'm sorry. *We're* sorry, okay?"

She locked gazes with Tori. A world of hurt and anger greeted her in that gaze. When Tori turned her attention to Sylvia and Juli, Tori said, "I've tried proving that nothing's changed since I married Gil. But you don't seem to get it."

"What's to get? Gil's got you all happy now," Sylvia said sarcastically, pasting an exaggerated smile on her face and wiggling her hands in the air like an overly enthusiastic Miss America.

Tori gripped the edges of the bench tightly. "You wouldn't know happy if it bit you—"

"You want to know what I said, Tori? That you were cock-tamed. 'Cause it's the truth. Gil has you so happy flat on your back that even when you're here, you're not," Sylvia shot back.

This was so not good, Adriana thought and tried to jump into the fray to stop it from getting any uglier. "Sylvia, that's enough."

"No. Let Sylvia go on. I'm dying to hear what other fascinating things she's learned from the highly refined and erudite crowd with whom she parties." Mimicking Sylvia, Tori put her chin up and crossed her arms.

With an angry bop of her head, Sylvia said, "And the corporate bloodsuckers you represent are better because . . . ?"

"Enough!" Adriana said loudly enough that several women in the immediate vicinity looked in their direction. By now her head pounded so badly that it hurt to open her eyes. She brought her fingers up to her forehead and massaged her temples.

"What's the matter, Adriana?" Juli asked softly, laying a hand on her shoulder.

A red haze swept over her as her temper finally erupted. "Our two friends seem to be in major bitch mode, that's what," she snapped and shrugged off Juli's comforting gesture.

Juli retreated into herself, which prompted reactions from the other two women. Tori wrapped an arm around Juli's shoulders, while Sylvia complained, "And I suppose you've just been a bucket of joy the last month?"

The barb struck a little too close to home. She had been miserable ever since Riley had told her he planned to marry Becca. "So you think I've been a witch, Sylvia?"

"If the broom fits, ride it." Sylvia mimed the flight with her hands.

Adriana waited for denial from the other two women, but silence greeted her. She glared at Tori as she consoled Juli. "Is that what you think, Tori? And you, Juli?"

"You didn't have to be mean to Juli," Tori advised, returning to her normally mothering mode.

"It's okay—," Juli began.

"No, it's not, Juli. You have to stand up for yourself," Tori said.

"That's right," Sylvia echoed. "You need—"

"For all of you to stop telling me what to do," Juli finally said, shocking all of them into silence. Which gave Juli the perfect opportunity to continue.

Pointing to Sylvia, she said, "You're always going on about men and sex and having fun. But I don't think you have a clue about any of the three."

"And you," Juli said, jabbing her index finger in the air in Tori's direction. "You try to protect me, but I don't need your protection. Other people do."

Juli paused for a second, hesitating as she gazed at Adriana. She leaned her hand on one of the lockers, took a deep breath, and then continued. "You lose your temper too much and bully everyone at the restaurant. And you're being a coward about Riley."

"A coward?" Adriana said calmly, but her voice escalated as she continued. "Funny thing to hear from someone who lacks any kind of backbone. You can't stand up to your mother about being a chef," she replied, her voice hard and with an edge sharp enough to draw blood. "And while we're at it . . . Sylvia. Tori. When's the last time you actually liked what you're doing?"

"What's that supposed to mean?" Tori challenged.

"Yeah," Sylvia chimed in.

She faced Sylvia. "Don't you get started. You won all kinds of journalism awards in college. Now you're busy reporting on what? Who's doing who and where?"

She whirled to face Tori. "You used to help people who really needed help. Now your clientele consists of the Fortunate 500."

Sucking in a quick breath, she immediately continued, unwilling to let anyone break in on her diatribe. After all, witch that she was, why let them have a say? "And Juli. Maybe I am in hypercontrol mode at the restaurant. But if I didn't take control, who would?"

Without waiting for a response, Adriana yanked her gym bag and purse out of the locker, and slammed the locker shut. She glared at her friends. "My broom awaits."

She stalked off, her body trembling and her throat

tight from fighting back her emotions. She hurried until she was on the path through Lummus Park, where she finally swiped her hand across the moisture on her cheeks. She told herself it was just from the heat and humidity of a typical South Beach night, tried to convince herself that what had happened tonight was typical of what friends occasionally did. They fought and behaved badly and then got over it. Especially since they had all agreed that you always took care of your friends since true friends were hard to find.

And true friends knew how to forgive and forget words spoken in anger. But many of the words tossed around that night had had the painful ring of truth, which would make them that much harder to forgive and forget. She dashed yet more tears from her cheeks and made a mental list of things to do.

1. Drop by the restaurant on the way home.
2. Update old PDA entries.

In particular, she probably should remove all entries related to Riley. It had made little sense to have them there in the first place, since she couldn't have forgotten Riley if she wanted to. But now . . .

She wanted to try and forget about Riley.

3. Add new PDA entries.

Maybe if she did that, she might be able to restore some control to her life.

12

Sylvia

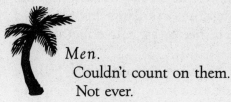Men.

    Couldn't count on them.

    Not ever.

Not one of them.

Not even Gil, as much as Tori would like to think otherwise.

It wasn't that she didn't want her friend to be happy, Sylvia thought as she took a break from the crush of bodies inside the nightclub by taking a step out into the hot and heavy Miami air.

She really did want Tori to be happy, even if it meant that her friend would leave them behind. The problem was that she worried about how Tori had unpredictably rushed things and possibly made a mistake by thinking that Gil was different from most men.

Men couldn't be counted on.

Men were dogs.

Take her Latino Bad Boy Carlos for example. For a

couple of months Carlos had been at every club or event Sylvia could think of. Then they'd had their first little encounter over a month ago.

She had wanted to spark his interest and had definitely succeeded. The next time she'd seen him, a week later, her Bad Boy had made a point of acknowledging her presence by coming over. They'd engaged in some temperature-raising verbal foreplay, not that she'd let him know how he had affected her.

Never let them know you're interested.

Their last time together, nearly two weeks ago, had been more intense. A few drinks and a dance.

A very slow and very sexy dance.

Her body still sprang to life as she recalled how his lean body had moved against hers. How his hand had rested at her side, close to her breast. Close, but surprisingly, not close enough.

He had been teasing her. Starting an itch. She had put an end to it quickly, retreating from the dance floor. She figured that if he was interested he'd follow.

Which he had.

So they had spent the next hour sharing a few drinks, some sexually charged banter, and an occasional touch. She had found him to be not quite what she expected from a Bad Boy, especially one she suspected was involved in the drug trade.

He had been funny.

Sexy.

Kind of sensitive.

Sexy.

She'd thought she'd done just enough to keep him interested. But in the last two weeks, Carlos had been around less and less. In fact, she got the distinct impression that he might actually be avoiding her.

Like tonight.

He was nowhere in sight as Sylvia took a long look down the line of people waiting to enter what she suspected was his favorite club on Collins. She turned and looked up the block to the people coming and going on Ocean Drive.

Not a sign of him, she thought, and wiped her hand across the damp skin at the back of her neck in frustration. Not even having her hair up in an elegant twist helped to battle the unseasonable heat and humidity of an October night.

She was hot.

Frustrated.

And running out of time.

While her editor had approved her going ahead with her investigative report—a meaty piece of journalism unlike what her friends had accused her of at the beginning of the week—she needed to provide Harry with the initial installment for the November issue within the next two weeks.

While she had first-person accounts of the designer drug scene in South Beach and a good number of interviews with patrons, bartenders, and even some club owners about their experiences, she lacked the real meat of the story—the drug dealers themselves.

If she couldn't get that, Harry might push the story back another month. If she was lucky. If not, he might shelve the story totally, which was why Carlos was so important. He could provide her entry into that part of the club culture.

She wasn't sure if he was actually dealing or just closely connected to those who were, but he certainly was in the mix somehow. She couldn't have been that wrong about him.

But then again, maybe she had been. After all, how else could she have actually begun to believe after their last few encounters that the Bad Boy might actually be . . . a nice guy.

As she looked around one last time, disappointment rose up once again. With a tired sigh, she walked back to the door of the club. The bouncer smiled and admitted her, earning a bunch of disgruntled comments from those waiting in line.

She ignored the comments and slipped inside.

The interior of the club was almost as hot and humid as the street. Possibly worse from the acrid smoke and nearly noxious colognes and perfumes being worn by the club's clientele.

Hazard pay. She was definitely eligible for it given the conditions in this club.

Parched and needing something to take the edge off her frustration, she stalked to the bar. Even though it was only Thursday night, people were getting an early start on the weekend and milled around the bar. Sylvia inched forward slowly, endured being jostled and elbowed, but when one man stepped on her new Fendis, she shoved back.

That freed a spot in front of her, and seeing an open bar stool, she quickly hopped up on it to avoid the worst of the crowd. The bartender inclined his head to let her know he had seen her and after, came over. "The usual?"

She shook her head. "Need something stronger. Tequila shooter."

"Trouble in paradise?" someone asked as he sat down beside her, impossibly broad shoulders brushing against hers, invading her personal space.

She shifted away on the stool just a bit and faced the intruder.

Not the Carlos she had been hoping for, but another Latino man. A stranger, although something about him was vaguely familiar. "Can I help you with something?"

He smiled—a cold smile that didn't reach flat empty black eyes. Average height, but heavily muscled. The charcoal gray silk suit he wore fit poorly, straining against his shoulders as did the expensive silk shirt below.

His smile also revealed a platinum tooth which had something engraved on it. As the lights from behind the bar caught the gleaming tooth, it glinted in the dark and she finally saw the writing. *Reaper.*

She didn't want to know how he had earned that street name.

"Heard tell you're the queen of gossip. Heard you needed the 411 on who makes the parties happen around here. Well, that's me. I'm a local celebrity," he said and spread his hands wide to emphasize the point.

The bartender, a young man named Manny who had been kind enough to tell her of his own problems for her story, quickly returned with the shooter. She raised it high in the air, forced a smile at the man beside her, and then quickly downed the drink.

"You heard tell right," she said once the burn of the tequila had stopped. "So you're a—"

"Party planner," he filled in for her smoothly, and with a finger that looked as heavily muscled as the rest of him, he motioned for Manny to bring over another round of drinks.

"Party planner," she repeated and chuckled. More like a bad-ass boy, but she had to admit he had her attention. If Carlos wasn't about to provide her information, maybe this bad-ass could. Not to mention that he had the kind of charm that thugs and gangsters sometimes possessed—Capone charisma.

Not that she would let herself forget for a moment that beneath the ill-fitting but expensive suit lurked menace. It was there in those dark fathomless eyes as he turned them on her once again and asked, "So are you interested?"

It was one of the first real breaks she'd had in her investigation, so she grabbed at it with both hands. Reaper, which was what he preferred to be called, considered himself a luminary of sorts and perfect fodder for one of her stories on men making South Beach rock. He seemed not to have a clue that her report was about something totally different, which was just as well.

Another shooter had him giving her details of how he helped provide some of the entertainment for the various parties around town, but he stopped shy of admitting that he dealt the designer drugs that were all the rage. He wasn't shy about admitting that he provided the women, however. Dozens of beautiful women to please whoever attended.

"If you ever get tired of your day job, I could get you enough work to keep you in that fine clothing you always wear," he said and motioned for Manny to provide yet another round.

"Well, thanks for noticing, Reaper, but I'd rather earn my money off my back."

Reaper leaned close. He smelled of Cuervo and Chanel Allure. Smiling that unnerving platinum-toothed grin, he raised his hand and ran a finger along the swell of her breasts. His touch was cold, making her shiver, but he misinterpreted it for something else. "Or you and me could hook up. I'd be better than that pretty boy Carlos. I've seen you around with him. He can't please you like I can."

She tried to extricate herself from what was already an awkward situation. "Sorry, Reaper, I'm unavailable until my infection clears up."

Stupid is as stupid does, she thought as he quickly ripped his hand away. He shrugged and said, "Well, when you're better, maybe."

He slipped from the stool and tossed a few bills on

the bar to cover their drinks. Leaning close, he said, "We'll definitely see each other around, Sylvia."

She nodded and watched him walk away, then turned back to the bar and waved to Manny to bring another drink, feeling as if she had to wash away the lingering effects of his presence. It took Manny a few minutes to return, for the crowd had gotten larger. More and more people lingered around the bar.

Reaper's stool didn't remain empty for long as someone slipped beside her, but she ignored him, looking toward the door for the ever elusive Carlos in the hopes of getting yet more information for her investigation. But as before, her Latino Bad Boy was nowhere to be found.

When Manny placed the shooter before her, she grabbed it and slugged down her final drink of the night. Slamming the empty shot glass on the bar, she opened her purse and was scrounging around for some cash when she heard a familiar voice from behind her. "Can I get you a refill?"

She didn't give Carlos the courtesy of looking at him. *Payback was a bitch.* "No."

"Really?" A sarcastic note tinged his voice at her refusal. "Don't need me anymore now that you've met my old friend Reaper, or pissed that I didn't take you up on your earlier invitations?"

She finally eyed him directly. Again, she told herself that was definitely a dangerous thing. His eyes were as dark a blue as she remembered and still had those odd flecks of teal and green. They were sparkling with humor at her pique.

"With friends like Reaper, you'd better watch your back. And what offer would that be?"

"If I recall correctly . . ."

He brought his big body barely inches from hers, until he could intimately whisper into her ear, "You're going to fuck me so deliciously slow that I will beg for the pleasure to end, then beg for more."

She gave a strangled cough at just how well he'd remembered, but wouldn't give him the benefit of seeing her surprise. She decided she needed another drink, raised her hand, and signaled Manny for another shooter, but when it arrived, Carlos covered her hand with his.

The pads of his fingers trailed from the back of her hand past her wrist and then up her bare arm. As he slowly ran them up and down the skin exposed by her sleeveless Gucci gown, he said, "What's the matter, Ms. Amenabar? Did your offer come with an expiration date?"

Looking up at him, she battled a surge of attraction. This man was clearly nothing but trouble, no matter how handsome. She only needed one thing from him, and it wasn't a quickie in some back alley. Lifting her chin a defiant notch, she calmly answered, "Let me finish my drink. Then maybe you and I can discuss what I want somewhere a little more private."

His smile broadened, displaying perfectly white and straight teeth. Movie star teeth. As perfect as his haircut and tan and the beautifully tailored and designer clothes he wore on an equally well defined body. Too perfect. Once again she sensed a mix of things underneath that exterior. Something rough and the lingering odor of eau de nice. A decidedly intriguing mix. Something not at all like the vibes she got from his friend Reaper.

In answer to her response, he released his hold on her hand and she slugged down the shot. Placing the glass back on the bar, she reached for her purse and some money, but Carlos was already taking care of her tab.

She didn't need his money, nor could she be bought so easily. She began to protest his actions, but he raised one hand to silence her. "Don't worry, *querida*. Somehow

I know that what you want will cost me much much more than a drink or two."

Slipping off the stool, she indulged herself by passing her hand across the side of his face. "And you would know that because—"

"You're a high-maintenance kind of girl," he answered and trailed behind her as she maneuvered through the crowd and out onto the street. Once on the sidewalk, he grasped her arm to stop her.

She looked over her shoulder at him. "My car's over there," Carlos said and inclined his head toward Ocean Drive.

"That's nice, but my destination is within walking distance." In turn, she inclined her head in the direction of Collins and he shot her a confused look, then shrugged.

Motioning with his hand, he said, "Lead the way."

13

Juliana

Something had to be done, Juliana thought as Adriana grabbed the day's receipts and her notes and stomped to her office to calculate the prices and print the list of the daily specials.

It was what Adriana had done every day since this past Monday's disastrous gathering. This was now the sixth day of the two of them not talking. It had been noticed by one and all in the restaurant. Even the bus-boys were jabbering away about it, worried that if the two *jefas* didn't soon settle their little *problema*, they would quickly be out of work.

She didn't believe in confrontations, she thought as she finished basting the *lechoncito* slow-roasting in the oven for their Sunday night dinner meal.

She closed the door to the oven and walked to her prep table, refusing to acknowledge that maybe, just maybe, she had to be a little more assertive. Which was not necessarily true.

She did stick up for herself.

So you told your mother that you're more than just a dishwasher? she chastised herself.

The argument with her mother was a years-old anguish she had managed to shove onto a back burner until her partner and friend—or maybe better to say partner-for-the-moment and *ex-amiga*—had made that hurtful, but truthful, comment the other night.

She leaned back against the edge of the table and stared toward Adriana's office. She could just avoid Adriana again today, only they couldn't keep this up for a variety of reasons. First, she wasn't angry enough at Adriana to not ever speak to her again. Adriana, as well as Tori and possibly even Sylvia, was just too important to her.

And secondly, she and Adriana had businesses to run. People relied on them for their livelihood. She couldn't allow their fight to jeopardize all that they had accomplished. They had worked too hard to let words spoken in anger destroy it.

So, as much as she hated confrontations, it was definitely time for one. She took a deep breath and then headed in the direction of Adriana's office.

She paused at the door and took another bracing breath before knocking. A muffled "Come in" drifted past the closed door and she charged into the office.

Adriana had been staring at her PDA, but quickly dropped it to her desktop when she walked in. She wore a tank top, shorts, and her bathing suit beneath in anticipation of her Sunday morning beach volleyball game.

Her friend seemed uncertain for a moment after she entered. Adriana was never uncertain, which just pointed out how badly the other night had affected all of them.

But regardless of how Adriana felt, Juli intended to

get it all out in the open. "I'm not weak and I don't lack a backbone. I just don't like fighting with people. And we can't keep on fighting and run our businesses properly."

Adriana leaned back in her chair, placed her elbows on the arms of it, clearly thoughtful for a moment. Then she leaned forward once again and said, "You're right. Completely right."

She looked Adriana over carefully and, after, shook her head as if to clear her ears to make sure she'd heard correctly. "You think I'm right? *Que tengo razon? Sin duda?*"

"Without a doubt. I was angry and hurt over so many things. I lashed out at you with the one thing I knew would hurt you. That wasn't fair. I shouldn't have hurt you just because I was hurting."

She hadn't known what to expect, but certainly not this absolute and total capitulation from her *amiga.* She sat down heavily in the chair before Adriana's desk. "So what do we do about it? About us?"

Adriana shrugged. "I don't mean to be a bitch at work. I'm just trying to do the best job that I can so that we're successful."

"*Lo se,*" she acknowledged since the hard lines of Adriana's body and the tight set to her lips made it clear how difficult it was for her friend to admit to her faults. "And we couldn't have accomplished all this if you hadn't pushed me. If I had to do it all by myself . . ."

Her voice trailed off at the end since she didn't need to finish. They both knew that without Adriana's business skills and determination the restaurant would have floundered by now and the hotel they had just opened would have never been a possibility.

"Don't sell yourself short, Juli. You'd have succeeded. Maybe not as quickly as we did together—"

"And you could have found another chef to share your dream, but you took a chance on me. That counts in my book," she jumped in, and battled the emotions welling up inside her. She loved Adriana, no matter all her faults. She had always been a true friend.

Adriana swiped at one eye and sniffled. "So what do we do?"

"Say I'm sorry and put it behind us, only—"

"Sometimes you can't take back something that hurtful. Especially if there's some truth there," Adriana finished. She rose, came around the desk, and held her arms open.

Juli stood, stepped into her arms, and they embraced.

Then Adriana sat in the chair next to hers. "What is it you want to do here that I've kept you from trying?"

She grasped her hands together, still a little fretful. "Desserts. I think we could really—"

"Who would we need to hire so you can try it out?"

"Just one person. Part-time," she answered, but quickly added, "unless we can't afford it."

Adriana shook her head and held up her hands to emphasize her point. "I'll find a way. If I pitch in with some of the paperwork for the hotel, we can lower our labor costs by cutting back on the temps we've been hiring."

"And where will you find this extra time? You've got a full schedule—"

"I can eliminate my volleyball games with Riley. It's not like they'll be going on for much longer anyway." Adriana didn't look at Juli as she made the statement.

Juli clasped and unclasped her hands together nervously. What she wanted to say was sure to be confrontational, enough to probably cause Adriana to erupt. But it had to be said. "You're a coward. The love of your life is slipping away and you're not only going to let it happen, you're going to facilitate it."

Adriana slashed her hand through the air angrily. "I do not want to discuss this. You got the time for your desserts. How it happens is my problem."

"It's *our* problem. We run this business together."

Adriana jumped out of the seat and faced her, tapping her chest while she spoke. "Riley is *my* problem and I will deal—"

Juli shot out of her chair and stood nose to nose with her friend. "Deal? You're not dealing with it or with your *mami* trying to control your life."

Adriana slapped her hands on her hips and shook her head as if amused. "And I suppose you're dealing with the way your *mami* refuses to accept that you chose to be a chef instead of a teacher?"

For a moment they both stood there, bodies stiff from anger, their breathing uneven with the emotions they tried to contain. And then suddenly, Adriana smiled and dragged a hand through her hair. "We are a sorry pair."

Juli wagged a finger at her friend and partner. "But you're the sorrier part of the pair. Admit it."

Adriana held her hands up in surrender and walked back around to her desk chair, plopped into it, and put her feet up on her desk. "I admit it. So what do I do about it, *amiga?*"

" 'It' being Riley, or your *mami?*" she asked and sat down once more.

Adriana pointed at her with one perfectly manicured finger. "Or your *mami*, remember?"

She chuckled. "I guess it's only fair. Your two problems to my one."

"Nope, to your two. While we haven't talked about it,

we never made time for that shopping we discussed so long ago." When Adriana finished, she grabbed her PDA. "Let's see. I'm free . . . tomorrow night. Are you?"

Taken aback, Juli stammered, "B-b-ut tomorrow's Monday. It's our—"

"Big night with the *amigas*. Do you think either of the other two is ready to talk? I don't know about you, but I haven't heard from either Syl or Tori all week."

No way she was going to hear from their friends before Adriana. In fact, she was probably the last person to hear, which made her sad and not for the first time. "No, I haven't heard from them."

"Then it's a date."

She shook her head. "No, it's not. The trade was, I let you make me all girlie-girl and you do something about Riley."

When she finished, she held her breath, anxiously awaiting Adriana's reaction. It wasn't what she expected.

Her partner slipped out the stylus from her PDA, tapped at the screen. After one final peck, she returned the stylus to its slot with a small flourish. "You are in for Monday night." Then Adriana met her gaze directly, "And as for Riley . . . I am going to feel him out. In a literal way, not in a physical one, much as I would like to feel some very delicious parts of Riley."

"So you *do* like him? It wasn't just our imagination?"

With a sigh and a hushed little laugh, Adriana replied, "I think I've liked him since the day he walked into my father's *bodega*. I was nine. He was older. I figured he didn't have time for a little girl like me."

Juli smiled, and with a knowing look, said, "You're not a *niñita* anymore, *amiga*."

Adriana smiled broadly and, in jest, examined herself

just to confirm her assessment. "No, I most definitely am not. So I will work on the Riley problem."

"And I will work on being less of a fashion victim. But what do we do about our *mamis*?"

With a wave of her hands, Adriana said, "*Chica,* one problem at a time. We're not Wonder Woman, *sabes.*"

14

Tori

Tori *quickly skimmed* through the pages of the *Miami Herald* as she and Gil sat beneath the shade of a large dark green umbrella at a table in front of the News Cafe. It was early still, so the crowds at the restaurant and along Ocean Drive were minimal. Some were older snow birds, power walking along the path in Lummus Park. Sitting around them in the café, a mix of Yucas—young urban Cuban Americans—were reading the papers beside a party crowd that hadn't made it home yet from a night of clubbing. In time, the party-goers would go crash in one of the hotels down the length of the street to sleep off the excesses of the night.

Tori, on the other hand, was wide awake and had just finished her fourth cup of coffee, after devouring one of the restaurant's cholesterol-laden breakfast specials.

After an early good-morning wake-up, she and Gil had decided to grab a bite before going to the beach for some wind surfing and relaxation. She hoped either the good sex, the good food, or some good waves might help take her mind off the fact that she now had no friends, no family, and possibly no work.

The no-family part she had anticipated. But she knew it would not last forever—maybe just until she and Gil celebrated their silver wedding anniversary.

The no-friends part. After nearly a week of having it always in the back of her mind, she still couldn't figure out how she had snapped and caused the equivalent of the worst train wreck ever with her friends.

As for the no-work part . . .

She still felt blindsided by the possibility that she no longer had a job. Well, either her or Gil. It was really up to them to choose who would stay and who would go.

She laid down the paper, grabbed the large white ceramic coffee cup in two hands, and stared across the street to the park, recalling what had happened at last Monday afternoon's partners' meeting.

Gil had joined the firm as a partner six months earlier, while she had been with the firm for over four years and clearly enjoyed the benefits of seniority. But the partners' speech about her seniority had come with a great deal of awkward bluster and commendations about her skills, as well as a lot of anxious coughs from her fellow *male* partners.

Why had she ever deluded herself into thinking that they had really let her into the club?

The no spouses policy had come as a shock since it hadn't been in either of the partnership agreements she and Gil had signed, but rather in some obscure procedure manual resurrected from who knew where. She had almost seen the dust come off the manual the head partner opened while a more junior partner passed around copies taken from the moldy tome.

To the older partners in her firm, marriage and children were the next most logical steps, and a perfect reason for getting rid of her. Children represented a major crimp on billable hours.

"You seem pensive," Gil said and placed his hand over hers.

"Shouldn't I be?" She put down her cup of coffee and slipped her hand into his.

"Let's wait for that second opinion."

"You mean that third opinion, don't you? You and I both looked at our agreements and that stupid manual. It'll be hard to fight. Even if we did and won, why stay where we're not wanted?" She gave an exasperated sigh and shook her head, annoyed with herself for having been so careless.

Gil scooted his chair closer to the table and leaned toward her. "Do you really mean that?"

Did she? Was she really ready to leave a position she had worked so hard to obtain?

Doubt and worry had been lingering in her mind since Monday night and probably had been largely responsible for the fight with her *amigas*. The harsh words from her friends had struck home, painfully reminding her that she had strayed far from her goals. But despite that, she liked the work she did, both for her corporate clients and for those who could not normally afford her services. And thinking about leaving the firm . . .

It had been just too much to comprehend at that moment. Maybe even now.

Shrugging, she looked away as she admitted, "I'm not sure."

Gil cupped her chin and gently forced her to face him. "I know this is about more than what happened at the office. Want to talk about it?"

Amazingly, she did. In a rush of words and emotions, she explained what had happened with her friends. The hurtful words they had exchanged and how she hadn't spoken to any of them since.

When she finished, he embraced her, filling her with more peace than she had ever thought possible. "I'm okay. Really," she offered, her voice husky to her own ears from the tears she suppressed.

Gil's sole response was to tighten his hold on her, and she in turn buried her head in the crook of his neck and allowed herself those tears, heedless of the people around them.

Once she had finished venting her grief and recovered some composure, she pulled away. Gil handed her a napkin to wipe the trails of tears from her face. "Everything will work out."

"How?" She dropped her hands into her lap dejectedly.

Gil grew silent for a moment, and then he said, "Fuck the ol' bastards. Let's both leave."

She reeled as his statement registered. "Leave? And go where?"

"Gonzalez and Rodriguez. Or Rodriguez and Gonzalez, although *G* comes before *R* in the phone book. Of course, since both names are so common that it's kind of like Smith and Smith, maybe we should—"

She silenced him by placing her hand over his mouth, unable to believe him. But knowing Gil, he had been thinking about this for a while, otherwise he would never have said it. Like her, he normally wasn't a spontaneous kind of person. "You're serious."

Beneath the palm of her hand she sensed his smile and it caused her to grin in response. "Really, really serious," she repeated with a laugh and when he nodded, she added, "It would serve the ol' bastards right."

"I saw this building on Collins, right at the corner of Fifth Street. Two brothers just bought it and are almost done fixing it up. There are a few floors available for rent."

He had a gleam in his eyes she hadn't seen in months at the office. "You haven't been happy at the firm?"

"Have you?" When she didn't answer him, he continued. "Being the newbie, I wasn't about to make waves. Plus I had a great fringe benefit, namely having you in my life twenty-four/seven. It made what went on at work less important."

She had been feeling the same way lately and didn't know why neither of them had discussed it. Why had it taken their partners' ultimatum and the fight with her friends to prompt this talk with her newlywed husband, with whom she was supposed to be sharing everything? "I haven't been happy for some time, but the partnership was just too good to pass up. And since you came into my life—everything's changed."

Gil grasped her hand beneath the table and kissed her on the lips. "I hope for the better, *mi amor.*"

She returned his kiss, but whispered against his lips, "Definitely for the better."

In answer, he grasped the back of her head and deepened the kiss until someone walked by, headphones blaring loud enough to be heard, reminding her of where they were.

She broke away from him then, heat rising to her face. She clasped her hands to her cheeks, but smiled sexily at her husband. "So are you game for a walk?"

A puzzled look crossed his features. "A walk? To where?"

"To check out the possible home of our new offices." She rose from the table and held out her hand.

Gil jumped up, took out enough money for the tab and tip from his wallet, then took her hand. Looking down Ocean Drive, he reminded, "We'll have to go right past—"

"We'll walk down Collins," she said, unable to go by Adriana and Juliana's place. At this hour of the morning, they would probably be there prepping for their Sunday meals. She wondered if they were talking, or still fighting.

Whatever they were doing, she wasn't up to seeing them either way.

That would have to wait until . . .

15

Adriana

Adriana and Riley sat on top of the small cement wall that separated the beach and volleyball courts from Lummus Park. The seashells and stones set into the wall scraped the back of Adriana's calves as she swung her legs. A gentle breeze blew in from the ocean, rustling the palm trees, while they waited for the earlier game to finish.

The first set of matches was running late. The mid-morning sun still lacked the bite that would come at noon and she hoped the earlier teams finished soon so she could avoid that stronger sun and heat, and because they had to be at her parents' for one of their usual Sunday get-togethers.

She wondered if Becca would be there and if today would be the day Riley made his announcement.

"So how has everything been?" Riley asked, the ex-cop in him obviously sensing that something was up. The breeze stirred a lock of shaggy blonde hair onto his forehead and he raked back the hair with his large hand.

With a shrug, she said, "I'm surviving."

"Just surviving? That sucks. Anything I can do?" His wide hazel-eyed gaze and innocent look said that he didn't have a clue that any of her problems had to do with him.

She opened her mouth, about to tell him. About to ask him when he planned to propose to Becca or if he had changed his mind. Only, Tom Banks, one of the players on the other team, jumped off the wall and motioned to the beach. "Hey. Court's free. Time to play."

Tom's partner, who happened to be his younger sister, ambled over and slipped her arm around Riley's waist. She was perky and petite, with the shape of a Barbie doll thanks to surgery. Adriana knew it wasn't nature because her boobs barely bounced while she played. She hated that the girl—since she was too young in her book to be called a woman—always made passes at Riley.

"Come on, Riley. Time to enjoy playing with me." As the baby doll spoke, she tugged on the front of Riley's tank top and batted her eyelashes.

Riley didn't get a chance to reply. "He enjoys himself all the time—*with me.*" She grabbed his hand and hauled him onto the court marked off on the sand.

Riley seemed a little too pleased with her pique, but she wanted to make sure his pleasure at her jealousy was short-lived. She took her time easing off her top and then her shorts, exposing the tankini she had on beneath her clothes. While it was way tamer than the thong contraption that Tom's sister barely wore, she hoped it was revealing enough to send both Riley's body and mind into overdrive. The suit exposed all her generous curves and the muscles she worked so hard to keep sculpted.

Riley seemed to be taking a steadying breath as he watched her, so she decided just to push it a little bit further. Just to test if he possessed immunity to her charms.

"Take your clothes . . . I mean, your shirt off. You'll be more comfortable."

Riley nearly choked at her faked Freudian slip, but smiled, although the smile quickly faded. He held the ball to his lean hip, hesitating.

She wished she could see past the dark lenses of the sunglasses he had put on in order to gauge what he was thinking, but the only thing visible was a reflection of the beach and sun and her. She wondered about his hesitation, and then cursed beneath her breath as she remembered his scars. Riley never took his shirt off in public since he'd been shot. How could she have been so senseless and thoughtless to have forgotten?

She grabbed the ball from his hip. Rising on tiptoe to Riley's greater height, she whispered in tones low enough so only he could hear. "I'm sorry. I forgot. You can keep—"

"You've seen what there is to see, so . . . Does it bother you?" he asked softly and laid a hand at her waist as he bent toward her, the gesture so intimate that it made her want to blurt out to him then and there that she didn't want him to marry Becca. That she wanted him to think about whether there were any possibilities for the two of them.

But she couldn't. Instead, she let out a wistful sigh and hoped he didn't notice as she said, "The only thing that bothers me is when you miss the set."

He lowered his sunglasses, exposing his hazel eyes. With a hint of playfulness, his mouth quirked into a smile. "You're a hard woman to understand."

Turning from her before she could say another word, he surprised her by pulling off the shirt and tossing it onto the sand at the edge of the court. When he faced her once more, the muscled expanse of his chest and midsection filled her vision, along with the network of fine white lines and the stellar-shaped scar too close to his heart.

Even though she had seen the scars before, they never failed to remind her how she might have lost him. Forever.

Just like you'll lose him forever if you don't say something, she reminded herself as she stood waiting for Riley on the court.

He came over, took the ball, and backpedaled toward the net. When he set the ball high into the air, she had no choice but to jump into action, tapping the ball over to their opponents, who executed a perfect series of sets and a spike that Riley deftly blocked, earning them the first serve.

"Good to see your mind's on the game," she joked, and her breasts accidentally brushed along his arm as she grabbed the volleyball for the serve. She shuddered at the shock of that contact.

"Or maybe on you," he shot back, his meaning clear and all too confusing when she met his gaze.

This was not "best friend Riley," or was she misreading his comment and signals? she wondered.

She forced her mind to return to the game and motioned to the other team that she would serve. The match began in earnest, only it was difficult to concentrate.

She had always found Riley sexy with his long lanky body and surfer boy looks. For a big man, he moved with easy grace and made even the most difficult of shots seem simple. They had been playing together for so long that she had almost forgotten what a good athlete he was and took the time to admire his abilities. As he saved one point with a diving bump shot and rolled in the sand to get back in place for the spike, she smiled. After the point had been won, she hugged him exuberantly. "That was awesome. Inspired."

He grinned, the hint of his dimple peeking out at her, and he returned her embrace by twirling her around. When he set her down, he whispered, "*You* inspire me. Now let's finish kicking some butt."

They won the next few points handily, taking the first game of the match. Pausing at the sidelines for a short break, Adriana handed him a bottle of water and Riley drizzled some into his mouth and then sprayed his face with a long squirt.

The drops clung to the strands of his shaggy blonde hair and on his face, glittering like diamonds in the sun. A few drops trickled down and landed on his chest. She reached out, smoothed them away, but found herself bringing her hand back once more to pass it over his well-defined muscles. Shooting him a half glance, she detected the tight set of his mouth as he rested his hand over hers.

Leaning close he whispered, "What is this about, Adriana?"

Her throat suddenly tightened. She had to swallow before she could answer. "I'm not sure. All I know is . . ."

The rules be damned, she told herself. She had to test the waters and see if they were as inviting as they appeared. So she made the dive, going up on tiptoe to take his lips in a tentative kiss. Pressing herself to him, she sighed against his mouth as he brought his hands to her waist and slipped them beneath the edge of the tankini top.

The kiss deepened, growing more intimate. She moaned into his mouth, and he took that as a sign and pressed closer.

"Yo, guys. We only have twenty minutes left on the court," Tom called out, and Riley ripped away from her.

"Sorry," he mumbled and handed her the water bottle. He jogged back onto the court, leaving her . . . frustrated, even more confused than she had been before.

That had definitely not been a "best friend Riley" kiss.

She squirted some water into her mouth and tossed the bottle into her bag. There were twenty minutes left to the match and then . . .

What was a girl to do? The only thing she knew to do—consider the facts as she knew them.

1. They were supposed to go to her parents'.
2. Becca would be there.
3. Riley still had to make the announcement.

But there was one last important thing to add to the list.

4. Riley had just kissed her like she was the only woman in the world.

Which, despite her list, left her dealing with her confusion for the next several minutes as they played.

When the game ended, she graciously thanked the opposing team and politely shook Riley's hand before heading to the sidelines. But Riley obviously sensed something hidden behind her deceptively calm exterior.

"Are you going to tell me what's up, or are you going to give me the silent treatment for the rest of the day?" he asked as he slipped on his shirt and watched her toss her things into her bag.

"What was that before?" She motioned back to the court where they had shared that delightful but troubling kiss.

Riley placed his hands on his hips and gazed at a spot in the distance before answering. "A kiss. An amazing kiss. Maybe one that shouldn't have happened."

She crossed her arms and shook her head. "Well, I'm glad that it happened. If I'm sorry about anything, it's that it took so long for it to happen."

Riley's jaw dropped open, but then he snapped it shut, stepped toward her, and placed his hand on her waist again. "You better be sure about this."

She covered his hand with hers, rose on tiptoe, and whispered against his lips, "I've never been more sure about anything in my life."

He smiled and closed the last little bit of distance between them. "Well at least that makes one of us."

16

Sylvia

She leaned back against the car, not yet ready to end the night with him.

When she juggled her keys, he grabbed them to quiet the nervous motion. Looking around the empty parking lot for a moment, he grinned and said, "Seems like we're all alone."

She shot a quick glance around as well and gulped. They certainly were. She had only the briefest of moments to consider if he intended to take her up on her months-old offer when he pinned her against the door of her car and kissed her.

No ordinary kiss.

It curled her toes and she imagined fireworks shooting off. But it was only her heart, crazily beating and bringing a rush of heat throughout her body.

Then she stopped thinking and hearing and wondering and just freed herself to the most amazing of kisses. Tender, but demanding. Forceful. Seeking. Enticing.

She answered him back, opening her mouth for him

to explore. She wasn't sure if she was moaning or he was or who was leaning into who and why he wasn't moving his hands . . .

And then he was, slipping beneath the vee neckline of her dress and lower. That hot and rough palm blazing a trail to cup her—

Sylvia bolted upright in bed, breathing raggedly. Her body throbbing from the dream.

No, not a dream. A nightmare, she thought, since she hadn't been able to get a wink of sleep in days without a replay of Thursday night's parking lot interlude, which had gone no further than his kiss.

No thanks to her.

With the way Carlos kissed . . .

She had been ready to have sex with him on the hood of her BMW. Not a very comfortable place, but then again, comfort had little to do with the way she had been feeling since he'd pulled away and left her wanting more. Left her with an itch that nothing—including everything she had ever learned from either *Cosmo* or *Latina*—had been able to cure.

Her mama was a witch, she thought, and not in a literal sense. She had cursed her and now that curse had come to life. She'd scratched and scratched and couldn't get Carlos out of her mind.

So *not* a good thing.

Not a good thing at all.

He was probably a criminal.

He would likely end up in jail soon, especially if her report caused the kind of stir she hoped it would cause. Which would sure show her fair-weather *amigas* how wrong they were about her journalistic intentions and abilities.

Immediately on the heels of that thought came one about how conjugal visits worked.

She groaned aloud at the fact that she was even think-ing about something so insane and fell back onto pillows damp with sweat from her dream.

There was no way she was going to be able to go back to sleep, she thought, and glanced at the alarm clock, which she never set on the weekends, or for that matter, on most other days of the week.

Both minute and hour hand rested tightly upon each other. As tightly as she and Carlos had been pressed together on Thursday night.

Ño. Noon.

Early, considering that last night's event hadn't broken up until dawn, late by even her standards.

For the rest of the world—the average people, who could only imagine the parties and social gatherings she wrote about—half the day was gone.

Juli would be busy overseeing the kitchen staff as they worked on the brunch orders and prepared the ingredients for the dinner menu.

Adriana would have long finished her morning vol-leyball game with Riley. After, she would either head out for a Sunday gathering with her family and Riley's, or go back to the restaurant to work.

And Tori and Gil? If they weren't visiting Tori's par-ents for either a quick visit or dinner, they might be doing newlywed things. Naughty newlywed things, she hoped.

That was, if things were normal with all of her friends. Which they weren't.

Poor Tori had been basically disowned by her family. For the moment anyway. She didn't think it would last long.

As for her other two friends, Lord help all their poor employees if the war that had started on Monday still raged.

Not that she knew.

Not that she cared, after Monday's debacle and the way they had all behaved rather badly.

But as for apologizing, Lord, it would be a cold day in South Beach before she did that. She didn't need friends who didn't believe in her. Friends who went off and did crazy things like get married without telling anyone. Friends who either just bitched or cowered all the time.

The phone rang and she leaned over to pick it up, but the caller ID said "Not available." She didn't know anyone who was a "Not available."

Except possibly Carlos, who should be "Not available" for a whole bunch of reasons.

Like being a Bad Boy.

Way too sexy.

Decidedly too nice.

She discovered that during their various encounters over the last few weeks.

She answered the phone and tried to ignore the way her body tightened with pleasure as he said, *"Buenos dias,"* in a deliciously husky voice.

"You sound like you had quite a night." She struggled for a neutral tone, but found that she sounded a trifle bit catty to her own ears.

"Jealous?"

She hung up on him, but he called right back. She let it ring a few times and picked up right before the answering machine kicked in. "How'd you get my number anyway?"

"I have my sources. Just like you, Ms. Amenabar."

"Sylvia, unless this is about the story. Is that why you're calling? About the story?" She braced herself to not be disappointed if he said yes.

"No."

Whew, relief.

"And yes," he added, jerking her emotions up and down like a yo-yo.

"So which is it?" she asked as she closed her eyes and slipped her hand down her body, still on edge from her dream. And now here he was, just a voice on the phone and yet . . .

"Carlos." She sighed his name as pleasure reawakened within her as she touched herself.

"Which do you want it to be?" he asked and she couldn't resist the challenge he presented.

"Are you in bed? Because I'm still in bed." *And throbbing because I was thinking about you, and you had to call and make it all that much harder to forget about you.*

A strangled groan came across the other end of the line and Sylvia smiled, pleased that he suffered, too. Before he could say anything else, she pushed him just a little bit further. "Are we having phone sex? And if not, do you want to be having phone sex?" *Because she definitely was.*

A louder groan this time and even more pronounced, as was the sound of a siren in the distance growing closer. A siren very much like the one she heard coming closer and closer in the street outside her apartment. Which quenched her passion like an ice cold bucket of water.

Shit. He's here, she thought, and jumped out of bed and raced to her window, where she looked toward the street. Two stories below, Carlos sat in his car, a perfectly restored blue and white 1962 Corvette.

"I'm sure you've been told that you look beautiful in the morning. Of course, I'm probably the first man to say that who hadn't just slept with you," he said, and she could imagine his grin all the way up in her bedroom.

She jumped back from the window. "How'd you get my address?"

"So, Sylvia," he replied, stressing her name so no doubt lingered that his call was not about her story. "Can you come out and play?"

Common sense told her to say no, but there was something tantalizing about him and not just on a sexual level.

During their last encounter, he had followed her without question to the small corner cafeteria on Collins. Shared a simple meal of Cuban sandwiches along with small talk about all kinds of things, including the fight with her friends. He had even grudgingly given her a maybe about providing information for her investigative report.

At the end of the night, he had walked her to her car and given her that amazing kiss, but nothing more.

Which made him a puzzle she was altogether too interested in solving to pass up his invitation.

"What did you have in mind?" she asked even as she headed to the bathroom for a quick clean-up.

"A spin on my boat."

His boat. A boat that he might use for something other than a Sunday outing.

If she hadn't already made up her mind to go, that would have clinched the decision for the reporter in her.

"I'll be down in a few minutes."

"I'll be waiting."

17

Juliana

The brunch rush was well under way. When it finished in a couple of hours, Juli would be able to take a short break before she'd have to start worrying about the early dinner crowd.

Normally she and Adriana would talk over business things and share a lunch with their staff. Sometimes they would go for a walk in the park just to relax before they had to get back to work.

Since this Sunday Adriana was due at her parents', she was all alone for that break.

All alone again.

She considered going home, but that would waste too much time, and what would she do when she got there? Watching more of her *telenovelas* or one of her DVDs seemed to hold little charm for her today.

Maybe she should check in with her *mami*. It had been too long since she had seen her. Maybe she should try again.

Excusing herself from the kitchen for a few minutes,

she went to Adriana's office and phoned her *mami*. She picked up after the second ring.

"Hello, this is Consuelo."

"*Hola, mami.* It's Juliana."

A moment's hesitation followed before her *mami* said, "*Mi'ja.* Aren't you at work?"

"Just taking a break, *mami. Como estas?*"

"I'm fine, *mi'ja.* I have the day off today."

Annoyance rose up in her. "*Mami,* you should always have off. You're retired, *sabes.*"

Another longer silence came, followed by her *mami*'s sigh. "*Mi'ja,* are you sure you can take this time to talk to me? Is it a problem—"

"I run the kitchen, *mami.* I *own* the kitchen. I am chief chef of *my* kitchen," she replied sharply, but instantly regretted her pique. "*Perdoname.* I didn't mean—"

"*Comprendo.* You have a lot of work. I shouldn't be taking so much of your time. I wouldn't want you to get in trouble."

"*Mami,* that's not it. It's just that—"

She didn't finish as she realized that the line had gone dead. Her *mami* had hung up. The quiet brown kitchen mouse had scurried away so as to not cause her any problems.

Her *mami* just didn't get it. Maybe she never would, Juli thought and headed back to the kitchen.

Only in her kitchen did she know just what to do.

18

Tori

The building wasn't on the corner of Fifth Street. Gil was not very good with directions. More like Sixth, in an eclectic area filled with residential, retail, and offices. The building had definitely been residential in another life. In this life, however, that wasn't quite apparent, except for the Art Deco–looking plaque on the face of the building that identified it as the Flamingo Apartments office complex and a Miami Beach landmark.

Unlike some of the worn-down buildings that lingered along the South Beach streets, this Art Deco wonder had been elegantly and lovingly restored. Not a crack or line marred the exterior stucco, which had been painted a lemon yellow. The façade along the top of the building had an Egyptian feel to it, and at the topmost edge, neon glowed below a railing that hinted that the rooftop might be available for use.

On the modest patch of carefully landscaped garden before the building, a discreet sign said, "Offices for Rent by Owner."

Gorgeous, Tori thought as she glanced at Gil out of the corner of her eye and wondered whether he had been serious about what he had proposed barely an hour ago. "It's nice, Gil. Really nice, only—"

She didn't get to finish as a rental moving truck pulled up at the curb. Two men and a woman spilled out of its cab and onto the sidewalk next to them.

Two nearly identical men, Tori realized as the group looked at them once they realized that she and Gil were examining the building.

"Hi. Matt Martino," said the one man. He was as tall as his twin, but with the more muscular build of a football player or wrestler. "This is my brother, Tony," he added and motioned to the other man as if it wasn't obvious from their features. When the woman with them slipped her hand into Matt's, he introduced her as well. "Jesse Rivera. She's the wonderful architect who did all the work on our building."

Tori and Gil introduced themselves and shook hands with the three.

"So, are you interested in renting?" Matt asked, obviously the more gregarious of the two brothers.

"Possibly," she answered, once again glancing at Gil out of the corner of her eye to try and gauge his reaction.

"If the space and price are right, we may be interested," Gil responded. When Matt held out his arm to invite them into the building, Gil slipped his hand to the small of her back and with a gentle push, urged her to follow Matt.

They all stepped inside into a cooler hallway that was, again, wonderfully done. The palest of pinks graced the walls. Sconces that were either excellent reproductions or carefully restored originals lit the hallway and stairs with soft pools of muted light. The terrazzo floor was a pale yellow shot through with bits of deep maroon and rose-colored marble.

Matt held his arms open wide as he explained. "My brother and I run a marketing firm. We have the whole first floor. Second, third, and fourth floors are free for now. Roof has a small garden area and is a common area available for all tenants. Elevators are at the end of the hallway." He held out the ring of keys with which he had opened the door. "Keys are marked. Feel free to look around for yourselves or I'm sure Jesse would love to show you around. She knows this building better than anyone."

Jesse stepped forward and when neither Tori nor Gil took the keys, she slipped them from Matt's hand. With a smile, she said, "Matt and Tony are just moving in themselves. We got the certificate of occupancy for the building about a week ago."

She motioned in the direction of the stairs, which were at the back of the hall right next to the elevator. The doors to the elevator had a geometric pattern worked into their steel surface, accented by strips of shiny brass. "We restored the doors and interiors of the elevator, but the lift mechanisms are all new."

Jesse opted for the stairs, however, leaning her hand on a steel and brass railing instead of traditional balusters. The railing had a geometric pattern that matched that on the elevator doors.

Tori followed the young woman, Gil behind her, as they toured the space on each floor until they were finally at the top level. Once they finished inspecting that floor, Gil was suddenly All Action Guy.

"I'm going back down to speak to Matt about the price," he said and didn't even wait for her reply as he exited.

Tori hung back, taking another look around the expansive floor, walking slowly from the main area to the offices on either side of the building. "We tried to keep an open feel in here," Jesse said as she remained in the center of the space.

"You did a wonderful job." She paused at the door of one office and looked inside. This one had a window, but most of the view was of the back of one of the hotels on Ocean Drive. The other small bit of view was worth it, though. Lummus Park, the beach and ocean were visible.

"Are you and your husband just starting a business or—"

"I can't really tell you just what we're doing," she jumped in, and walked back to where the other woman stood. "We're kind of in limbo right now. Or maybe I should say, I'm kind of in limbo. What about you? Do you work with Matt and Tony?"

Now that Tori was able to give her attention to something other than Gil and the building, she noticed what an attractive woman Jesse was. Mid-twenties or so. Latina. Jesse was dressed casually, much as she was—low-rise jeans and a cropped tank top that exposed her trim figure.

"That would be a sure recipe for disaster," Jesse answered with a laugh. "Actually, I work for an architectural firm in downtown Miami. I'm trying to make partner, but it's not easy."

Tori let out a harsh sigh and clasped her hands before her. "Don't I know it."

"Just what are you and Gil?" Jesse asked and motioned for Tori to take another look at the office at the front of the building.

As Tori strolled there, she said, "Partners at a law firm in downtown Miami." She mentioned the name of the firm and Jesse seemed surprised. "That's one of the biggest, so why are you—"

"Here?" Tori said and held up her hands. "Because Gil and I eloped—"

"You eloped?" Jesse let out a little hoot of wonder. *"Dios,* how I wish I had the courage to do that. Matt and I . . . We've been together since high school." She shrugged uneasily, jangled the keys, and then added, "I'm not sure just where we're at right now, relationship-wise."

"It's a long time to be together. I wish I could offer some advice, but Gil and I have only been together for about eight months."

Jesse rolled her eyes. "Girl, you move fast, don't you?"

Tori stepped into the office, looked out the window with its views of Collins and beyond, the downtown Miami skyline. A gorgeous view, but nothing like that from the skyscraper in which her firm was located. Her firm, she thought, realizing just what she had been asked to give up, first by the old relic partners, and now by Gil.

"Having second thoughts?" Jesse asked.

When Tori turned around, the younger woman leaned on the door to the office, an inquisitive look on her face. "My whole life I toed the line," Tori said. "Followed the rules my parents laid down for me."

"The whole Cuban gotta-be-successful theme, I imagine. I know it well myself."

Tori sat on the ledge of the window and as she spoke, clicked off each thing on a finger. "Top of my class in high school, college, and law school. Made it into a top firm and worked my *culito* off. Made partner days before hitting thirty. And then along came Gil."

She paused for a moment, took a deep breath before continuing. "What happened with Gil . . . It was spontaneous and rewarding. Fun. Sexy. Ama-a-a-z-z-ing. And right for me. I knew it almost immediately."

"And so you went with it. For the first time."

Tori snapped her fingers. "Like *that,* everything changed. Or maybe it had always been that way and I didn't know it. I started feeling not right at work. My parents drove me crazier than ever. Worse, my friends . . . my friends and I had a big blow-up and aren't talking and—"

"Now you're like most of us mortal women who are sometimes lost and unsure of what they're supposed to be doing with themselves," Jesse said. She stepped up to her and held out her hand for a shake. "Welcome to the real world."

Tori laughed as Jesse had intended and shook Jesse's hand. "*Gracias,* I think."

"So what are you going to do?"

The sounds of the elevator doors opening made her pause for a moment, but as Gil walked into the office, she said, "For the first time in my life, I'm not really sure," and rose to meet her husband.

19
Sylvia

"*Expecting a go-fast*, weren't you?" Carlos asked, referring to the speedboats used by drug runners in the Florida waters and Keys to slip past the Coast Guard.

She hated that he could be so right about her when she couldn't seem to get anything right about him.

His boat was a thirtysomething-foot sailboat, and while she knew little about boats, she couldn't fail to notice it was well kept and clean as a whistle. The fiberglass and brass fittings gleamed with the sun. Everything above deck seemed neatly in order.

Carlos opened a door along the railing and stepped down onto the deck of the boat. He turned to hold out his hand and help her down as well. Once she was settled, he walked forward a few feet, unlocked some kind of hatch to open what appeared to be the cockpit of the ship.

From the deck beneath her feet to the cockpit to the

steps leading to a lower deck, everything was made of teak, which glowed with a warm, rich finish.

Carlos faced her. "You can stow your bag below until we reach our destination."

She grabbed hold of the teak railing and walked down slowly, mindful that even though they were docked, a passing boat might cause some sway. The area below was spacious, with deep navy cushions on a bench that wrapped all around the back and to one side. A large plasma television and sophisticated electronic equipment filled a built-in unit on the opposite side. She tossed her small bag and purse on one bench, and looked toward the front of the boat—a roomy galley and, beyond that, a stateroom.

A huge bed filled the middle of the stateroom and she told herself not to imagine what it might be like if that's where they ended up later in the day and well into the night. Possibly even for breakfast.

Down, girl, she warned herself.

As she climbed back up to the deck, she heard assorted noises from one side of the ship. She assumed Carlos was untying them from their mooring. A moment later there came the even hum of an engine as she reached the deck.

Carlos had slipped on dark sunglasses and sat in the captain's chair. He motioned to another chair beside him in the centrally located cockpit and reached down, closed the door leading below deck. She took the seat and watched as Carlos used motor power to pull the sailboat from its slip and out into the waters of Biscayne Bay. Once they were clear of land and moving along at a steady pace, a little bit of a breeze kicked up. Spindrift occasionally came up over the bow of the boat, refreshing as it landed on her sun-warmed skin.

"Where are we going?" she asked over the noise of the engine and the ocean slapping against the hull.

"Just past the barrier islands, where we'll hopefully get more wind and let out the sails."

She nodded, not that he was really paying any attention to her. His sole concentration right now seemed to be getting them clear of the boat traffic near shore. It was only after they were past one small island that he finally killed the engine and looked at her.

"Have you ever sailed before?"

When she shook her head, he grinned, his smile a bright slash against the darker color of his skin. "Then get ready for the ride of your life."

Standing, he closed up the seat he had been using, jumped up on the deck, and removed the covers on the sails. Slipping the ropes through a winch, he returned to the cockpit and soon had the sails up and in place.

Carlos gripped the wheel tightly as the sails unfurled and caught the first stir of breeze. With a lurch, the boat moved forward slowly, but gradually picked up speed as Carlos tacked back and forth to catch wind in the brightly colored sails.

The wind rushed against her face, more forcefully than before since the boat moved so much faster. The bow dipped into the waves now and again, sending seawater spraying onto the deck and sometimes as far as the cockpit.

She let out a little scream of excitement as one dip sent a rush of ocean water at them and he faced her, his grin even broader than before. The muscles of his arms bunched as he steered. She could stop guessing why his hands were so rough and why he looked so fit. Manning and maintaining this ship would require strength and lots of manual labor.

They sailed back and forth in the bay for what

seemed like only minutes, but when Carlos finally turned them back to shore and a calm slowed the ship, she glanced at her watch and realized they had been at it for well over two hours. Once the sailboat had come to a virtual stop, Carlos lowered the sails and jumped back up onto the deck to stow them away.

"Can I help?" she asked, and when he nodded, she scrambled up beside him.

Patiently, he explained where everything went and how to hitch the sails and ropes into place. Once the sails were covered again, all the ropes secured, and the anchor tossed overboard and set, he asked, "Are you hungry?"

She hadn't eaten a thing since last night. "Famished. Want me to rustle up some food?"

He waved off her offer. "It's all made. But I'll toss up some cushions so we can sit here on the deck and enjoy the day."

With that, he jumped back into the cockpit, undid the door, and almost immediately popped up with the cushions, which he passed to her. After, he went back down and returned with her bag. "Thought you might need this for sunscreen and stuff."

She wanted to ask him if he meant reporter stuff, but didn't want to possibly ruin what had so far been an enjoyable day. From the ride to the marina in Coconut Grove in his vintage Corvette to the sail, he had been courteous and charming. "Thanks," she said and took her bag.

When he left and she heard the sounds of activity in the galley almost directly below her, she grabbed the cushions and laid them up against the glass of the cabin.

She sat down, leaned against the cushions, and waited for him.

Carlos exited onto the deck with food-laden plates

and cutlery in hand, which he passed to her. Then he returned to the galley and a moment later, joined her on the deck, a bottle of wine and glasses in one hand, a basket filled with bread in another.

He sat cross-legged on the cushion beside her and they laid everything out between them.

The plates held a cold lobster salad, perfect for the heat of the day. The wine was white and perfectly chilled. After he filled the glasses, he raised his glass in a toast. "To meeting each other."

She clinked her glass with his and repeated his toast.

Handing him a plate and then taking one for herself, she forked up a bit of the salad. It was delicious and very familiar so she asked, "Where did you get it?"

A blush crept over his cheeks. "Now I know you had a fight with them—"

"Just leave it at that." She wasn't quite ready to talk with him about her friends again. She thought that topic had been exhausted the other night.

"Eventually you will talk to them. You love them. They're your friends."

While he might be right, she would rather discuss him, something they really hadn't gotten to on Thursday or during their ride. Come to think of it, every time she tried to learn more about him, he managed to deftly turn the conversation around until she was talking about herself instead. "So who are *your* friends?"

Carlos shrugged and forked up a little bit of the salad. "Hard to know who your real friends are when—"

"You're a drug dealer?"

He put down the forkful he had been about to eat. "Why do you think that's what I am? What if I was something else?"

"Like what?" she pressed, seriously wanting to know more since she couldn't fight her fascination with him.

Carlos met her gaze, but his eyes weren't visible behind the mirrored shades he wore. It wasn't a surprise when he didn't answer her question and instead asked one of his own. "What kind of information do you need for your story?"

It didn't deter her.

"Do you mind?" she asked as she took hold of the arms of his sunglasses, but didn't wait for his answer to ease them off.

His eyes were that amazing color she remembered and it fit somehow. In this environment, the blue of his eyes perfectly matched the ocean and sky behind him. His skin was barely a shade lighter than the lush teak on his boat. She gently closed his sunglasses, tossed them on the cushions, and brushed back a lock of his thick unruly black hair.

"Why do you do it?"

His eyes hardened, glittering like sapphires, and his lips thinned into a tight line. "Why do you think?"

She shook her head and sighed in frustration. "This is getting us nowhere."

Carlos pursed his lips and said, "You're right. So let's stop playing games."

She arched one eyebrow to stress her point. "Meaning?"

"If I give you the story you're after, will you fuck me?"

She was glad she had gotten rid of his sunglasses. It made it easy to see from his eyes that he was testing her. Pushing her to see how she would respond. But she had only one response to give. "No. Never. *Nunca*. Is that clear enough?"

Carlos smiled and his eyes lost their earlier chill. "Glad to hear that. So what do you want to know?"

She found herself asking not about what she needed for her story, but about him. He had been born in Cuba, but escaped during the Mariel boatlift with his family. The rest of his life had been spent in Miami. After working his way through college, he had tried a variety of jobs until he had finally found his niche in the club scene. It had been easier to do back then during Miami's wilder heyday.

She stopped asking questions then. She suddenly didn't want to know what he had done. How he had come to be what he was today.

"Do you mind if we just . . . take a break?"

"Sure. Get comfortable. Finish the wine." He refilled her empty glass to the very brim with the last of the wine.

"Why, Mr. Carlos," she began, and teasingly adopted her mother's slow Southern drawl. "Do you think a little alcohol will help loosen my inhibitions?" She batted her eyelids dramatically as she finished.

"Maybe," he said with a dimpled grin.

Locking her gaze with his, she beamed him a sexy smile and slowly took off her T-shirt to reveal the top of the tiniest string bikini she owned. Thin straps kept two scraps of black fabric barely covering her breasts. "Maybe," she repeated. "Hurry back. I need someone to oil my back."

The plates and cutlery rattled in his hands and with a gulp, he hurried down to the galley.

Sylvia peeled off her shorts, and then because she wanted to try and shake him up as much as he flustered her, she undid her bikini top and slipped it off.

Pulling the cushions down until they were flat on the deck, she lay on her back to wait for him.

She heard the tread of his sneakered feet coming up the stairs followed by a thunk as he obviously hit something on his way over the railing. Going onto her side and propping her head on her elbow, she looked at him and coyly asked, "Are you okay?"

Carlos rubbed his shin as he sat. "I see you've made yourself comfortable."

Continuing with the coy act, she looked down at her breasts, and then back up at him. "Do you mind?"

He shifted his gaze, which up until then had been fixed on her body, out to sea, and in a strangled voice replied, "Mind? No. You're very beautiful, but I'm sure you've heard that before."

His discomfort struck her as curiously ingenuous. Part of the niceness factor she had noticed in him before. It made her regret playing games with him. Raising her hand, she cupped his cheek and gently urged him to face her. "Not from anyone who mattered," she said, surprised by her own words once she'd uttered them. They were too painfully truthful.

The blue of his eyes darkened. He cradled her cheek as well, stroked the line of her cheekbone tenderly. "*Querida*, how I wish I could do more, but not right now. Not just yet."

His hand trembled and he dropped it to his lap. She kneeled before him and grasped his hand as it lay there. With her other hand she traced the defined edges of his full lips and said, "Then just kiss me for now."

She didn't know if she moved toward him or he toward her. She only knew that suddenly she was in his lap and there was no stopping for even a breath. They just kissed and kissed and then kissed some more until she shook in his arms. But it wasn't enough and even though he seemed reluctant to touch her, she had no such reservations.

She undid the one button on his white guayabera shirt that had kept it closed all day and slipped her hand beneath the fine cotton. His skin was warm and so soft. She inched her hand slowly to his side and encountered a harder ridge of skin followed by something too smooth to be normal.

Pulling away from him, she met his uneasy gaze for only a second before shifting the shirt to the side to reveal the scars along his ribs and lower. He had been shot. At least twice. Two irregular scars—the smoothness she had felt—marred his skin. The ridge began at those imperfections and moved downward, below the waist-band of the board shorts he wore.

She ran her fingers along the scars again, but he grabbed her wrist and pulled her hand away.

"What happened?" The wounds had been serious enough to almost kill him.

His blunt answer explained nothing. "Someone didn't like what I was doing."

"They tried to kill you." An edge of concern colored her voice and she forced herself to regain control.

"This is what's out there. This is what you want to know about," he urged and cupped her cheek.

"It's what I want to stop by writing about it," she explained and laid her hand on his chest, needing to feel the life there, beating beneath her hand.

He covered her hand with his and smiled, but it was a sad smile filled with regret. "The pen being mightier than the sword? I promise that I will give you the infor-mation you need. But I need a little more time. *Por favor,* just believe in me. I'm not what I seem."

She nodded, even though in her heart she knew she couldn't back down with her story. But she would be careful, she thought as she crawled into his lap and let him hold her, because she couldn't bear to think about doing anything that might hurt him.

They sat on the deck, wrapped close together as the sun dipped lower in the horizon. Eventually, Carlos excused himself to start the motor back up and return to the marina. She watched him go, but stayed where she was, needing the distance from him. She had to restore some order to her emotions since her Bad Boy seemed to have so much more depth and integrity than she had ever expected.

He was a surprise and she didn't quite know how to handle him.

20

Adriana

After the volleyball game, Riley and Adriana returned to the restaurant only long enough for her to make sure Juli didn't need help and grab her purse.

Normally, she would have driven herself to whichever parents were hosting the Sunday-night gathering, but Riley had offered to give her a lift and, after, bring her home. Considering their too brief kisses at the beach, she loathed to leave him.

But Becca was probably meeting him there, her conscience reminded. Becca. His soon-to-be fiancée. But he had kissed her. Adriana. Not once, but twice. And they hadn't been brotherly peck-on-the-cheek kisses.

She wished she had stopped to tell Juli, but her partner had been busy in the kitchen when they had popped into the restaurant. She itched to grab her cell phone and dial Tori, ask her what would be the right thing to do. Then she realized that if she wanted to know about what to do to make a man notice you, the person to call would be Sylvia. Sylvia would know what to do.

But she couldn't call either Tori or Sylvia. They were still not talking to one another.

"You okay?" Riley asked and grabbed hold of her hand.

"*Sí*, I'm just . . . Thanks for driving me." *Lame, Adriana. Totally Lame.*

"I'm headed back this way later. It's silly to take two cars," he answered.

"Will Becca mind? I mean, the two of you—"

"Becca won't mind."

Becca won't mind, she repeated in her mind. Was it because Becca thought Riley was so in love with her that he wouldn't think of another woman?

But he'd kissed me twice.

She glanced at him as they drove. A strong breeze swept through the T-top of the Viper, ruffling the longish strands of his blonde hair as they drove along the causeway and headed to her parents' home in Coral Gables. She wanted to brush back that hair, smooth it into place.

A girlfriend would do that. Only she wasn't his girlfriend. She wasn't quite sure what she was since they'd been friends for so long, only . . .

Riley had kissed her. Twice.

She sighed and dragged a hand through her own hair, holding it in place from the wind as Sylvia's favorite adage came to mind.

Men are dogs.

Which meant that maybe she had read just way too much into why Riley had behaved the way he had today. Maybe Riley was a dog as well and she had made herself available. So maybe Becca had nothing to worry about except that she was marrying a man who was being unfaithful to her even before the wedding.

Only Riley had not asked Becca to marry him yet.

And he had kissed her. And she was a total idiot for putting so much emphasis on two simple but not quite chaste kisses.

She forced herself to forget about them and instead worried about whether her ever-observant mother would notice that something might be up. Because if she did think her daughter was up to anything that wasn't by the book, Adriana would surely hear from her *mami*. That was the last thing she needed at the moment.

As she had told Juli earlier in the day, one problem at a time. Her *mami* was a problem she didn't want to deal with today.

Taking a few deep steadying breaths, she girded herself for the upcoming visit and thought she was ready for it as they pulled into the driveway of her parents' home, which was located near the famed Venetian Pool. Her parents had renovated a slightly run-down and typical Miami home into a Mediterranean palace.

The money for the transformation had come from the import/export business that her parents and Riley's parents had founded nearly twenty years ago. They had built that business into one of the nation's largest Hispanic food distributors. Riley had joined the business a few years ago after being shot while on the job as an undercover detective. Her parents had expected her to join the business once she'd finished her MBA, shortly after Riley's shooting.

Only she hadn't.

She had followed her own path. Her *mami* had never really forgiven her. One problem at a time, she reminded herself, and with another deep breath, slipped from Riley's car and waited for him as he came around from the driver's side, his hair wildly windblown. She gave in to her earlier yearning and ran her fingers through its thickness to straighten it out.

In return, he smiled, bent, and pinned her against the side of the car with a kiss that made her nearly light-headed and had her straining up on her tiptoes to answer it.

Until there came a cough, and then another, a little more loudly, before she heard her *mami* call out, *"Mi'ja.* I thought I heard a car."

Riley jumped back from her.

Heat erupted across her cheeks. Leaning her head against Riley's chest, she murmured, "I'm doomed."

Things went downhill from the initial debacle at the front door.

As they sat down for the meal, Riley's mom asked whether Becca was joining them.

Riley stammered an excuse about Becca having to work, finishing with, "You know how these modern women are."

Her *mami* jumped on that comment first. "Really, *mi'jo?* And how is that? I'm sure my working-woman daughter would love to know."

Forks clattered to plates or stilled in midair.

Riley's jaw worked up and down a few times as he struggled with an answer. Finally he blurted out, "You know, always working with no time left for anything else."

Meaning, in manspeak, with no time left for me, Adriana thought, but didn't say a thing. She didn't have to—her *mami* did.

"De verdad? Is that how your mother and I were? With no time for our families?" she challenged, and Riley's mother chimed in with, "Becca always seems to have time for you."

Riley's jaw clenched tightly and a nervous tic began in one muscle as he struggled for a response, but his dad jumped into the fray, sparing him.

"Leave the boy alone, Gladys. Can't you see he doesn't want to talk about his fiancée," he said. "She still is your fiancée, right?"

"Bill, please. If I remember correctly, Riley hadn't quite gotten around to asking her. Isn't that true?" While his mother said it in an innocent tone, the look she exchanged with Adriana's *mami* spoke volumes—clearly this had been a much discussed item between the two women.

When her *mami* met her gaze from across the width of the table, Adriana knew she had to jump in and save Riley. Poor little thing didn't stand a chance with both mothers plotting against him.

"Riley was nice enough to drive me here today after we absolutely creamed the team we were playing against. *Papi,* you should have seen the game," she said, which prompted her father to ask all kinds of questions, volleyball being his favorite game after dominoes. In Cuba, he had played on a club team and a few of their members had participated on the Cuban Pan-American squad B.C.—Before Castro.

Everything good in Cuba had always been Before Castro, she thought and steered her father toward that topic, which did what she wanted—kept them all talking about politics and other things and not about Riley and Becca.

Or Riley and her.

Although she knew that once the men left to share some cigars and brandy and she went with the *mamis,* the topic was sure to arise as sure as the sun would set.

So since she wasn't driving and needed the Dutch courage, she had more than one of her *papi*'s wonderful daiquiris, let herself enjoy not just the food, but the pleasure of Riley sitting beside her. Especially when he slipped his hand into hers and smiled gratefully for rescuing him.

She was, therefore, feeling quite able to handle anything as the *mamis* asked her to help them clean up. She did and found herself corralled into the kitchen for the equivalent of the Spanish Inquisition.

Her *mami* plopped her into a chair, stepped away, and returned with a cup of Cuban coffee. "Drink. After, we want to know what's happening with Riley and Becca."

"Riley and Becca? *Ño*, how am I supposed to know what's happening with Riley and Becca. I don't even know what's happening with Riley and me."

Adriana hiccuped and covered her mouth with her hand. *Maybe she'd had one too many of her* papi's *daiquiris.*

"You and Riley. So that wasn't some kind of . . . accidental thing I saw at the door?" her *mami* asked, circling her finger around to hint that she needed more information.

Riley's mom, Gladys, piped in with, "An accident? Did you fall, dearie?"

Adriana waved her hands for them to stop. "Yes, I accidentally fell and landed on Riley's lips."

"Well, it's about time," her *mami* said, shocking her into silence.

"It definitely is, don't you think, Carmen?" Gladys confirmed with a nod of her head.

"B-b-but, Riley's engaged," Adriana said out loud, their unexpected responses making her play devil's advocate.

"He hasn't asked Becca to marry him. If you want my opinion, he's not ever going to," Gladys said and glanced at her *mami*, who nodded in agreement.

"So why did he tell us that he was going to?" Adriana asked.

Both *mamis* looked at her as if she had two heads.

Her mother wagged her head in chastisement. "I thought I had raised an intelligent girl. One who went after what she wanted."

"She's just confused, Carmen. She doesn't know men as well as we do," Gladys said, reaching out and laying a comforting hand on Adriana's *mami*'s shoulder.

"Men are dogs. He's going to ask her to marry him, but he's busy kissing me."

In a strategic move so smooth a four-star general would have been impressed, she suddenly found herself flanked on either side by one of the *mamis*.

"*Hija*," her mother began as she slipped her arm around Adriana's shoulders. "Riley hasn't asked her because he realized he didn't love her."

"He loves *you*, Adriana. He has since he was a little boy," Gladys offered, to try and comfort her.

"You're saying this because for as long as I can remember both of you—"

"Have wanted you and Riley together," Gladys interrupted, and laid a hand over Adriana's as it rested on the tabletop. "You're like a daughter already."

She looked up and met her mother's gaze. "*Mami*? Do you want that as well?"

The look on her mother's face seemed pensive. With one hand, she brushed back Adriana's hair from her face. "*Hija*. All I've ever wanted is for you to be happy."

"What if it doesn't work out? I not only wreck Riley's chances with Becca, I'll lose one of the very best friends that I have." She hated to hear the whine in her voice. Whining was a sign of weakness and she wasn't weak. Confused maybe, but not weak.

"If Riley was your husband, would you let him run around with a beautiful young woman? Do you think he will stay your friend for long, *mi'ja*?" her mother urged.

Adriana couldn't deny what she had already thought on her own. Before she could say anything else, however, her mother said, "Go after him, Adriana."

"But *mami*—"

"*Go after him.* I've always been proud that you've never been afraid of a challenge, so don't disappoint me now."

Riley pulled up in front of her condo, but Adriana didn't want their time together to end. Plus she had the comments of the two *mamis* still ringing in her ears. "Would you like to come up for some coffee?"

He grinned and nodded, as if aware that it was about more than coffee. "Coffee? Sure. That sounds great."

He wheeled the car to a free spot in the lot, parked, and then they both went up to her apartment.

Once they were inside, she turned to him to ask what kind of coffee he wanted, only the look on his face said coffee was the last thing on his mind. "Riley, we need to talk," she said as he placed his hand on her waist and drew her close, clearly intending to kiss her.

Riley looked down at her from his much greater height and grinned. "Talk? Adriana, do you realize how long it's been since the day I walked into your father's *bodega* and first saw you?"

Dios mio, she couldn't believe that he remembered that day, but was incredibly pleased that he did. "Twenty years, Riley. It's been twenty years."

His smile grew even broader and he bent his head, brought his lips to brush against hers. "Twenty years of talking," he said as he began a lazy exploration of her lips with his.

"Hmm. *Sí.* Twenty, but—"

He silenced her by deepening the kiss, forcing her to respond. Bringing her close by encircling her waist with his strong arm until she pressed tight against him.

"Riley," she said, but his name was part protest and part plea for more.

"After twenty years, it's time we put our lips to better use, don't you think?" he asked as he broke apart from her for just a second.

Her head whirled and her body screamed that this was what she'd wanted since she'd gotten old enough to realize that the funny little kick her stomach did every time she saw Riley was something special. So it was a little hard to say no to him. She was still uncertain about that path on which they were embarking.

"Are we crazy to do this?" she asked, although she didn't stop kissing him as she said it, slipped her arms up around his neck, and crushed herself to his wonderfully hard body.

"Would it be crazier for us to not find out? To spend the rest of our lives wondering?"

"Yes," she answered without hesitation.

"That's what I thought," he said. He scooped her up in his arms and walked to her bedroom.

21

Juliana

Like the quiet little mouse her mother had raised her to be, Juli watched and didn't say a thing.

She didn't say a thing on Sunday when she noticed Riley pick up Adriana for their morning volleyball game. Didn't say a thing when Adriana left with Riley; and now, in the bright sunny light of a Monday morning, she observed quietly as Riley and Adriana stood on the sidewalk in front of the restaurant, locked in a more than friendly embrace.

She'd done it, Juli thought. She had gone and tested the waters with Riley. Adriana had gotten lucky just as Tori had gotten lucky. About time, considering how long Adriana had known Riley.

With a smile, she walked back into the kitchen to finish up the morning preparations. As she did every morning, she instructed the two sous chefs and their assistants on what to get ready and how, finalized the list of the daily specials, and gathered the receipts for Adriana's review.

Adriana. She hadn't come into the kitchen yet. Juli wondered if her partner remained lip-locked out front with Riley, with whom she had clearly spent the night. Juli was certain that Riley wore the same clothes she had seen him in yesterday morning.

Which meant that Adriana had probably not done her regular morning jog with Tori—not that Juli had been expecting that she would anyway. The two women had not done their jog since the blow-up last week. She grinned. That explained why Adriana had so much extra energy for Riley this morning.

She had barely finished that thought when her partner breezed into the kitchen, a broad smile on her face.

Only Adriana normally didn't "breeze." She hurried, strode, occasionally stalked, but never ever breezed. And she went right to the coffee machine, where she cheerily called out, "How is everyone this morning?" as she prepared two coffees.

Sylvia would say their friend had been cock-tamed, but Juli preferred to think Adriana had found love. Or at a minimum, very serious *like.* Definitely lust.

"Buenos dias, amiga," Juli said as Adriana breezed over and placed a cafe con leche before her on the prep table. "I can see that it was a—"

"Very good morning. An amazingly incredible morning," Adriana said with a smile before taking a sip of her coffee. "Hmm, this is really good. Really, really good."

Juli shook her head and chuckled. "It's the same as it is every morning, only . . ." She paused and leaned closer to Adriana, who also shifted near. In low tones, and with a little bit of a giggle, she said, "It's because of the sensual overload from spending the morning making love. At least I'm assuming that's what you did."

Adriana held up her hand to confirm it. "Guilty as charged. It was . . . marvelous. Extraordinary. I wish he hadn't just left for work because if I could, I'd start all over again."

Juli experienced the joy in her friend's smile, and then reality brought her crashing back to earth. Selfish and painful reality. With this sudden change, Adriana would not want to spend less time with Riley. Which meant that the plans they had made yesterday to allow her to experiment with her desserts would likely fall by the wayside.

"Oh, no. Don't even think it," Adriana said as she realized what Juli was worrying about. She wagged a finger in her face to stress her point. "You and I had an agreement. More than one if I remember correctly. First, we're going shopping tonight."

That took Juli back for a second. "You mean to tell me you're not going to call Tori and Sylvia for tonight? Tell them everything about you and Riley?"

Adriana wrapped her hands around her large mug of coffee and hesitated. When she spoke, some of her earlier vivaciousness had fled, and Juli regretted being the cause of it. "I'm sorry—"

"No, you're right. Normally, that's exactly what I'd do. Only . . ."

Adriana nervously clasped and unclasped the mug for a second. "First, I made you a promise and I mean to keep it. Second, I'm still pissed at them. And last, but maybe more importantly, I'm not really sure of what's happening with Riley."

"You're sleeping with him, but you're not sure?" Juli asked, the old-fashioned girl in her reacting out of habit.

"*Ay,* Juli. It's complicated, you know," Adriana said with a bit of wistfulness in her voice.

"*No se, sabes.* Men and me—unmixy things."

Adriana chuckled as she repeated her words from the other day. "No longer, *amiga.* Not after tonight."

"Why? Do you think playing fairy godmother will turn me into a beautiful woman?" Juli said with a sharp snap of her fingers.

Adriana brushed back a lock of Juli's hair that had escaped the ponytail she usually wore in the kitchen. "You already are a beautiful woman, both inside and out. You just need a little help with the packaging because a lot of men just can't see past the brown paper wrapping to the wonderful gift that lies beneath."

Adriana's words brought tears to Juli's eyes. She eased around the corner of the table and enthusiastically embraced her friend. Her friend forever, she thought, harsh words aside. Earlier fights forgotten. After all, that was what friends did sometimes. They fought and they bitched, but true friends got over it. Even grew stronger afterward.

"Tonight, then," she said as she finally released Adriana, reached for the receipts, and tried to get back into the routine of the day. Which they did, going over all the specials and pricing them. But when they were done, Adriana looked up from the list and said, "When do you plan on looking for a chef to help out so you can tackle the desserts?"

For yet another time that day, she was surprised. "I thought we might not be doing that with you and Riley—"

"Spending time together? You're right to think that I don't want to lose time with him, which had me thinking . . ."

Juli waited anxiously for Adriana's next words.

"*Mami* and I had an interesting talk on Sunday. After she realized Riley and I were maybe interested in one another."

"A real talk. Where you talked and she—"

"Listened. Really listened and, granted, pushed a little for me—"

"To leave Riley alone, right?" She couldn't imagine that Adriana's very controlling mother would approve of Adriana doing anything like possibly breaking up Riley's engagement.

Although, could it be an engagement if Riley had never asked Becca to marry him?

"No, like telling me to go for it."

" 'It' being—"

"Riley. She said I was intelligent and she was proud of how I went after what I wanted. We talked some more and I was thinking—*Mami* has nothing to do now that she's 'retired.' " She mimicked little quotation marks as she said "retired" because they both knew that her mother occasionally dropped by the business founded by all the parents to make sure things still ran smoothly.

"Am I following this right, because the logic sure appears to be *un poquito* circular."

"*Mami* has too much time on her hands to think about things, thing number one right now being me and Riley. I need time for Riley. *Mami* is a great organizer and knows how to run a business backward and forward. For some reason, she's suddenly mellowed, so—I want to ask *Mami* to help us."

Juli plopped down heavily on her stool and searched her friend's face to see if she was joking, but it became obvious that Adriana was totally serious. "You want to let your *mami*—"

"Help out in the hotel. *Mami* will be glad I asked. We'd save money on the temps and be able to get you help. You'll have time for your desserts, and I get time with Riley."

"And if it doesn't work? How will you deal with your *mami*?" Juli asked, but laughed as Adriana rolled her eyes. Her friend had been battling with her mother for years. How much worse could it get?

On the other hand, if it actually worked, it could make things much better, and not just businesswise. Maybe Adriana and her *mami* would finally learn how to get along. Be able to talk to each other.

She had often regretted that she and her own mother had drifted so far apart. Sunday's call had just confirmed how they could no longer talk. She wished she could change that and bring them close once more, the way they had been when she was a child.

Realizing Adriana's plan might just be something workable, she asked, "So do you think I should start with some kind of flan, or pastry?"

22

Tori

Tori stood at the window of her office, staring out at the unobstructed view of Biscayne Bay, admiring the cerulean of the sea that almost melded into the bright blue expanse of a cloudless afternoon sky.

So clean. Tidy. As her life had been before. Before Gil. Before last Monday's partners' meeting and the fight with her friends.

Her friends. How she itched to pick up the phone and call. Adriana would dissect the problem and give her a myriad of answers. Sylvia would urge her to tell the ol' bastards, "Fuck off."

With a smile she remembered the call from Sylvia a little over a month ago when she had bluffed her editor into assigning her an investigative report.

An investigative report.

Guilt welled up inside that she hadn't come to Sylvia's defense during Adriana's tirade a week ago, but then again, Sylvia didn't need anyone defending her. She did a good job of that herself, only . . .

Sylvia hid behind that self-confident façade. Much as Adriana did. Much as she had done pre-Gil. The only one of them truly open with most people was Juli. Juli, who couldn't see her own self-worth because she had yet to get over disappointing her mother.

Tori crossed her arms and wondered if her parents would be disappointed if she walked away from this partnership. Would they even care? she asked herself.

But the answer that came to her was the same one that had come to her over and over again since Gil had dropped his bombshell yesterday morning.

Her friends. Her family. Gil. They all wanted only one thing for her—that she be happy.

As she gazed at the vast expanse of the bay visible from her window, she wondered why she had taken cases she didn't want to handle while turning away others worth battling over.

Although the comment had stung, Adriana hadn't been all that far off the mark when she'd said that lately her clientele consisted mostly of the Fortunate 500.

She wondered why it had taken the ultimatum dropped on them last week and Gil's subsequent bombshell to make her realize how unhappy she had been and how her "colleagues" would never really let her into their club.

And why she suddenly didn't give a shit that they hadn't.

In the scheme of things, she had done what she wanted—she had made partner.

Now it was truly time to take charge of her life.

A new horizon loomed before her. Another journey to be started.

Only this time, she wouldn't be making the journey alone. She had Gil now. Eventually her family would get over their snit about the elopement.

Maybe even her friends again. Once they had all thought about the unkind but truthful comments they had lashed out with in anger, they would make up. True friends couldn't stay angry forever.

A knock at the door broke her from her reverie. "Come in," she called out and Gil walked in, hesitant. He waited by the door, but she smiled and held out her hand to him.

"Are *you* ready?" He slipped his hand into hers.

"Have *you* made up your mind? Do you know what you want to do?" He searched her face, looking for her answer.

A smile and a kiss provided it.

23

Sylvia

She'd slept with him.

"Slept" in the real sense.

Not in the we-had-mind-blowing, mattress-denting-sex sense.

But rather, the spooned-tightly-together, spend-the-night-kissing-and-talking sense.

They had kissed so often her lips were sore, she realized as she ran a hand across them. It started a tug deep inside her.

Sweet Lord, she was ready to hump a doorknob and didn't have a clue why she hadn't had her way with Carlos last night.

Maybe because he wouldn't let you? her conscience reminded.

She stopped doodling on the pad before her and grimaced as she saw that she'd written his name over and over again. Outlined it and done little curlicues.

Sweet Jesus, what was she? In grade school?

"Got something for me, Sylvia?" her editor said, his

balding head poking around the edge of her cubicle before the rest of his rotund body followed.

"I've made . . . progress with my contact."

" 'Progress' being a euphemism for 'slept with him,' I'm gathering." He backed up that statement with a leer.

"You're a pig, Harry. Do you know that?"

"You were the one who said no straight man could resist you. What am I supposed to think?"

Unfortunately, she had no argument for that. He'd trapped her quite effectively with her own words. Outrageous words used to bolster her place in the world, defend her worth, only they had backfired on her in much the same way that her outrageousness had failed to gain any ground with Carlos.

Probably because he saw right through that defense.

She rose, shuffled some papers on her desk until she located the ones she wanted, and handed Harry the first part of her story, hoping it would be enough. "You're supposed to think that this is brilliant and put it in next month's magazine. Part two will be ready for the following month." That would hopefully give Carlos the time for which he'd asked. Also give her some breathing room before Harry started pressing for the second part of the article—the one Carlos had a major hand in providing. Reaper's contribution had been only a small part, which she had already included in part one.

Without waiting to see what Harry would say, she glided out of her cubicle and headed to the coffee machine, needing the boost to keep her going until tonight.

Tonight being the night she normally went out with her friends, but she suspected that wouldn't be happening this particular Monday night.

Which left her with nothing to do. A very rare occur-rence.

Hitting the buttons on the coffee machine, she thought about her plans for the rest of the day. She had checked the calendar of events and except for the opening of a new show at the Bass Museum, her day would be pretty light.

As for tonight, she could head out to the clubs, but on Monday nights, the crowds were generally nonexistent, so she usually avoided them. She wondered whether Carlos did the same. Was business slow for him as well?

If he avoided the clubs also, maybe they could have dinner. Share some time as they had yesterday.

Except, of course, for one big problem—other than knowing where his boat was in Coconut Grove, she didn't have a clue how to reach him.

The beep of the machine alerted her to the fact that her coffee was brewed and waiting for her. She added a ton of milk and four spoons of sugar, hoping to drown the institutional taste of the brew. Taking a sip, she realized her efforts were futile. It still tasted as bitter as something designed for removing paint.

After pouring it down the drain—where in retrospect it actually might do some good—she returned to her cubicle, made a call so a photographer would meet her at the Bass Museum later that day, and then left for South Beach, where she was guaranteed an excellent cup of coffee.

David's was a small cafeteria on the corner of Collins, a block away from Ocean Drive and the Versace mansion. One section of David's consisted of an old-style lunch counter. She and Carlos had shared their first meal there. The other part of the restaurant was mostly kitchen, with a half wall and counter open to the outdoors. Day in and day out locals stopped by to pick up Cuban coffees and sandwiches.

She had a craving for something Cuban, she thought as she wheeled her BMW into an open spot just a few doors down from David's. Of course, the craving wasn't for food, but she'd make do before heading to the museum.

As she rounded the corner onto Collins, someone came barreling around the same corner headed for the outdoor counter. Hard hands grabbed her as they collided. She knew who it was even before she looked up. "Carlos."

"Sylvia. What are you doing here?"

She smiled up at him, for even with her height and heels, Carlos was still a few inches taller. He was dressed casually today, in jeans and a form-fitting T-shirt that showed off the sculpted muscles of his chest and arms. She looked him up and down and said, "I had a craving."

He bit his lower lip before smiling. "Something Cuban, I hope?"

"Of course, but weren't you going somewhere?"

Carlos held his arm out and she slipped her arm into his as he said, "It can wait."

24

Adriana

Adriana hovered in the background as her hairstylist, Andre, listened to Juli's list of requirements.

"I need to be able to keep it out of the way while I cook. And not too short, because it makes my face look way fat."

Andre picked up the thick strands of Juli's long black hair with some disdain and tsked as he walked all around her while Juli continued with her prattle.

"And easy to take care of because I don't want to be fixing it all the time."

Andre finally stopped directly before Juli and with one slash of his perfectly manicured and buffed nails, silenced her. "*Basta.* Do I tell you how to cook?"

At a shake of Juli's head, he said, "So do not tell me how to cut hair."

Adriana covered her mouth with her hand to hide her amusement. As Juli gazed into the mirror and met her gaze, she shrugged as if to say, "Temperamental artists. What can you do?"

With another wave, the hairdresser motioned for Adriana to go away while he did his work.

The almost frightened look on Juli's face nearly made her change her mind about leaving, but Juli had to take this first step. It had occurred to her that afternoon that a few new outfits alone wouldn't do it. Juli needed a complete change. Something that would make her see herself in a totally different light. A new hairstyle was just the thing.

So she'd begged a favor of Andre and he had snuck Juli into the last slot for the night.

So here they were, with a nearly petrified Juli about to be clipped and primped to within an inch of her life.

Adriana wanted to stand right there, to make sure Juli was all right, but Juli's words to Tori from the week before came flashing back. *"You try to protect me, but I don't need your protection."*

So she backed away, ready to trust that Juli could take care of herself.

She grabbed one magazine and then another, skimming through the pages but not really seeing anything since she was too busy trying to get a glimpse of what Andre was doing to her friend. Impossible to do so, as Andre constantly moved around Juli, snipping away with his scissors and razor. The only thing Adriana could see was the growing pile of jet black hair on the clean white floor tiles.

She cringed and thought back to all the years she had known Juli. In all that time, Juli's hairstyle had always been the same—a long thick curtain of hair hanging down to midback. When she was in the kitchen or working out, Juli wore it tied back in a ponytail. The rest of the time it flowed down the middle of her back, almost like a living, breathing part of her.

Biting her lower lip, Adriana wondered if maybe she hadn't made a big mistake. Maybe this would be a little too much for Juli to handle right now, what with all the other changes going on. The whine of the hair dryer pulled her attention to her friend, only now she could see absolutely nothing.

Andre's back hid what was going on. In one hand he held a round brush, which he worked through Juli's hair while he dried it with the blow-dryer in the other. Over and over he worked the brush, and then he shut off the dryer and stepped away.

Unable to contain herself any longer, Adriana tossed the magazine down and walked over to stand behind her friend.

She experienced a moment of shock and almost did a double take to check it was Juli because she looked so . . . beautiful. Gone was the plain brown wrapping, at least hairwise.

Andre had pruned away years of hair, but a rich mass of it still hung down to just below Juli's shoulders. Certainly long enough so Juli could still pin it up or French braid it if she wanted. Blue-black highlights glinted in her hair from the salon lights. Andre must have treated it somehow since Juli's hair glistened with rich color.

As long as the hair was, Andre had cut in layers all along Juli's head as well as some wispy bangs in the front. They framed Juli's exotic, almond-shaped brown eyes and accented the higher slant of her cheekbones and the sharp, perfect slash of her nose. And her lips. Even without lipstick, the way the wisps of hair curled in at her jaw made her face appear thinner and brought out Juli's full lips. "You're gorgeous."

Adriana said it with awe and Andre chimed in with, "I am the best, am I not?"

"*Sí.* You are," Juli replied a little breathlessly as she used the mirror Andre had provided to check out the hairstyle. With her free hand, she touched the strands, almost as if not believing it was truly real. Then she smiled. A broad smile filled with . . .

Adriana didn't know just what emotion graced Juli's smile, but she was radiant. As Juli thanked Andre and rose from the chair, a new attitude filled her posture.

"Ready to go shopping?" Juli held out her hand to Adriana.

Adriana grabbed hold of Juli's hand and walked beside her to the register, where Juli whipped out her card and paid the bill, including a handsome tip for Andre. When she was done, she looked at Adriana for guidance. "Where to?"

Glancing at her watch, Adriana said, "We can't make Bal Harbour, but there's a few shops within walking distance on Collins."

"I'm game," Juli replied, and it was clear from the spring in her step that she truly was.

They hurried up Collins until they reached Armani Exchange. A possible place for some casual things, Adriana thought, but she worried about sizes. If things were cut too small, she might be hard-pressed to find anything that would fit Juli's generous, size twelve body. If that happened, it would undo all the good from the haircut.

That made her take a moment to look in the display windows before saying, "Not what I had in mind."

She tugged on Juli's hand and led her back across the street and up a few blocks to another shop, with a broader selection of jeans, shirts, and leather. Leather would look great with Juli's new cut and coloring. Something not quite Goth, but definitely edgier.

Once inside, Adriana was a whirlwind, going from

one rack to the next to pick out a few shirts and a leather jacket. Returning to the shelves lining the walls, she grabbed a pair of jeans and held them up to Juli's hips.

Juli looked down at them and said, "But I already have jeans—"

"That look like one of our *mamis* should be wearing them, and which we are going to have a party to destroy." Satisfied that the jeans might fit, Adriana pushed them into Juli's already full hands. "Please go try them on."

Juli did as instructed and trudged down to a fitting room. She entered and Adriana walked toward the room more slowly, taking one last look through the racks before stopping before the room into which Juli had disappeared.

She waited. Clothing rustled and hangers clattered behind the door. Then nothing. She waited some more and glanced at her watch again. They were running out of time tonight for trying another store. She only hoped the clothes she'd chosen would be a good start.

The doorknob finally turned and Juli stepped out. A totally new and transformed Juli. The jeans were tight and low-rise, unlike the baggy high-waisted ones Juli usually wore. The fit accented her well-rounded hips and her legs, which were amazingly long for Juli's average height.

The shirt was the color of a full-bodied red wine. Adriana had chosen something form-fitting but not tight. That would have been too much for Juli to handle right away. She had made a good choice. The deep vee of the neckline showed off Juli's full cleavage, then tapered in at the waist before flaring back out just above the waistband of her jeans.

Juli self-consciously held her hands before that bare gap of skin. Adriana reached out and moved away her hands. "Don't worry. You look great."

Juli glanced down at herself and said, "I look fat."

"No, you don't. Now try on the leather jacket. It won't be complete without the jacket," Adriana urged, and waved Juli back into the fitting room to retrieve the garment.

Juli eased the jacket off the hanger and slipped it on. Like the shirt, it extended just to her waist. Juli tugged at the front of it, trying to get it to close, but Adriana reached out and stopped her.

"It's supposed to be that way. You don't want to cover up."

"I don't?" Again Juli pulled at the jacket front uneasily.

Adriana grabbed hold of Juli's shoulder and urged her to stand before the next fitting room door, with its full-length mirror. She gently turned Juli around to look at herself.

Silence reigned for a moment, and then the attitude Adriana had sensed earlier in the hair salon returned to her friend. Juli looked over her shoulder and with a grin said, "I guess you were right about the not-covering-up part."

Walking up behind her friend, Adriana laid a hand on her shoulder. "It's a good first step."

The stores in the upscale Bal Harbour mall were all having sales. Perfect for getting some additional items for Juli's new look. Sneaking out right after finishing the morning routine, Adriana headed to the mall, intending to surprise her friend with something totally different, something she was sure Juli wouldn't pick for herself.

The stores were crowded. She had only a short hour to try and find another outfit. She zipped through the racks of sales clothes and spotted a dress in a rack across the way that would be perfect for a night out.

Racing into the aisle, she failed to see the woman swinging around the edge of the other set of racks and headed in the same direction as she was. They collided and both dropped some of the items they'd been holding.

Adriana bent and collected her things as well as picking up some of the woman's items and returning them to her, which was when she noticed it was none other than Becca. *Riley's Becca.*

Surprise flickered on Becca's face as she realized who had handed her the items. "Hi," Becca said regally, inching her head up just a notch.

Adriana just stood there, craning her neck up to meet Becca's six-foot-something arctic blue gaze. Tall, spare of frame, and bottle blonde, Becca was about as different from her as could be.

"Hi," Adriana finally said, juggling her own items and feeling awkward. A natural way to feel, considering she was sleeping with Riley and, as far as she knew, Riley was still Becca's Riley. Only . . .

Now he's my Riley as well, she thought. Raising her head a notch and trying to put forth a friendly smile, she said, "How have you been?"

"I've been better," Becca replied, her voice tight and her manner curt.

Better to get this over with, she thought. "Look, Becca. I'm sorry if—"

Becca silenced her with a haughty wave of her hand. "No need, Adriana. I should have realized that any man who has a woman for a best friend is either gay or in love with her."

The other night sure as hell proved Riley wasn't gay,

she thought, but she was still unprepared for handling the whole Riley's-in-love-with-me thing.

"Regardless. I'm not sure what's happening—"

"That makes two of us," Becca again jumped in, but some of the tension fled Becca's body for a moment before a defeated slouch crept in. "He was never really with me, you know. Even when he was, I could always sense his heart was elsewhere."

"You think I was that elsewhere?" Adriana asked, both surprised and puzzled by the other woman's candor.

With a careless shrug, Becca said, "I'm successful at what I do because I can sense what my clients like. I should have heeded what I sensed whenever Riley looked at you. Or for that matter, when you looked at him."

Whenever Adriana had been around the two, she had tried to keep her own emotions contained, but apparently she had failed. Maybe she had been failing for years as she had tried to keep her feelings about Riley to herself, fearful of what would happen if she did give voice to them. Despite that, she felt guilt—but only a twinge of it—about what had happened between Riley and Becca. "I'm sorry things didn't work out with you two."

"Be real, Adriana. Or are you as self-sacrificing as Riley?"

"What? What are you talking about?"

"Are you willing to give him up because you think that's what's best? The way he was ready to give you up because he thought someone else might make you happier?"

Anger colored Becca's words, but there was pain as well, which made Adriana temper her next words. "I never poached while you were together. If you would have made Riley happy . . . yes, I would have stepped aside."

Becca laughed harshly and slung the clothes from one arm to the other, clearly uncomfortable with Adriana's revelation. "Then you're a better woman than me. So I guess we both know who Riley wants."

"I guess we do."

25

Tori

If she craned her neck just right, an even bigger sliver of the bay became visible from the window of her new office. Or possibly the Government Cut. Tori wasn't quite sure. Regardless, the view was nothing at all like that from her old office. On the street below, traffic traveled along Collins no matter the hour. Across the way, a grocery store catered to an assortment of people all day long.

She should know. She had found herself staring down at the street and at that market more than once during the last few days, wondering if she'd done the right thing.

Turning from the window, she examined her new space. Gil had graciously given her this office rather than the one that faced the back of the hotel on Ocean Drive.

Nothing here was similar to her old place, other than the three framed documents on the wall—her college and law school diplomas, and her certificate of admission to the Florida Bar.

She walked to her new desk and ran her hand over

its smooth surface. Modern in style, but made of rich mahogany, which gave it warmth. Her old desk had been all chrome and steel. Someone else's idea of contemporary chic, but utterly cold and uninviting.

Low mahogany file cabinets sat along the entire wall beside her desk, providing a spot where she had put pictures of her family and friends, along with a few knick-knacks, a hardy pothos plant, and a commemorative desk ornament given to her in thanks for her work in a large and highly successful litigation a few years back.

On her desk rested a picture of Gil, her appointment planner, and the phone from the new system she and her husband had purchased.

They had been doing a lot of purchasing the past few days in an effort to get their new office ready for the big party celebrating their opening. They had scheduled the party a month away and hoped that by then they would have something to celebrate—like a new client, or one who had decided to transfer work to their new firm. After all, both she and Gil had had their share of clients with whom they had worked closely. But when they had tendered their resignations that fateful Monday, they had not had a chance to do anything other than pack up their personal papers and items.

After the meeting, a partner escorted them back to their offices. The partner had supervised the file clerks who had helped them pack and make sure that none of the things leaving could be considered the property of their old law firm.

She should have expected they would react swiftly and aggressively. It was just the way they were, which made her wonder why for so many years she'd been so eager to be part of their fold.

With their cars filled with boxes from their offices, she and Gil had gone home, but hadn't bothered to unpack. It made little sense. Instead, they had walked over to the building on Collins and Sixth, looked over the lease from the Martino brothers. Finding it fair, they had signed on as their first tenant.

By midafternoon on Monday, they had unpacked the boxes from their cars. By that night, Jesse Rivera had come by and offered suggestions on how to best use the common space in the office. She had also provided the names of a few furniture people she knew whose prices were reasonable—which she and Gil discovered as they visited their showrooms on Tuesday to select furniture for the new space. By that afternoon, they had purchased new computers for themselves and for the secretaries and clerks they hoped to hire. They also selected and paid for a new phone system, and placed an order with a printer for announcements and invitations.

For the first time in their married life, they had not made love on Tuesday night. They had just been too tired after the long and grueling day.

The same had happened on Wednesday after another trying day of furniture deliveries—they had bought "gently used" furniture (as the salesperson had noted)— and setting up the computer network for their office.

The network was set up through a barter arrange- ment with a friend of Jesse's who needed someone to go over a contract he'd been asked to sign.

So, technically, they had a client—unfortunately, not one who would help restore some of the personal funds that had been severely depleted by the expenses they had incurred over the last week.

And so now it was Thursday and they faced the daunting task of creating a potential client database from both their contact lists so they could send out announce- ments of their new law firm. Invitations to the party would follow in two weeks and would hopefully serve as a second reminder that she and Gil were now open for business.

Gil.

She walked to her office door and glanced across the way to her husband's office. She caught a glimpse of him now and then as he went from his desk to the cabinets along one wall. When he popped out to place something in one of the file cabinets outside his office, he saw her and came over.

"You okay?" he asked, sensing her unease.

"A little worried."

Gil laid a hand on the side of her head and stroked her hair. "I know this is a shock. Believe me, I hadn't planned on leaving this firm so quickly after the last."

Which had made the decision even more difficult for him. Clients grew nervous when their lawyers bounced around. He had already lost some from his first move and might lose more from this one. "I know and I'm sorry."

"There's nothing you need to apologize for."

She wished she could feel the same way. In the last few days, she'd blamed herself more than once, thinking that if they had waited a little while to get married, Gil's situation wouldn't be as bad and maybe the partners might not have reacted the way they did.

When she remained silent, Gil stroked his fingers through her hair and then cupped her cheek. "You know what I think?"

At the shake of her head, he said, "You decided to break the rules and now all this has happened and you feel guilty. You feel that if maybe you had been anal and conformist, you wouldn't have been punished."

"*We* wouldn't have been punished," she clarified, and he nodded.

"It is a 'we,' *amorcito.* We're in this together and I, for one, wouldn't change a thing. It may be rough for a little while we get established—"

"*If* we get established," she jumped in again.

"This isn't the Tori I know talking. This is some other Tori."

Totally Depressed and Despondent Tori.

"Things have been so sucky lately," she said and took hold of his hand.

Nodding, Gil slipped his arm around her shoulders and drew her close. "I know. We pissed off your family. You and your friends had that big blow-up. But this will all pass."

As if some mischievous god somewhere had heard him, a knock came on the open door of their office. When they broke apart and turned toward the sound, her *mami* and her sister, Angelica, stood there. Her *mami* had a huge potted palm in her hand, while her sister pushed a stroller with her little niece.

"*Mami?* Angelica?" Tori walked over hesitantly, a little disbelieving that they were actually standing there.

"I called the office to see about having lunch and your secretary said we could find you here," Angelica said.

Gil came to stand beside her. Her mother thrust the plant at him and then launched herself at Tori. "We came to help, *mi'ja.*"

"That is, if you don't mind a little drool and can forgive that my typing skills are a little rusty," Angelica said, and wiggled her fingers as if they were on a keyboard.

From beyond her mother's embrace, Tori looked up at Gil and noted the smile on his face, his cocksure knowing smile with its irresistible grin.

She shook her head and said, "Don't get all know-it-all on me."

To save her from her mother, he said, "*Mamacita,* don't I get a hug?"

In a blur, her mother released Tori and threw herself at Gil, who embraced her and then led her mother to his office so that the two sisters might have a moment.

Tori stepped up to her sister and hugged her hard. "Thank you," she said, somehow knowing Angelica was responsible for her mother being there.

"*No problema,* sis. I've been trying for weeks to make them see reason. I'm sorry it took this long for them to come to their senses. By the way, *papi* will be by after work, although I'm not sure how he can help."

Tori stepped away from her sister, wiping at moist eyes. "Were you serious about typing?"

Her sister grimaced. "I had hoped that the office work part of my life was over, but for you—anything. After all, *mi'ja* needs a good role model."

She hugged her sister again and said, "She already has one."

26

Juliana

It took a little getting used to, Juliana thought as she strolled through the market, checking out the offerings for the day while some of the men checked her out.

Nevertheless, a good thing, she realized, walking with a new, sexy swagger in her step. To think a haircut and a few outfits could do the trick! After their short Monday-night shopping expedition, she and Adriana had gone shopping again midweek during a break. They had picked up a few more everyday items, as well as a couple of dresses and suits for special occasions.

Today Juli wore a pair of black low-rise pants and a black lace shirt to match. Nothing fancy, but heads turned. On her feet were a pair of stylish yet comfortable sandals instead of her serviceable sneakers. She had always worried that too much black coupled with her dark hair would make her look like Morticia Addams.

Dios, had she been wrong. Black made her look more slender and brought out the wonderful highlights in her hair, which, as Andre promised, was incredibly easy to handle.

Adriana had also insisted on her ditching the comfortable but totally unflattering fleece sweats in exchange for more fashionable exercise clothes. After missing the regular Monday night workout, Juli and Adriana had snuck one in this morning instead of the jog that Adriana usually did with Tori.

Adriana and Tori hadn't seen each other since the fight nearly two weeks ago.

Juli thought she'd seen Tori yesterday at lunch, although it didn't seem likely, since their friend rarely left her busy job midday. Juli had considered mentioning it to Adriana, but sensed that her friend was still hurt about Tori. Not to mention that Adriana seemed totally besotted with Riley.

Was that a good thing? Juli wondered as she finished her walk through the market, arms laden with groceries for that day's specials.

She always loved going to the markets. Loved the hubbub and activity. Normally she would go unnoticed except for an occasional wave from a friend.

But that had changed.

Now as she went by, the little brown mouse hiding in the corner had vanished. She had to admit she liked this kind of attention, since she had lacked it most of her life.

The few men with whom she had been involved—there had been something missing with them. She had known it and they had known it. It was why after a few dates and the inevitably awkward first night, the relationships had gone nowhere.

Not that she expected it would be radically different now. The outside packaging might have changed, but inside . . .

She was a force to be reckoned with. A renowned chef and an artist with passion for what she did.

Passion didn't exist for one thing alone, it occurred to her as she left the marketplace and drove back to South Beach.

Either one was passionate or one wasn't.

She knew it wouldn't happen right away, but she intended to allow her passion for cooking to extend to other areas of her life.

Like shopping. She decided that she liked shopping with Adriana. Maybe they could go again together next week, especially if Adriana's mom started working in the hotel as they had discussed.

Adriana hadn't raised the idea with her mother yet. She planned to do that at a special Sunday gathering. A gathering where Becca would not be present.

Juli had her suspicions about that. Riley had always been a stand-up guy. His suddenly being involved with both Adriana as well as Becca didn't seem like the kind of thing the Riley she knew would do.

But she had other concerns, namely the desserts she would prepare once they found someone else to help out in the kitchen. She had a few different recipes in mind. Age-old ones learned from her *mami*. In time she hoped to add a more modern flair to them as well as whip up some new items. Maybe even take a class or two to help brush up on her skills. It had been a while and she felt a little rusty around a puff pastry.

As she pulled up to the curb in front of their restaurant, Juli wondered whether Riley would be coming by tonight the way he had almost every other night. Not that she minded. It made Adriana happy. Everyone could see that.

She only hoped it would work out, because when Adriana was unhappy . . .

Watch out.

27
Adriana

Juli and she had snuck in an early-morning workout, but that didn't mean that afterward, Adriana couldn't slip back next to Riley, who was still asleep in her bed.

In her bed!

She tossed off her clothes and snuggled back under the covers after making sure her alarm was set. Riley might not need to be at work until nine, but that was late for her.

Sensing her presence beside him, he rolled over and slipped his arm around her waist. His skin was warm from sleep and as he slung one leg over hers, she could tell he was waking up quite nicely. She placed her hand on his thigh as he pinned her to the bed and ran her hand up the smooth line of his hip.

"Buenos dias," she said softly as he nuzzled the side of her face with his. The soft whisk of his morning beard tickled.

"Hmm . . . very, very good." He planted a kiss at the

side of her mouth, worked his way down to her jaw, and then ever lower, brushing one kiss at a time on her body until he found her breast and kissed the tip of it.

She cradled his head to her, loving the way he could stir her to passion.

"Touch me, Adriana," he whispered against her skin, and she encircled him, caressed him slowly.

In the past week, she'd come to know he liked that. Liked being touched and touching her. Loved building the passion with words and kisses and caresses before taking her, gently, despite his size and the power she sensed coursing beneath her hands.

That was Riley. She had always known that about him. He was her protector. Her friend. And now her lover. Formerly Becca's lover, which made her stiffen in his arms.

He sensed it immediately and stopped, shifted back up to look down at her, his head propped up on one arm. "What's wrong?"

"*Nada*," she lied and decided it was time to get up.

She was rising when he reached out and grasped her arm. She had no choice but to sit there on the edge of the bed, waiting for what he would do next. He ran his hand down the middle of her back before coming to sit behind her. "This is about Becca, isn't it?"

She laughed harshly before she said, "I guess I should have asked about her before now, only . . . I was afraid of what you might say. I was afraid that if I did ask, this might all end."

Riley muttered a curse and fell back onto the pillows, raked a hand through tousled blonde bed hair.

She looked at him, pulling up the sheet to cover her nakedness, for she felt guilty and vulnerable and knew that all he had to do was look at her in a certain way and she would forget all that and sleep with him again.

Only, Riley wasn't looking at her. He stared straight up at the ceiling, his jaw tight, a muscle jumping along the straight line of it with his tension.

"Riley?"

"I guess I should have said it before now, but I was afraid as well."

Shooting him a confused look, she asked, "Said what before now?"

He struggled with her question, then finally said, "I remember the first time I saw you. I thought, *She's a cute little kid.* You were nine. I was a very mature thirteen." He gave a self-deprecating chuckle.

"I thought you were way cute, too."

Riley smiled and blushed, but continued. "Then you were suddenly fifteen and I thought, *Don't look. You're nineteen and she's jailbait.*"

He glanced up at her, his gaze so intense her stomach did a little flip-flop inside.

"And then?" she asked, desperate to hear more.

"You were eighteen and needed a date to the senior prom . . ."

"I said no to everyone who asked me," she confessed.

He seemed startled for a moment, but then shook his head as he realized why. "Because of me?"

She nodded. "No one else was as good as you."

Riley blew out a harsh breath. "I took you to that prom and you were so hot. For a moment I thought, *Go for it,* then reason jumped in and said, *Don't touch.*"

"I wanted you to touch. And now . . . You can look all you want, Riley. And *por favor,* please touch if that's what you still want."

"After I told you about Becca . . . about asking her to marry me . . . I realized I didn't know if I could go ahead with it. Because . . . I couldn't imagine not having you in my life."

A moment of relief filled her, but she still needed more. "I will always be in your life, Riley. Just in a different way."

He finally faced her and the emotion in his gaze almost hurt. "But not in the way I wanted. I realized it that day as you pulled away from me. I knew what we had—"

"What do we have? We've known each other forever. Been friends forever. Now we've slept together, only . . . I still don't know what we are."

He surged up off the bed then, cupped the side of her face in his large, gentle hand. "I wish I knew. All I do know is—I can't imagine life without you. And now . . . all I can think about is how I feel when I make love to you. When I slip inside you."

She placed a kiss on his palm. Covering her hand with his, she said, "Is Becca out of your life? Is it over with her?"

He nodded. "I broke it off with her a few weeks ago. I didn't think it was fair, since I couldn't give her all of me."

Smiling and with a more playful tone in her voice, she said, "Thank you for telling me—although it might have been nice if you had told me before, so I wouldn't have been feeling all other-womany."

She lay down beside him, nestled into his side, her hand in the center of his chest. As he brought his arm around her back to draw her close, he said, "I'm sorry. I was just too confused, and what happened was so sudden . . ."

She slipped her hand over his mouth to silence him. "I'm confused as well. I guess we just need not to rush this. Take one step at a time."

"I guess I should go, then. Give you time to think about this." He began to slip from the bed, but she grabbed hold of his arm to keep him beside her.

"No way, Riley. You are not running from me now."

He looked down at her, an almost relieved expression on his face. "Are you sure? The honorable thing to do—"

"You're talking to someone who's spent the whole week worried she broke up your engagement."

He arched one sun-bleached brow upward. "Which means . . . ?"

"I've been holding back. Emotionally and physically," she admitted, a mix of playful and serious in her voice.

He grinned and made to rise again, but she knew he was only kidding as he said, "Well then, I'd better go because I'm not sure I can handle having all of you."

She sat up, brought her lips to his, and whispered, "Well, Riley Evans, you are just going to have to try."

Which he did. Multiple times, until the alarm clock went off, warning her that she had to get up to go to work.

She groaned as she smacked it off. Riley never took his hands or mouth off her body. She playfully shoved him away. "I have to shower, *mi amor.*"

"Good, so do I," Riley advised and followed her into the bathroom, where he proceeded to handle her again and again until she finally protested that she wasn't going to be able to walk, much less last through a day of work.

"Are you always this amorous?" she teasingly asked as she toweled herself dry after she had finally been able to shower. As she stroked the towel over her body, he swept her into his arms for one final kiss as he said, "Only with you, love. Only with you."

After, they both dressed and headed down together, Riley to downtown Miami and Adriana to the restaurant. As she stuck her head in through the open window of Riley's Viper for a last kiss, he asked, "Will I see you tonight?"

"I'll be done by eleven," she answered and felt his answering smile against her lips before he pulled away.

Riley met her gaze. "I'll come by the restaurant to walk you home."

Home. She liked the sound of it on his lips. Liked the way that he thought being with her was home. *Home is where the heart is*, the old adage said, and as she watched him drive away, she realized just how true the adage was.

Being with Riley felt like being at home. But as safe and secure as that felt right now, after as many years as it had taken for them to finally give it a try, she knew she needed more time to see if this was right.

She wanted to be sure her home truly was meant to be with Riley.

28

Sylvia

It *had been nearly two weeks* since Sylvia's lunch with Carlos. Since then, he had pulled another disappearing act, which hadn't left her feeling all too comfortable, for a variety of reasons.

For starters, Harry was on her tail every day about how the second installment of her story was progressing. She had handled it by showing him her notes from various law enforcement types about the problems with tracking down the drug dealers and bringing them to justice. She had also interviewed a prosecutor regarding the challenges he faced when trying cases against defendants who could mount legal defenses so expensive that the prosecutors and police couldn't compete.

She wouldn't even begin to consider her disappointment, on a personal level, over Carlos's absence. She'd thought they had connected during the time they had shared, but obviously not enough that he wanted to take it further. Actually, the more she thought about it, the more it occurred to her that for every overture she had made to move their relationship of sorts to the next level, he'd effectively pushed her away, both physically and emotionally—as if he didn't really want her to get any closer.

No matter how he had asked her to believe in him, to believe he was not what he seemed, maybe she had been right all along to think he was involved in drug activities. Which meant the last thing she needed was any kind of relationship with him.

She told herself that the only thing she needed from Carlos was his answers to the questions she had for him.

Only, he was MIA. And she was tired of waiting around.

Friday night was always jumping, especially when combined with the opening of a new club. She had a VIP invitation and didn't waste that opportunity.

Dressed to kill in a cream-colored Versace gown, she arrived at the club near the Delano as soon as the doors opened for the VIPs. Together with the photographer, she worked the crowd for her stories. This was one of the more prestigious opening parties she'd been to, probably because the club was partly owned by two well-known Hollywood celebrities.

There were a number of rock and cinema stars popping in and out, and since she was the It Girl, they made a point of coming by to tell her about their latest project or the businesses in which they had investments in the Beach. She took notes and made sure the photographer snapped their pictures, promising to get them a good spread in the magazine. One after another they came by until finally it was just the locals.

The one advantage of the locals was that she knew which of them was into what. Knew which ones were sure to know Carlos and so she asked, but by the end of the night, she was no closer to figuring out where he was or what he'd been up to.

Frustrated, she walked out of the club for a breather, and as she had done what now seemed like so long ago, searched the street up and down, but found no sign of him. After her break and a few last interviews, she told the photographer he could leave for the night. Being a family man, he took her up on that offer, clearly eager to get home to the missus and rug rats.

She watched him go and tried not to feel sorry for herself that she had no one waiting for her, except maybe her mama. No dad. No friends. No lover to keep her warm at night.

Shaking her head, she walked back in, intending to find a spot at the bar, have a free drink or two, and then head home—probably alone, although she had noticed one of her old male friends in the crowd. He would probably accommodate her if she desired.

Only, emotionless accommodations like that had long lost their luster. That was the reason why it had been well over a year since she'd had sex. What was the point if, at the end of the whole thing, a big empty hole still existed inside?

Carlos had filled that hole with just his kisses, damn him. And damn her for being so wrong about him, she thought, and slowly threaded through the crowd until she reached the bar.

The bartender was familiar from another club, which had closed its doors a few weeks ago. "Hey, Jimmy. Glad to see you again."

"The same," he said as he took a moment, made a cosmopolitan, and set it in front of her. He motioned to the drink. "Did I get it right, Sylvia?"

"That you did, Jimmy. Only, do you think you can keep them coming until I can't say no?" She reached into

her purse, pulled out a C-note, and slipped it into his
hand. Although the drinks were free for VIPs, she wanted
Jimmy's extra attention so she could work up a nice case
of alcohol-induced happiness.

He pointed at her. "Done."

She slammed back the cosmo and hadn't even put the
glass on the counter when Jimmy placed another in front
of her. She grabbed that one as well and was about to
slug it down when a hand roughly grabbed her arm.

Thinking that it was Carlos, she turned to blast him—
only it was his friend the Reaper. "Do you mind?" she
said calmly and tried to pull her arm away, but he only
tightened his grip and smiled.

Not a friendly smile, only Sylvia didn't care what
bothered him. She pulled at her arm again, a little more
forcefully.

He just tightened his hold even more, to the point
that she flinched from the pain of his grip. "You're hurting me, Reaper."

"Word has it you're looking for Carlos."

"I haven't seen him."

"Neither have I, and I'm looking for him as well." He
motioned to a steroid-fest man of muscle who came to
stand right behind her, his back flush with hers so she
could not escape.

Jimmy came over. "Is everything okay?"

"Just fine. Would you like a drink, Reaper?" she asked
her captor, trying not to escalate the situation.

"That's mighty nice of you," he answered, smiling
again with his platinum-toothed grin.

Hoping to calm him down so that he would release
his hold on her, she asked, "What can I do for you?"

"I see you've been spending a lot of time with Carlos.
Are you and him hooking up?"

"We went out a few times. Nothing special."

As Jimmy placed the drinks before them, Reaper finally released her.

"But you're looking for him? Seems to me that makes him special." Without waiting for her answer, Reaper said, "Just tell Carlos I'm waiting for him to ante up with the cash he promised. We can't be holding his shit forever."

Reaper snared the glass of scotch before him and belted it back. Slamming it on the surface, he left, taking Mr. Muscle with him.

Sylvia observed his passing, noting that the crowd seemed to part before him, as if sensing his menace. She could well understand it and rubbed at her arm, noticing the red imprints of his fingers on her skin.

A chill went up and down her back and she shivered.

"You okay?" Jimmy placed yet another drink before her.

"I don't think so." She gulped back the drink with shaky hands and winced as the liquor burned the back of her throat. Heat traveled down her stomach. "Whoa, Jimmy. That was a strong one."

"Figured you needed it," he said, and leaned close to her, bar towel in hand. "Are you in some kind of trouble?"

"Not me. A friend. Do you know Carlos?" Sylvia asked softly.

"Can't say that I do. You know how it is. People drift in and out."

She pressed on. "Big good-looking Cuban guy. Dark blue eyes. Shoulders out to here." She held her hands wide to emphasize the size of him.

"Look around, Sylvia. That description fits a good number of the guys in here tonight."

At his request, she did just what he said and peered around inside the new club. Sure enough, there were at least half a dozen men or more in the general vicinity who fit the big good-looking-Latin-guy moniker. But not one of them was Carlos.

With an exasperated sigh, she pushed back from the bar and slipped off the stool. "Guess I'll call it a night. But if someone happens to say he's Carlos, tell him Sylvia is looking for him."

Jimmy nodded, grabbed her glass, and wiped down the bar where she had been sitting. "Does he know how to reach you?"

Unfortunately, he seemed to know more about her than she did about him. "Definitely," she said and walked out of the club, but all the time, she kept looking for the only tall broad-shouldered Latino man she was interested in.

But he was nowhere to be found.

She only hoped she would reach him in time to relay the message from the Reaper.

29

Tori

"Just another manic Monday."

The line from that Bangles song bounced around in her head since she had heard it playing on the radio on her way to pick up files from their old law firm.

She shouldn't have been surprised that they would play dirty, barely on the edge of ethical.

She and Gil had gotten the files, all right—just their contents, tossed into the boxes they had gone to pick up that morning. Granted, the papers were basically in order, but it would take a while to separate the individual files and locate things like the firms' and clients' reference numbers, which would have aided in entering the files into their new computer system. Not to mention the cost of file folders and the time and effort to label them.

While they could do nothing about it, she and Gil had agreed to let the various clients who had transferred their work know the condition of the files or lack thereof. It was a fairly small community, and hopefully word of mouth from one company to the next would bring to light what had been done.

Those clients who had come over had done so mostly in the past week, after receipt of the announcement regarding the opening of the new firm. Confidence grew that in the next few weeks, and with the invitation to their grand opening party, a second round of clients would follow.

Surprisingly, once the Martino brothers had graciously placed another plaque on the face of the building with the firm's name on it, they'd had an eclectic and interesting number of walk-in clients. Store owners in the area and artists. A few people needing help with possible malpractice cases from a county health services office just down the block.

As she lugged in the last of the boxes from the firm and placed it on top of the desk in the empty cubicle, Tori realized that with the work they had now, she and Gil wouldn't need to worry so much about their financial situation. Little by little they would be able to dig themselves out of the hole created by the expense of setting up the firm.

But it would be a slow dig. Especially since, with the work that had just been transferred to them, they would need more than Angelica's part-time help.

"Is that the last of it?" her sister asked, gently bouncing her baby against her chest as she grew fidgety.

"Is she okay?" Tori asked, still not up on everything baby, even with her sister bringing in her niece to the office every day. It had been one of the conditions of Angelica helping out and Tori had been fine with it. They didn't have many clients coming up to the office anyway, and even when they did, they could quickly make the office client-ready. But just as that had been one of Angelica's conditions, Tori and Gil had had one of their own—that they pay Angelica for her labors.

Which had pleased everyone involved, except maybe their *mami,* who had thought Angelica should help her sister out of the goodness of her heart. That might have been fine in the first few days, when all they had done was address and mail announcements and set up the computers, but after that—when it became clear that they needed someone to do more, which Angelica was well capable of—there had been no question about payment.

Her sister, Angelica, had become their first employee.

Even better, Tori and her sister had found a new place in their relationship. After the past few years, when they had gone in such different directions, the time together had given them the opportunity to get to know each other again.

The baby grew even more fidgety, bordering on frustrated. "Do you need to do something with her?" Tori asked as she grabbed hold of the manila file folder that Angelica suddenly thrust before her face.

"I need to feed her, if that's okay. I tried to do it before you and Gil came back, only—"

"It's okay, Angie. Do you need to warm up the bottle? Although, we don't have a microwave. I guess we should get a microwave so you can heat the—"

"I'm still breast-feeding, *hermanita,*" Angie explained.

"Oh." Tori hadn't thought about it since, in the two weeks after opening the firm, she had never seen Angelica feed the baby. Angie probably waited to do it until Tori and Gil were either gone or busy, as Angie had probably tried to do today.

Tori nervously fingered the manila folder. "Well, why don't you come into my office so you can have some privacy? I'm just going to go through my messages."

Which hopefully would take longer than the time necessary to feed one hungry infant.

Without waiting for her sister's reply, Tori whirled and

strode into her office. Angie followed and, once inside, closed the door.

She sat at her desk and Angie took a seat in one of the chairs before her.

While Tori quickly flipped through the emails to prioritize them, Angie undid a few buttons on the front of her blouse and her bra, released one breast, and brought the baby to it. After, she rearranged the clothing as best she could, so Tori could barely see more than where the edge of the shirt covered her niece's little mouth as it worked at her sister's breast. But she could still see the way her niece's cheeks moved while she suckled. Enough to distract her for a moment.

"It's not bothering you, is it?" Angie asked, and shifted yet again to try to obscure what was happening.

At which point Tori decided that it was useless to avoid the whole thing. Especially since she was kind of fascinated. She tossed her messages on her desk, where another manila folder already sat, rose and walked around to sit in the chair beside Angelica.

Reaching out, Tori gently ran one finger over the baby's soft fuzzy cheek and marveled at it. "Makes you realize your priorities, doesn't it?"

To which her sister replied quite emphatically, "Oh no, *hermanita*. Don't even think it."

Surprise made Tori pull her hand away abruptly. "Oh no, *hermanita*. Not for me. Don't you think I've got enough pandemonium in my life?"

"Yes, I do. Which is the only reason I even considered working again. What with the living-with-Gil thing, followed by the eloping-with-Gil thing, all I could think about was, *Mi hermanita* is drowning, and I better be there to toss her the line."

"Really? You did it for me?"

Angelica rolled her eyes and, when the baby fussed,

picked her up and succeeded in getting a loud burp before returning her daughter to her breast to finish feeding. "*Chica,* it may not have been easy following after you—Wonder Woman that you are—with everyone always comparing the two of us. But I was always proud of what you did. Plus, it pushed me to do better."

Although Tori had sensed it was difficult for her sister, this was the first time Angelica had ever said it aloud, put it out there for them to talk about. Tori was not going to pass up the opportunity. "I didn't mean to make it hard for you. I've always been proud of you, too, even though we both wanted such different things in life."

"They weren't really so different. I think we both just wanted to be happy with what we were doing," Angelica admitted. "So, I'm happy being a mom and even, *Dios me libre* for saying this, working again."

"Well, I want you to know not only how much I appreciate it, but how satisfied I am with the job you're doing."

Angelica playfully pointed a finger in Tori's face. "Better watch that, boss, or I'll be asking for a raise soon."

Tori laughed, stroked her niece's face again, and then returned to her desk to go through the messages. "It's kind of nice to see some business already."

"Certainly is, but you better check that other folder on your desk. I think that needs your immediate attention." Once again Angelica lifted her daughter to her shoulder and burped her.

Tori moved the messages to the side and opened up the folder her sister had mentioned. Inside were the three invitations to her *amigas* for the firm's party.

She hadn't sent her friends the announcement. She hadn't heard from them in three weeks, a sure sign that they weren't ready to speak about what had happened.

Not that she hadn't wanted to talk to them. Not a day

had gone by that she hadn't been tempted to pick up the phone.

But so many harsh words had been exchanged, many of them with the ring of truth. They were the hardest to forgive, and Adriana and Sylvia weren't normally the forgive-and-forget types.

As for Juli—who knew what she was thinking? Tori assumed that Juli and Adriana had reached some kind of truce—otherwise, working around them would be horrendous. Not to mention that of all of them, Juli needed support more than the others. Sylvia and Adriana could well take care of themselves.

Tori had been lonely without the company of her friends, without the company of women in general. In a way, she'd been lucky to have contact with Jesse Rivera. The architect had a real sense of the problems she was facing and had been a good sounding board, and immensely helpful in getting the office up and running.

If she and Gil ever decided to buy or build a home . . .

Tori stopped herself right there. The *mami* pheromone pouring off her sister was making her think about a home and what would follow to fill its rooms. As Angelica had succinctly pointed out, Tori's life was already enough of a roller-coaster affair without adding yet another complication.

Angelica.

Tori's sister had been an excellent help in the office as well, and they'd had their share of girl talk during the downtime in the office, which had somehow lessened the impact of missing her friends. But not entirely.

She juggled the invitations in her hands. They were the last ones to go out. If she didn't send them out soon, her friends would never be able to make it to the event.

Unless she had them hand-delivered. That would give

her a little more time. Maybe by the following Monday . . .
maybe things would be different.

Maybe by then she would be able to deal with facing
her friends.

Slipping the invitations back into the folder, she
looked up and met Angie's inquisitive gaze. She held out
the folder to her sister and said, "Do you think you can
remind me about this next Monday?"

"Tori—"

"Next Monday, Angie. Let's just leave it at that for
now."

30

Adriana

After finishing off the last of the morning paperwork for the restaurant, Adriana grabbed her PDA from where it sat forlornly on the edge of her desk. Lately she had little time for keeping it current, and yet, she still managed to make all her appointments. Ones with the travel agents and the advertising company. A few interviews with prospective sous chefs and assistants to help Juli in the kitchen.

But the PDA beeped to let her know she could no longer avoid it.

8:35 a.m.: No voice messages. No missed calls. One text message waiting.

Scrolling through the menu to get to the message center, she wondered who had left the message. At this hour, everyone who had to reach her was close by and just had to walk over—Juli and the rest of the staff, the hotel manager, and her mother, who she would drop by later to see.

Anticipation surged through her as it occurred to her that the message might be from either Tori or Sylvia. It had been three weeks since she had heard from them. She tried to contain the little surge of excitement that maybe it had been long enough already for them to be feuding. That maybe one of them was messaging a desire to get together again.

Only, the message wasn't from either of her two friends, but from Riley. A different kind of excitement raced through her.

8:25 a.m.: Text message from Riley.Evans—Lunch after the game?

Right. Lunch.

She knew just what Riley meant by that, and it didn't involve food, although . . .

Tapping her lips with a finger, she thought about the delicious dulce de leche sauce Juli had whipped up that morning and how it might be of better use on Riley than on the ice cream Juli planned to make.

Typing away with the stylus, and with wicked thoughts running through her head, she quickly text messaged back: "I've got just the thing for you to eat."

Chortling as she imagined his reaction, she rose and slipped the PDA into its holder on her belt, intent on meeting her mother in the hotel's office.

She hadn't taken more than a step or two when the PDA beeped, announcing that she had another message.

Riley, so soon? she thought and grabbed the PDA. Sure enough, it was from him.

8:41 a.m.: Text message from Riley.Evans—I'm not sure I can wait until lunch. Are you free for breakfast?

Chuckling and considering how nice it would be to go back to her apartment and meet Riley for "breakfast," she was so distracted she almost walked into the wall by the front door of the restaurant.

"You okay, Adriana?" her lunchtime hostess asked from where she sat at a table on the veranda while inserting the sheet with the daily specials into the menus.

"Just fine," Adriana answered and continued walking out the door of the restaurant and down and around to the entrance of the hotel. She paused there for a moment, pulled the stylus from her PDA, and text messaged Riley: "Sweets are bad for breakfast. You'll have to wait until later to see if you like the way the sweets taste. On me."

But instead of putting away the PDA, which had now started beeping to remind her of her eight-forty-five meeting with the hotel manager, who stood just feet away and stared at her quizzically, Adriana stopped the alarm and waited.

A second later, her PDA beeped.

8:46 a.m.: Text message from Riley.Evans—You're an evil woman, Adriana Martinez.

She chuckled and fired back one last salvo: "But you like it. A lot. Now leave me alone so I will be free for a very long lunch."

With that, she walked over to the hotel manager and they quickly ran over the occupancy for the day and any special requests. Adriana prided herself on their hotel being one of a kind when it came to premier service for its guests.

Just one last thing to do with the manager. "How's my mother doing with the paperwork?"

The manager beamed a smile. "Carmen is amazing. She got the hang of most of it in just a few days. Even made some suggestions on where we could get better pricing for the uniforms and linens."

Adriana nodded, thanked the manager, and slipped inside the office, where her mother still labored over getting acquainted with the paperwork for the hotel. Her head of dark brown hair was bent over the papers. She sported bifocals, which made her look older, but nowhere near her sixty-four years of age.

"*Mami,*" Adriana said to alert her mother to her presence, since her mother seemed so engrossed in her work.

"*Mi'ja.* I didn't hear you come in. How are things this morning?" She rose and motioned for Adriana to sit.

"Fine, I think. How are things with you?"

Her *mami* removed her glasses and snapped them shut. She shuffled them back and forth in her hands while she spoke. "I must say I've always been proud of all you've accomplished here—"

"Really?" Adriana jumped in, because for the most part she had gotten the impression that both of her parents had been disappointed with her choices.

Her mother fidgeted nervously before answering. "*Sin duda.* Only, you must understand that your *papi* and I had been hoping you would take over the business we worked so hard to create."

Wasn't she sorry now that she had even opened the door to this discussion again? Only, maybe it was about time to finally put it to rest. Leaving it out there, festering, had done no one any good for years.

Just like letting the harsh words with your friends fester is doing you a world of good? the little voice in her head interjected, but she tamped it down. She could deal with only one issue at a time.

"I'm sorry you feel that way. I'm sorry that I've disappointed you, but Riley is there now . . ."

"Having you and Riley together is so wonderful," her

mami jumped in, with an almost beatific smile on her face.

"But I don't know if Riley and I are forever, *mami.*"

"Stunned" would have been a good word to describe the look on her mother's face. But of course, she had seen that look once before—the day she put her foot down and told her parents she wouldn't come to work for the family business.

"B-b-but, *hija*. The two of you have known each other for years. You've gone through so much together . . ."

"There will still be so much more to go through together. Work. Other things." Riley's shooting alone would have been more than enough to break many couples apart and yet they had survived somehow. And they hadn't even been a couple at the time.

"*Mi'ja*, I see the look on your face when you come back from being with Riley. It is the look of a very satisfied woman," her mother said, leaving her embarrassed into silence for a moment before she replied, "*Mami, por favor.* What Riley and I—"

"Do is what Riley and you do. Didn't I know you would say that? You're very predictable at times."

Predictable! Predictable being the equivalent of boring, which is what she had accused Tori of being oh-so-long ago, only Tori had gone and unpredictably upset the whole balance of things. Come to think about it, what she had done with Riley—and of course to Riley—was no way, no how predictable!

"*Mami*, I just like things to be in order and under control.

Her *mami* raised one perfectly waxed eyebrow and pursed her lips for a moment. But just a moment, since her mother would never be accused of keeping her thoughts to herself. "Seems to me your major complaint with me is that I tried to control too many things."

"Including me," Adriana interjected, but when her

mother shot her a commanding glare, she crossed her arms and slunk down in her chair, suddenly feeling all of five years old again.

Her mother surprised her by rising from behind the desk and coming to sit in the chair beside her. Laying a hand on her arm, her *mami* said, "If I tried to keep things in order, it's because you were so important to me. You were my miracle baby."

The tone in her *mami*'s voice was so different, so melancholy, that it pulled at her heartstrings. "Of course I'm your miracle. All *mamis* think their kids are a miracle."

"But you really were," her mother said earnestly. "I never expected to have you. After what happened in Cuba, the doctors said I couldn't have any more children."

She faced her mother, searching her features for some clue, but just one emotion appeared on her face—pain. The same pain Adriana had seen all her life every time someone mentioned Cuba. Every time there was something on the news or certain songs played. Only, her mother had never wanted to talk about what had put the pain there—a pain so strong that it still lived over forty years later.

"What happened in Cuba?" Adriana asked, prepared to have her mother turn away the question much as she had all of her life.

Her mother looked down at her hands. She still gripped the glasses in one hand and now she juggled them again, back and forth, back and forth. When she stopped, she took a deep breath and then met her gaze. "Your father and I were so young and idealistic. I was working as a secretary at a big Cuban perfumery company. There were some there who were involved in the civic resistance in Havana. We fell in with them."

Her *mami* paused, took another long breath. "We would gather information, money, and medicine. Guns sometimes. The guns would be buried at the beach in Varadero and we would go get them. Hide and clean them. Pass them along when we were instructed."

Her mother had been a rebel? Her straight-laced, anal, and totally by-the-book mother? she thought, but said nothing as her *mami* continued.

"Your father and I had been married for just a few months when we began our little adventure. There were so many things we didn't expect, including that one day I'd be caught passing some information."

There was no emotion as she said that, but her *mami*'s entire body stiffened and the color drained from her face. Adriana laid a hand over her mother's. "What happened?"

"What happened?" her mother repeated and issued a lengthy sigh. "What happened to so many others as well. I was beaten. Tortured in a variety of ways all night long."

Adriana schooled her own emotions, sensing from the fine trembling beneath her hand that her mother barely had the control she'd prided herself on all of Adriana's life.

"But they let you go."

Her mother nodded and looked away once more. "There were people with connections. Priests and others who interceded, and I was just a young foolish girl. I had learned the error of my ways."

"So they let you go?" Adriana pressed again, hoping that was where the story ended, but in her heart she knew it wasn't.

"Before they set me free, one of them decided to teach me a lesson. So he beat me some more and while I was lying there nearly unconscious, he raped me."

Cold created a lump in the middle of Adriana's chest, so large it was almost impossible to speak. "*Mami,* I'm so sorry . . ."

"No, don't pity me. It was a consequence of the decision I made, much as you will have to live with whatever decision you make about Riley."

Unwilling to fight with her *mami* because it would be like kicking a wounded animal, she said, "Why was I your miracle?"

With a sniffle, her mother said, "When I got home I was bleeding badly. It turned out I had been pregnant. Stupid little me—I hadn't even guessed it. The rape and subsequent miscarriage caused a great deal of scarring. The doctors in Cuba said they didn't think I could have another child. But then you came along, *mi'ja.*" Her mother cupped her chin and gave her a watery smile.

She smiled as well and embraced her mother. "I wish you had told me sooner, *mami.* I might have been able to understand things better."

"I didn't think, *mi'ja.* This is America and we are safe here. No one would do the same to you, and you were such a good girl. You never fell in with the wrong crowd."

Trying to lighten the mood, Adriana said, "Maybe because you did such a good job. But why do you tell me this now?"

Her mother shrugged. "Because I made a bad mistake. One that changed my life forever. Now I see you, so uncertain. I know you're on the verge of making a mistake, but in truth, I don't know whether the mistake is loving Riley or leaving him."

Adriana had resented her mother's controlling nature for so long, but even despite that, she'd been able to recognize that a great deal of her mother's advice had been wise. Unwelcome, but wise. This counsel was no different.

"I love Riley. I think I've loved him from the first

moment I laid eyes on him. But I keep on asking myself, why has it taken so long for us to get together? What if that delay is because somewhere inside we know we're not really right for each other?"

Her *mami* nodded and gripped her hand, squeezed it tightly. "No matter how much you hate it, you're a lot like me. The me who left Cuba and became afraid of taking chances."

She almost reeled from her mother's comment. "Are you telling me to—"

"Take another chance. You've started this thing with Riley, and unless you totally free your heart of all doubts, you won't ever be able to know whether or not it was meant to be."

She wanted to deny it, but a part of it hit too close to home. She realized there was another chance she had to take. One that would also change many things in her life.

"Gracias, Mami. I really appreciate your advice. I'm glad you told me about what happened."

Her mother smiled and embraced her once again. "I'm glad as well."

"So tell me what to do so Juli can have more time for her desserts."

31

Juliana

"*No way, no how. I am not* that desperate!" Juliana emphasized her statement with a bang of the sauté pan on the range.

"So let me get this straight," Adriana began, and she cringed. It was Adriana's determined tone, and in all the years of working together, Juliana had never been able to refuse that tone. But you're a new Juli, she told herself. A new and more empowered one, who can resist.

"Okay. Number one. I asked my mother for her help."

She couldn't counter that one, so while tossing some onions and sour orange juice together to put on top of boiled yuca as a mojo, she said, "*Sí.*"

"My *mami,* who we all know has tried to control my life forever. I asked that same *mami* to help *us* so we could cut costs and find a way for *you* to have time to make desserts." Adriana accented each point with an emphatic wave of one perfectly manicured hand, which made Juli glance down at her own hands as she finished the sauce. Her nails were no longer a mess, but nicely trimmed and polished.

"You're ignoring me," Adriana warned. "Don't ignore me, Juli."

Undaunted, she mixed some of the citrus and onion topping into the yuca and urged Adriana to continue. "Go on."

"So my *mami*—and again I stress my *uberanal mami*—is helping us out by doing some paperwork which will allow us to save enough money to hire a part-time assistant for you. May I stress at this point that while my *mami* and I have reached some kind of truce, it may not last, and even if it does—"

"We still need an assistant, and that will cost money," Juli jumped in, fully aware of where her partner was going. "Unless, of course, we do as you suggested, namely, ask my *mami* to help out. May I remind you that my *mami* hates what I do."

Juli motioned the sous chef over to finish the yuca by plating it and adding the main part of the dinner—the succulent citrus-marinated pork. Wiping her hands on the apron hanging from the tie around her waist—her slightly narrower waist due to three weeks of workouts with Adriana, some dieting, and the sudden desire to buy more clothes in a smaller size 10—she tossed over her shoulder at her partner, "It will *never* work."

Adriana grabbed her arm so she couldn't make a getaway or start on some other cooking project.

"If you don't give it a try, you won't find out. Think of all the benefits, Juli."

Arms akimbo, she asked, "Name one."

"Name one," Adriana repeated and for a moment, Juli thought her friend might not be able to pull it off until she said, "Your *mami* might finally realize you're not just a cook, but a chef. An artist."

The thought came unbidden, but once there, it was hard to displace.

She might just stop being disappointed in me.

What would it be like if she and her *mami* could be friends again, as they had been when she was younger? Back then it had been the two of them against the world.

"Juli? Does this mean you're considering it?" Adriana asked at her delay.

"It depends." She walked away from Adriana and stopped by the prep table as she picked up some orders to double-check that her assistants were properly preparing the meals. After a quick glance around her kitchen, where everything appeared in order, she finally met Adriana's gaze.

"What does it depend on?" her friend and partner asked.

"You telling me how that dulce de leche sauce tasted at lunch. I have to get my vicarious thrills somehow," she replied and wiggled her newly waxed brows playfully.

Adriana turned a bright shade of red, close to the auburn shade of her hair color, but chuckled, her hazel green eyes glittering with humor. "I think you've been possessed. So what's next? Some hot guy knocking on our door asking if you can come out and play?"

Grinning, she said, "You just never know. So tell me, was Riley sweet enough?"

Juliana's *mami* stood before her, looking timid and unsure of herself. Her gaze darted nervously around the kitchen, taking in all the early morning activity. Her mother usually behaved this way around strangers, and even more so around those for whom she worked.

But with her, *mami* had always been so much fun and full of life, replete with interesting *cuentos* about her life as a *niñita* in Mexico. Many of the *cuentos* revolved around how her *mami* had sat in the kitchen, watching her own *mami* cook for the family and listening to stories about their ancestors, learning for herself the many recipes, so that when she, too, had a family, she could cook for them and tell them the stories.

Passing on those *cuentos* and recipes had not only kept the family's histories and traditions alive, but birthed in her the love of cooking and the desire to spread those traditions through her art.

Only, her *mami* had never seen it that way. Since the day she had graduated from college and announced to her mother that she wasn't going to get the master's degree she needed to teach, but instead become a chef, that wonderful warm and loving relationship had deteriorated rapidly.

Her *mami* had told her that she'd cooked too many meals and washed too many dishes to see her daughter end up doing the same thing for the rest of her life.

She had hoped that her mother would eventually change her mind, but as more and more time went by, there had been less and less talk, and more and more bitterness.

Which was why it was so hard for her to believe that her mother actually stood there, waiting anxiously to work with her in the kitchen. *"Mi'ja*, I don't know what you want," *Mami* said in Spanish, since she had always been more comfortable with her that way. In a restaurant where most of the staff either was Latino or spoke Spanish, it wasn't an issue.

"I'd like some time, *Mami,*" she began. "Time to try different things, which means I need someone to help with all the other things we're doing."

"So you want me to cook?" Her *mami* said "cook" as if it were a four-letter word, which maybe it was to someone who'd had to do it all her life.

"Not really cook, *Mami*. Prepare some things. Make sure the other chefs and assistants are doing everything right. That all the dinners are ready. Keep an inventory of supplies we need. Just like you used to do when you ran the Hendersons' house."

The lines furrowed into her mother's brow from years of worry deepened. "I can't tell them what to do, *hija.*"

"*Sí*, you can, *Mami*. I'm the boss and if you agree, you'll be my chief assistant. They'll do what you say."

The lines lessened only a little. To try and ease her misgivings, she laid an arm around her mother's shoulders. "Don't worry, *Mami*. Once you see the routine, you'll know just what to do."

Her *mami* nodded, but appeared unconvinced. Juli didn't hesitate, however. She called her staff over and introduced her mother. After, she got her *mami* all set up with her own uniform and apron, and provided her with a list of things to have the staff do for the rest of the day.

Then she settled back to complete her own routine, but all the time she kept an eye on how her *mami* was doing.

At first, her *mami* was the quiet little mouse she'd taught her daughter to be, unobtrusively watching what happened, darting out occasionally to do as Juli had asked, and after, scurrying back to a corner or out-of-the-way place to do other chores while she watched. She barely said a word unless someone directed a question to her about their work.

Glancing out of the corner of her eye, Juli caught her mother's concerned countenance as she observed one of the chef's assistants working on a sauce. Clearly her *mami* was unhappy with what was going on, and Juli could understand why. The assistant, a relatively new hire to replace another young woman, who had left a week before, stirred just a bit too fast and with little regularity.

She was about to handle the problem, certain that her *mami* wouldn't, when her mother hurried from where she had been working, approached the assistant, and gently laid a hand on the young woman's arm. While she did so, she muttered a totally familiar refrain. "Slowly, *mi'ja*. Always in the same direction, otherwise you'll curdle the sauce."

She smiled as she recollected her *mami*'s patient voice as she had schooled her as a child. The patience was still there, and the young woman responded to it, agreeing with the suggestion and altering her actions.

Her *mami* smiled and picked her head up, noticed her sitting at the stool, preparing a list of delicacies to be ordered. Their gazes met across the width of the kitchen and Juli nodded her approval at her *mami*'s actions.

Maybe it was her imagination, but she detected a slight straightening of her *mami*'s slightly bowed back and a more determined thrust to her chin. While she returned to her list of the foods and contemplated preparing the dishes containing them, her *mami* fluttered about the kitchen, taking note of everything going on, even picking up a knife and helping prep some of the ingredients they would need for that night's meal.

By late afternoon and the end of the lunch rush, Juli was tired, and a quick glimpse at her *mami* revealed that she appeared to be dragging as well. "Are you hungry, Mami? Do you want to grab a bite and maybe go for a walk to get some fresh air?"

Her *mami* walked over to the prep table where Juli was just finishing up some delicate touches to the frenching on some lamb chops for that night's dinner menu. Easing onto a stool beside her, her *mami* quipped, "A walk? *Hi'ja,* maybe that's what a *jefa* like you needs, but poor li'l me has been on her feet all day."

Juli smiled. "Well, I wouldn't want the labor unions coming after me, *Mami*. How about I fix us up a little something I was going to try on tomorrow's menu. You can tell me what you think."

With her mother perched on a stool near the stove, she whipped up a variation on a Cuban steak, complete with yuca fries and a tasty mojito sauce for dipping both steak and fries. After, the two slipped to a small table at the back of the kitchen where the staff normally grabbed their meals from what had been prepared for the day.

Sitting down, Juli patiently answered all her *mami*'s questions, hoping that doing so would help her mother understand her better.

They followed that routine for the next few days, until the routine got interrupted by a visit from a local news station doing a story on the restaurant and the newly opened hotel above it.

The reporter and camera crew toured both the hotel and restaurant, but decided to film a longer portion of the feature in the kitchen.

Juli and Adriana stood side by side, but the reporter clearly intended this segment to be about Juli and the food. As the reporter questioned her about the various awards she had won as well as the occasional negative critiques, she answered as best she could.

"The key is to not let either the praise or negativity take away from your passion for what you do." After she finished, the reporter closed up the segment.

When she finished, the reporter turned to her and smiled. "That was great. Thanks for taking the time. I know how busy you are."

"My pleasure," she said. After the crew had left the kitchen with Adriana, who was taking them to the hotel, her *mami* approached.

She laid a hand on her shoulder and smiled. "How exciting, *mi'ja.*"

"*Gracias, Mami,* but I think I was a little nervous," she admitted.

"You did well, Juliana. Very well," her *mami* said with a nod and returned to the prep table where she had been working.

With each day that passed, her *mami* seemed more and more familiar with the routines and how her kitchen functioned. Maybe even understood just how much Juli did as the head chef. Even maybe appreciated that everything belonged to her in part—that she worked for herself and no one else dictated to her.

By Friday her *mami* walked into the kitchen in the morning with her shoulders straight back and her head aimed high. Held tight to her breasts was a thick black book of some kind. Tucked into that book and haphazardly sticking out at random spots were little pieces of paper. "*Buenos dias, Mami.* What have you got there?"

Her mother walked over to the prep table where she sipped her cup of coffee while she reviewed her plans for that day's meals. Her *mami* laid the thick book on the table and lovingly ran her hand over its surface. "Recipes," she said, reverence in her voice. "*Our* recipes."

Juli put down her coffee, her hands a little shaky as she did so, reached out for the book, but hesitated. "May I?"

Her mother urged her on with a wave of her hands and a "*Como no?*"

Much as her mother had done before, she ran her hands carefully over the surface. Gently, she opened the book and flipped through the pages. Two different sets of handwriting. One in an older, harder-to-read style littered with misspellings. The second in her mother's more familiar script with careful notations and precisely written words.

She didn't recollect ever seeing the book. Her mother had always been a hands-on instructor in the kitchen. When she looked up at her *mami*, it was almost as if her mother knew what she was thinking.

"Your *abuelita* passed it on to me at my *quinceañera*. I thought to do the same, only . . . I didn't want you chained to the stove the way we had been." She finished with a shrug and a slightly discomfited look.

"And now?" Juli asked as she pored over the pages of the book, her mind racing as she contemplated making some of the more traditional recipes and melding others with the *nouvelle cuisine* for which the restaurant had become known. Especially some of the desserts.

"Now? I think I better understand what you do, *hija*. Who you are. I'm sorry I didn't want to try and understand before."

The admission surprised her and made her pause in her examination of the book. Meeting her mother's gaze, Juli said, "*Gracias, Mami.* I'm sorry I couldn't explain it better. So this book is mine now?"

"It's your turn to add your recipes. For when your daughter turns fifteen."

She smiled and hugged her mother effusively. Sitting back down, she motioned to the book and said, "So which one should we try first, *Mami*?"

"The almond-flavored flan was always one of my favorites. It's been so long since I made it." Her mother sat next to her, quickly began flipping through the pages, and as she did so, Juli noticed one piece of paper toward the back of the book.

She pulled it from the blank pages and her mother pointed at it. "Oh, I meant to tell you about that. I saw it in the paper last night and thought you might be interested."

She read the announcement carefully clipped from a

newspaper. A local university, well known for its cooking program, was holding a series of classes in various disciplines. Registration was still open to the public and the classes began the following week.

"*Gracias, Mami.* I think this will be very helpful," she said and once again embraced her *mami.*

Then the two of them tucked their heads together as they had for so many years over her homework and went to work on selecting a recipe to prepare for that night's dinner menu.

32

Sylvia

She walked up Ocean Drive, heels tapping against the cement of the sidewalk, dodging the late night crowds lingering at the various clubs and restaurants. A full moon silvered the fronds of the palm trees in the park and along the drive, its light so bright it seemed to dim the neon embellishments on the buildings.

Despite her workouts, her legs ached from all the walking she had done today thanks to Carlos. She hadn't seen him in the nearly three weeks since their lunch together. For the last week she had been worrying about getting Carlos the message left to her by the Reaper.

She had checked as many places as she could think of and spent the better part of the night cruising all the "it" clubs for some sign of him. She had even gone by his slip at the marina earlier during the week, only his boat hadn't been there.

Which could mean one of two things. One, that Carlos was avoiding the Reaper, or two, that he'd gotten what he wanted from the same gentleman and was busy plying his wares in places she knew nothing about.

But regardless of which of the two, the faith that she'd had that Carlos was really a good guy had waned. Call her idealistic, but in her book, good guys didn't deal drugs.

Frustrated at what had turned out to be a total waste of a Friday night, she turned up Eleventh Street toward Collins and went home, dog tired and depressed.

She had just slipped into bed when she thought she heard a knock on her door. Sitting up, she listened carefully and heard it again.

She walked to the door of her apartment, wondering how someone had gotten past the doorman without being announced, and the knock came again. Peering through the peephole, she realized none other than Carlos himself stood on the other side of the door. "Go away," she said through the thick metal of the door.

Her phone rang and she picked it up. "Let me in before the neighbors complain."

Sylvia wanted to hang up, but suspected that would do little good. "I have no desire to see you, Carlos."

"Your messages say to the contrary, *mi amor,*" he countered quickly.

Damn. "I just wanted to let you know one of your friends is looking for you—the Reaper. Charming name and an even more charming man." She hoped that Carlos didn't fail to note the sarcasm in her voice.

"You're okay, aren't you? He didn't hurt you, did he?"

She glanced down at her arm. By now the imprint of the Reaper's fingers had disappeared. She didn't want to escalate whatever was going on between the two men. "No, he didn't hurt me," she lied, but Carlos sensed it.

"You've got until the count of three and then I am kicking down this door."

"Won't work. I was—"

"One."

"Guaranteed that the lock and mechanisms—"

"Two."

"Are the strongest on the market."

"Three."

A moment of panic rose up as she imagined him crashing through the door and the neighbors calling the police, so she flung it open to find him standing there, that irresistible grin on his face, cell phone in hand. He'd clearly had no intention of going through with his threat.

"I wish it was always that easy to break in." He sauntered through her doorway, leaving her standing there openmouthed that she had fallen for his bluff. She needed to take lessons from Tori on developing a poker face.

Closing the door, she followed him to the center of her living room, where he stood, arms akimbo, examining her apartment. His gaze traveled over the modern decor with its nearly austere lines. "Nice digs."

She stalked over until she stood before him and mimicked his stance. "What do you want?"

The grin broadened and a wicked glint entered his gaze. "No, *amor,*" he began and took a step toward her. "The question is, what do *you* want?"

He stood close enough for her to feel the heat from his body. As he exhaled, his breath brushed her forehead. "All I want, *Mr.* Carlos, is to let you know that a gentleman—and mind you that term is used in the loosest of senses—by the name of Reaper has a message for you."

"No need for you to repeat it. I know what he wants," Carlos replied curtly.

She paused, waiting for something else from him,

something like an explanation. But when nothing was forthcoming, she said, "You asked me to believe in you."

"I'm still asking the same thing."

She strode away from him angrily and plopped down onto her pale beige leather couch. "My editor was on my ass about the article. I had no choice but to give him the first installment since you apparently are what you seem."

With an almost arrogant swagger, he followed her to the couch and then sat down beside her. "Really?"

"Really. So start talking or start walking."

He chuckled at that, picked up his hand, and trailed his fingers along the skin exposed by the skinny straps of her pajamas. Each pass of his finger seared a nerve ending, but she didn't give in to his allure.

Shrugging away his touch, she reminded, "Talk or walk."

Carlos did neither. Instead, he settled back into the sumptuous cushions of her couch. "I seem just like what I am. A man trying to do what he can."

"More riddles aren't going to cut it." She gazed into his eyes as she tried to figure out what was up with him.

"What did you think I was when you first saw me?" he tossed out for her consideration.

"A drug dealer. Or someone with connections to drug dealers."

He raised one dark eyebrow as if to say, "So?"

"I don't do drug dealers or any other kind of criminal for that matter," she clarified, but he chuckled yet again and shifted on the couch until he sat nearly on top of her.

"Really? Because it seems you were very eager on a number of occasions to do me. Or was I misreading the signals?" he challenged, and caressed the line of her collarbone with his rough fingers.

She shivered from his touch, and imagined him touching her in other places—so *not* good. Her mother had gotten into trouble this way—giving in to the attraction of a Latino Bad Boy like Carlos. She readied to push him away, but he replaced his fingers with his mouth.

Electricity sizzled along her nerve endings, shocking away any thought she might have had at that moment. The voltage surged higher as he dropped his head, nuzzled the edge of her pajama top with his nose.

"I think the signal is green for go, Sylvia."

He didn't wait for her answer, shifting their bodies until she lay tucked tight beneath him, his one leg between hers, pressing upward intimately. He brought his hands to her waist, slid them beneath the hem of her shirt and upward until he cupped her.

Her moan—a needy, lust-filled moan—broke through to restore her sanity.

I am not like my mother. I will not give myself up to someone who isn't worth it.

Shoving him away roughly, she tumbled from beneath him and onto the floor. Scrabbling away quickly, she stood in the middle of the living room, hugging herself tightly. "Leave," she said forcefully.

Carlos sat up and stared at her, but not in the way she had expected. A hint of admiration flickered in his gaze, which gave her second thoughts for a moment.

"Is that what you really want?"

She wanted him to be for real. A good guy. One she could depend on. Maybe then she could give in to her other wants, but not before. Nodding, she said, "That's what I want."

He walked to the door, but hesitated when he reached it. Turning, he said to her, "The lock might be the strongest, but you didn't have your chain on. Make sure you put the chain on before you open the door to strangers."

With that he exited, leaving her to wonder if she'd just heard him right.

Put the chain on? Had those really been his parting words? Where was his grand exit? His plea that she give him another chance?

She hurried to the door, tempted beyond belief to call him back and force him to tell her why he did what he did. Not because of her story, since at this rate part two would likely never get done. But because she was still dying to find out more about him.

As she stared at the chain dangling there, it seemed to mock her. So she reached up and slipped it into the slot to safeguard the door, but it brought little closure to her emotions.

Days later, as she sat in a chaise lounge, soaking up the sun next to her mama during their regular Sunday visit, she thought about the state of her life. Again.

Carlos.

The interview.

Tori.

Adriana.

Even timid little Juli.

Sylvia's list of things to worry about had grown exponentially, she thought, and immediately Carlos jumped to the front of her mind and the top of the list once more. Some evil portion of her brain inserted Reaper right behind Carlos, bringing yet more anxiety.

"Mama, what was it like with Pablo?" she asked because she never, ever called her father anything other than Pablo, and because if Pablo was anything like she imagined him to be, he was a lot like Carlos. As she waited, she took a sip from the strawberry smoothie her mother had had waiting for her. She'd been thankful for the beverage since she was dehydrated from a night of excessive drinking.

"Like, honey? Can you define 'like' for me?" Her mother lowered her Chanel sunglasses, apparently to better gauge Sylvia's answer.

Sylvia rubbed the cool glass across her forehead to ease the pounding there. Closing her eyes against the light that was still too strong despite her own sunglasses, she answered her mother. "When you first met him, were you attracted to him?"

Chuckling, her mother wrapped her cherry red lips around the straw and took a pull of her own drink before responding. "Baby, there wasn't a woman around at the time who wasn't attracted. He was quite a looker. Still is."

Her mother's words made her shoot up from her reclining position on the chaise lounge. "You've seen him? Recently?"

"I told you he was up in Palm Beach. You might not want to see him, but—"

She held up her hand to silence her mother. "Don't say you still have a thing for him." *The way you still have a thing for Carlos despite thinking he's a criminal?*

Her mother leaned closer to her and in conspiratorial tones, said, "Honey I guess you still haven't gotten the itch, but believe me, when you do . . . it never goes away."

"Never?" Fear created a knot in her already shaky stomach since her mama's words unfortunately struck a sympathetic nerve.

Her mother emphatically shook her head. The large gold earrings she wore tangled in her loose blonde curls. "Never. Of course, now I'm smart enough to know that as good as it feels when you scratch that itch, there's hell to pay afterward."

Didn't she know it, and she hadn't even slept with her Bad Boy, she thought and took another long drag on her smoothie.

"Why, baby? Do you have something to tell me?"

"No, Mama. Nothing at all," she lied, and not too well at that, she thought. "You raised me better than to believe in any old man." She ducked her head down to avoid her mother's stare, but it was impossible to miss her mother's hoot of delight.

"Sweet Jesus, it finally happened! Who is he?"

"The totally wrong man, which is why you will never, ever get to meet him."

Again her mother chuckled, but laid a hand on her leg in a gesture meant to comfort. "Don't feel bad, honey. Unless you're going to become a nun, there's just no way to avoid it. And maybe not even then." Her mother began to prattle. "After all, look what happened in that *Thorn Birds* movie. Poor little girl . . ."

Sylvia shut it all out. She had too many real things to think about, like Carlos and Reaper and the second part of her story, which seemed to be limping along. Which her editor would definitely be pissed about. While she normally would turn to her friends for commiseration, well . . .

They were also on her list of problems.

Her mother hadn't helped at all. If anything, she added another worry—that thirty years from now she would be sitting there wondering where Carlos might be and what might have happened had she scratched that itch.

In the interim, she had to do something other than bemoan how everything had gone wrong. She had a list

of other names she had garnered from her earlier interviews. Tomorrow she would start lining those people up
and do something to finish her report. It was too just
important.

Nothing, especially a man, was going to stand in the
way of her getting what she wanted.

33

Tori

Sunday with la Familia . . .
and most of Little Havana

It *was supposed to have been* just another
Sunday dinner at her parents' house. The first
since she and Gil had eloped over two months
ago.

She had expected her family would be angry with
that development. She had expected it would take several
weeks, if not more, for them to be able to accept her
actions and get back to the regular routine of family life.
As upset as she had been with their initial reaction, she
had been prepared for it, could even understand the reasons for it. Nevertheless, it wouldn't have changed her
decision to elope with Gil.

Nor would it have changed her mind had she envisioned the debacle at her law firm.

With the same single-minded focus she had applied
to everything else in her life, marrying Gil had been the
thing she'd wanted to accomplish most.

Turning to look at him as he sat beside her, watching
the beehive of activity that had erupted in her parents'

home, she had no regrets about how she'd accomplished that goal.

Not a one—except maybe that they weren't home in bed right now rather than enduring the passage of well-wishers all day long.

She hadn't expected this little wedding celebration today. Her family's small cinder block home was packed with family, neighbors, and friends. But not *her* friends.

People milled all around the living room, where the television sat blessedly silent, a testament to the importance of this gathering. Her father had slipped on his Sunday going-to-church guayabera and looked tropically elegant in the fine white linen shirt.

Her *abuelita* had replaced her everyday pink sweater with a black beaded one Tori had given to her at Christmas. She held court at one end of the living room, surrounded by a gaggle of other black-clad neighborhood widows.

In the kitchen and dining room, the remaining party-goers helped themselves to the delicious foods her mother and sister had prepared for the celebration. The roast pork—her favorite. Appetizer-sized Cuban sandwiches and pastelitos of assorted varieties. Finger sandwiches with a deviled ham spread. Fried yuca, tostones, and ripe plantains.

To wash down all those foods and others too numerous to list, ice cold mojitos and her father's specialty—wicked whiskey sours.

She sipped on one of those now as she considered how nice this was and how unexpected.

As unexpected as how her family had come to her aid following her abrupt departure nearly three weeks ago from the law firm. They had been a godsend, but even more, it had given her the opportunity to reestablish her relationship with her sister, with whom she had drifted apart in recent years as the paths of their lives had taken different directions.

But no longer. The Rodriguez sisters were together again and truly enjoying it. Those renewed bonds of sisterhood had helped fill the void left by the absence of her friends from her life.

Her friends. Her sisters by choice and not by birth.

Every day something brought one of them to mind. She had pondered picking up the phone and calling. Finding out what was happening in their lives. Apologizing for the words that had driven them apart.

The urge had grown stronger over the last week or so, and today, with all her other *familia*—and come to think about it, most of Little Havana buzzing in and out of this celebration—she felt overwhelmed by the need to see her friends. Only . . .

She couldn't think of how to start the conversation. Funny, given that as a lawyer she was supposedly gifted with the ability to take words and shape them into whatever argument she needed to make a point.

"*Mi'ja,* you're looking too serious," her mother admonished as she came to stand beside her. Like her father and grandmother, she, too, had dressed for the occasion—a pale beige raw silk suit that perfectly accented the dark brown of her hair and her hazel eyes.

Craning her head around to search for the source of her upset, her mother set eyes on one person—her childhood nemesis and resident neighborhood ne'er-do-well—and said, "Don't tell me that good-for-nothing Julio—"

"No, *Mami.* Not at all. I'm just . . . missing *mis amigas.*"

"*Ay, mi'ja,*" her mother said in total understanding and embraced her. "I knew we should have invited them, but Angelica wasn't sure you wanted them here. You haven't invited them to the office party."

Gil, who had been busy listening to one of her neighbors, picked up on their conversation and excused himself. He faced the two women. "Who haven't you invited?"

She took hold of his hand. "My friends."

"Oh," was all he said, having heard only the barest of explanations from her about what had happened, but knowing how deeply wounded she'd been.

"There's still time, *mi'jita*. Almost two weeks until the party. If you mailed the invitations—"

"*Mami*, I appreciate the advice. Just let me think about it," she said, as if she hadn't been thinking about it since Angie had placed the folder with the invites on her desk.

Nodding, her mother backed away and headed over to take care of Tio Francisco, who reached for yet another whiskey sour, but was swaying like a palm in a strong breeze and about to tip over into Señora Lopez from the bakery around the corner.

Chuckling, she faced Gil after he gently applied pressure on her hand to draw her attention.

She looked up at him. His face was serious. Way too serious for a day supposed to be about happy celebrations. "What's wrong?"

"I don't want to be the one responsible for you losing your friends."

There was no doubting the hurt and concern in his words. Shaking her head, she said, "*You* are not the reason, Gil. Believe me."

He nodded, but his full lips were set in a grim line. "You've told me that, but I can't help thinking that if—"

She gently placed her hand on his lips. "Don't go there. What happened with *mis amigas* was bound to happen eventually. We had all been holding stuff in for way too long."

"But I was the catalyst," he mumbled from beneath her hand.

Maybe he had been, she acknowledged to herself. But the truth of it was much as she had already told him. It would have happened eventually anyway.

"You know that saying about setting something free . . ."

"The lame one about having it come back to you if it's meant to be yours?" he finished for her.

She was about to complete her thought when her *abuelita* came over with one of her friends from the senior center. She and Gil welcomed her *abuelita*'s friend and made polite conversation for a few minutes. After, they resumed their earlier conversation.

"Maybe it's not so lame. If we were truly meant to remain friends, we'll come back together. This fight we had . . ."

She hesitated and then met Gil's inquisitive gaze. "We needed to get all that out in the open. It had probably been festering for way too long and keeping us from really being honest with each other."

"Sometimes being honest can be a tough thing."

She sensed uncertainty in the tone of his voice.

"Afraid to be honest with me about something?" She wished that they were alone for the discussion.

When he met her gaze, it was almost as if it was just the two of them. The look in his gorgeous eyes. The way he brought his suit-clad body to hers and blocked out everything else going on around them.

"I've been feeling guilty for weeks about everything that's happened—your friends and family. The law firm. And yet selfishly, if I had to do it all again—"

"Please tell me that you'd do it. Because if I had to do it all again, I would."

The lines of tension around Gil's mouth evaporated with the smile he gave her. He snapped his fingers to stress his point. "In a second, *mi amor*. I wouldn't trade any of it for being without you."

She smiled, closed the few inches between them, and kissed him hungrily. It took a long while before the wild clinking of glasses shattered the moment they were sharing. That and ne'er-do-well Julio shouting, "Get a room!"

It prompted congenial laughter and as she pulled away from Gil, she affectionately wiped the remains of her deep coral lipstick from his mouth. "Ready to go home?"

He snapped his fingers again in answer.

She noticed her mother at the far end of the room, anxiously watching her. When their gazes met, her *mami* quickly avoided hers by scurrying out the door into the kitchen. "Give me a moment. I want to go thank *mami* for everything."

She tried to hurry across the room, but as she passed one person or another, they offered congratulations once again and so quite a few minutes passed before she got to the kitchen.

Her *mami* stood at the table, loading up another platter with pastries from Señora Lopez's bakery. She walked over and laid a hand on her mother's shoulder to draw her attention. "*Mami*, I just wanted to say thank you."

Her mother continued transferring the sweets from the bakery box to the plate, but not before shooting a teary look over her shoulder. "It was my pleasure, *hija*. It's good to see you so . . . happy."

She sensed something behind her *mami*'s words, something painful, and tried to ease that distress. She wrapped her arms around her mother and hugged her tightly, whispering as she did so, "I've always been happy, *Mami*, thanks to you."

Her *mami* started crying in earnest then, turned, and wrapped her arms around her. She held her in return and patted her *mami*'s head as she buried it against her chest.

"I'm so relieved, *mi'ja*. Your *papi* and I only wanted the best for you, but you seemed so *infeliz* as a child. Working so hard. Always trying to be the best."

"But that's what you wanted. You wanted me to be successful."

Her mother continued without a pause at her comment. "When Guillermo came along, I thought, She's gone crazy and it's all my fault. I should never have given her that gift certificate for that nasty store, only Angelica said it would help and—"

"*Ay, Mami. Por favor.* That gift certificate was the best thing you could have given me," she urged. At that, her *mami* popped her head up and examined her with reddened eyes.

"*De verdad?* You weren't angry?"

She shrugged. "Well, I was at first, because it seemed like all of you thought I was boring and predictable and, well, unhappy. I wasn't unhappy, but I wasn't happy either."

A puzzled look erupted on her *mami*'s face, and Tori tried to explain. "It's like I was on a treadmill and I wasn't falling off, but I wasn't gaining ground either. Even after making partner, I was just stuck running in place."

"But now you're running, right?" her *mami* asked with a remaining touch of concern on her face.

"I'm speeding along. Gil makes me happy, *Mami*. So does the new office. So does everything you've done for me in the past few weeks." She hugged her mother once again, just to make sure her *mami* understood.

"I'm so glad, *mi'ja*. I felt so guilty."

Tori chuckled and to lighten the mood said, "If you want to feel guilty about something, how about that your gift turned me into a sex maniac?"

"*Gracias a Dios,*" her mother replied.

"You're happy about that?" she questioned, slightly puzzled.

Her *mami* looped her arm through Tori's and led her back out into the other room. As she did so, she whispered, "Of course, *mi'ja.* With all that sex going on, I may just get another grandchild real soon."

Things were back to normal, Tori thought and smiled.

34

Juliana

The class wasn't hands-on, but that was fine by her. She was there more for a refresher course and some inspiration to apply to her *mami's* and *abuelita's* traditional recipes so she could make them her own.

It was a small class, with only a dozen people sitting at the long tables in the room. At the front of the room there sat a peninsula with a large work area and stove top. Above the peninsula an oversized large mirror tilted at an angle over the workspace so that the students could watch whatever went on down below. Behind the peninsula, a refrigerator, sink, and another work area completed the setup.

Juliana eased into a spot in the second row of tables and waited as the other spots gradually filled up just as they had the past two weeks of class.

When the teacher walked in a few minutes early, followed by the students who were assisting him, he placed his knives on the larger worktable behind the peninsula, and after, he surprised her by walking to stand before her. "*The* Juliana Marquez? I wasn't sure it was you after the last class."

She nodded, blushed, and tried to avoid the inquisitive looks directed her way by her classmates. Holding out her hand, she asked, "We've met before, haven't we?"

He smiled at her comment. "One of the Taste of South Beach demonstrations. We talked for a bit. Right after that article in *Gourmet* magazine. You look . . . different, but really good."

He continued holding her hand long after it was necessary, which surprised her. Although she had noticed how cute he was, up until now he hadn't seemed to notice her in any way other than as just another student.

Trying to remember the day they met, she peered up at him. She vaguely recalled meeting him, but should have had a better recollection because he was handsome in that clean-cut American Boy Next Door way. She had noticed that last class and he'd popped into her mind more than once during the week.

He had a nice square jaw and cleft chin. Intense green eyes with short-cropped dark brown hair. "I'm sorry I didn't remember meeting you right away."

He actually seemed crestfallen at that and so she quickly added, "But I'm glad we got a chance to reacquaint ourselves."

He smiled and she glanced around. They were the center of attention of the whole class.

Her blush deepened. "Professor—"

"Vince," he corrected and finally released her hand.

She motioned with her head to the other people in the room, and almost absentmindedly, he seemed to recall that he had others waiting on him. "I'm sorry, class. Tonight we'll be discussing puff pastry and its many variations . . ."

As he walked to the peninsula and the class commenced, she jotted down a few notes, observing carefully as he began the preparation of the basic dough. Not that she didn't know how to make puff pastry, but she'd been dissatisfied with the flakiness of some of her latest attempts.

Intently she watched his hands prep the dough. Roll and fold it over and over. He had strong hands with blunt-shaped fingers. He moved his fingers deftly as he worked, his actions sure and without hesitation. Over the last few classes she'd intently watched his hands as he'd worked, impressed with his adroitness.

Now, she found herself imagining those hands elsewhere, busy doing other things. Propping her head on one hand, she let herself daydream about the two of them in a scene like the one in *Ghost,* but with pastry dough instead of clay. Their hands intently worked the dough, and then each other.

It took a long moment for her to realize that class had finished. People were leaving and the professor stood before her, an amused grin on his face.

"Good thing this class isn't for credit. Am I that boring?"

"No, not at all," she stammered and quickly closed up her notepad. "I was just—"

"Thinking about pastry?" He had crossed his arms, which stretched the materials of his white chef's jacket across his broad shoulders. He still smiled and clearly he didn't believe her.

What would Sylvia do? she asked herself. Or Adriana? Or Tori? "Actually, yes. Although not quite in the way you would imagine." After she said it, she tried to give him a sexy grin.

A gleam entered his eyes and his smile broadened considerably. "I imagine that your plans for the pastry dough are much more interesting than mine."

Rising from the chair, she slipped the straps of her

purse over her shoulder and stood next to him, invading his space. "Definitely."

Picking up on her cue, he brushed back a wispy bang from her face. "Care to have coffee and compare ideas?"

"Most definitely," she confirmed and glanced past him. The rest of the class was long gone, as were his student assistants.

What to do?

Sylvia would say, "Would tonight be too soon?"

Dios mio! Had she just let that come out of her mouth?

"No, not at all. I just need a few minutes to change."

She nodded, although surprised by his quick acceptance of the invitation. "I'll be waiting for you by the front door."

With a wave, he quickly strode out of the room and she also left, but waited for him by the entrance of the school building.

When he arrived a few minutes later, he'd changed from his chef's clothes to a faded pair of jeans and a pale blue button-down shirt. He looked even more Boy Next Door in these clothes and downright delicious. The jeans fit him like a well-worn glove. She wondered if the material would be soft beneath her hands if she touched it—whether beyond that there would be hard muscle, since he looked to be in good shape.

"One car or two?"

The college where the classes were being held was a little out of the way from both South Beach and her home. Besides, at this hour, most of the places she'd choose to stop for a coffee and dessert would be closed. Which left only one choice she normally wouldn't make, but the new Juli dared to take a risk. "I live just off North Road and have a mean cheesecake in the fridge. Why don't you follow me?"

They walked down the steps together and into the parking lot, where only a few cars remained. He accompanied her to her car and then walked to his.

She drove her Jeep Cherokee to the exit of the parking lot and waited there until Vince pulled up behind her in his equally serviceable Chevy Blazer.

Hesitation settled within her for a moment, but she drove it away, telling herself she was a modern confident woman. She could handle inviting a man to her house for some coffee and dessert. Women did things like this all the time, she thought, and pulled out of the parking lot.

Vince followed at a conservative distance. As she drove, she checked the mirror every now and then to make sure he still followed, telling herself that if this night wasn't meant to be, Fate would make sure they got separated. Then they would have to do it all again next week. Only it would happen all over again and again and again, as in *Groundhog Day*.

She watched too many movies, she suddenly realized. Maybe because while her friends were usually out and about, she was home alone, devouring a *telenovela* or one of the DVDs in her vast collection.

Home loomed suddenly just a few houses up. She must have been on autopilot because she didn't remember getting there, but here she was with Vince's car still right behind her.

Fate.

She pulled into her driveway and Vince drew up right beside her. After stepping out of her car, she waited by the walkway to her front door.

Vince bounded out of his car like an overeager puppy. "Thanks for having me over," he said while he followed her up the path to her home.

She smiled and teased, "I have an ulterior motive for bringing you here."

He rubbed his hands together playfully. "This is the most interesting proposition I've had in a while."

Crooking her finger, she invited him to follow her and he did, hurrying behind her until they were in her kitchen.

"Nice," he said as he looked around the spacious and well-equipped area.

"Gracias," she replied, walked to the fridge, and removed coffee beans from the freezer.

Vince settled himself on a stool at the breakfast bar at the island in the middle of the kitchen.

She quickly put up a pot of coffee and returned to the fridge for the cheesecake she had promised him earlier. "Can you give me a minute while I heat up some sauce?"

"Let me help." He hopped off the stool and was instantly at her side, taking the cheesecake from her hands.

She looked up at him. He was tall. She liked that.

"Thanks." She motioned to the island where he had been sitting. "Cutlery is in the third drawer."

"And plates?" he asked as he followed her instructions.

She pointed to a different spot in the kitchen while she removed more of the dulce de leche sauce Adriana had loved so much from the fridge and took it to the stove to warm it. "Plates are in the cabinet above the fridge."

As she heated a bit of the sauce in a small pot, she watched him out of the corner of her eye. Vince located everything, prepared two slices, covered the cheesecake, and returned it to the fridge.

"Whoa!" he said as he opened the door. "Major sweet tooth?"

She stirred the sauce and with a smile said, "Minor sweet tooth. Major need to whip up some desserts for the restaurant."

He eyed her up and down, and grinned. "You didn't strike me as the type to overindulge in sweets."

Confused, she examined herself. The low-rise jeans she and Adriana had picked on their first shopping expedition were now a little loose on her. Exercising with Adriana during the last month had clearly had an impact, as had being a little more careful with what she ate.

"Now me, on the other hand," he began and walked over, pulled her stirring spoon from her hand. "I lo-o-ve sweets." He swiped at the spoon with a finger and stuck his finger into his mouth. "H-m-m-m, delicious."

"Really?" She was flustered by him. By the way he saw her. She hadn't really gotten used to the fact that some men found her . . . sexy.

Vince repeated the action of swiping some sauce from the spoon, only this time, he held out his finger for her to taste. She took his finger into her mouth. The sauce was sweet, but beneath, his skin was salty. Tasty.

She met his gaze as he eased his finger from her mouth and passed it over her lips.

"You're very beautiful." He stepped closer, invade-your-space closer.

Heat raced over her and she felt the blush on her face from his intense perusal. Still uncomfortable with her role as Sex Goddess, she said, "Most men haven't thought so."

He brought his lips to within an inch of hers and whispered, "Those men were fools."

With those words, he pressed his lips to hers for the briefest of kisses before pulling away and returning to the island for the plates with the cheesecake. Plates in hand, he came back to where she stood, openmouthed.

"You'd better watch the heat on that sauce. Wouldn't want it to burn."

The sauce wasn't anywhere close to burning, whereas she, on the other hand, definitely sizzled from the heat of his attraction. It was a little disconcerting to be up close and personal with someone who found her . . . desirable. More so when that desire was mutual.

She told herself it was just a physical thing as she turned to the sauce and stirred. She dipped her finger in to test its warmth and found it perfect. Just warm enough to create a different sensation on the tongue from the chill of the cheesecake.

Facing him, she spooned a little of the sauce over the pieces he had cut and he returned to the island while she grabbed the coffeepot and set it on the counter before him. "Cream?"

He nodded and she brought out the little cow-shaped creamer and placed it on the island, and then sat beside him.

Vince poured coffee for each of them, and after, they started talking about the reasons for the nearly half dozen desserts in her fridge—the only things in her fridge actually—and how she was trying to develop some new recipes for the restaurant.

"So I needed a little inspiration in the kitchen and decided to take your class," she finished by saying.

"Inspiration?" he said with a grin and looked around. "And we're in the kitchen. So how do you want me to inspire you?"

She had no doubt what Sylvia would have done, only the granite island would be too hard and cold, and then whenever she walked into her kitchen she would be able to think of nothing else but the two of them doing it on the counter.

She wasn't ready for that. "Not like that. At least not yet."

He chuckled and she looked down at their plates, which were both empty, the cheesecake obviously having pleased. She held up a finger. "Hold on a second."

Returning to the fridge, she pulled out two individual-sized flans she had whipped up and placed them on the island. After, she got fresh cutlery and plates.

A smooth caramel-colored sauce slipped from beneath the edges of the ramekins as she inverted one on each plate. With a little wiggle of the ramekin, the flan slipped free. She lifted the small baking dish to reveal the dessert as it sat on the plate.

"Inspire me. Tell me what you think."

He dug into the dessert as she also did once she'd prepped her own. The flan was smooth and creamy, with just a hint of almond. The sauce bathing it, traditionally a caramel flavor, held a trace of coffee flavor from the liqueur she had used.

As she'd asked, Vince discussed the dessert, noting many pros and only one con—the size of it.

"Size does matter, doesn't it?" She blushed as she realized the double meaning behind her words.

Vince, gentleman that she was discovering him to be, said nothing except, "So you've got another dessert, don't you? Bring it on!"

She did as he asked, taking out one dessert after another, listening to his comments, appreciative that he would take the time to share and critique her work.

As the last bite slipped past his lips and they finished their discussion, he smiled and then wiped his mouth with a napkin. "That was good, only, you're not playing fair."

Guilt welled up inside and she faced him. "You're right. It's very presumptuous of me just to sign up for your class and then have you—"

He raised his hands and waved for her to stop. "That's not the reason why."

"Then what is?" she asked, puzzled by his words.

"You've kept the best dessert from me."

He scooted his stool over until they were sitting there, knees touching. Shifting to the edge of his stool, he raised his hand to cup her cheek.

"But we're all out of—"

She didn't get to finish as he brought his lips to hers once more. Unlike before, he was in no hurry to move away. He kissed her over and over again, pausing for only a moment to say, "Now this is what I call sweet."

And this is what I call inspiration, she thought and gave herself over to his kiss.

35

Adriana

Juli, Consuelo, Adriana, and her *mami,* Carmen, sat around the prep table, partaking of an early morning cup of cafe con leche. In the two weeks since Consuelo had joined her daughter in the kitchen, it had become a ritual of sorts, giving them an opportunity to share some time together before the day got hectic. All around them, the kitchen staff had begun prepping the ingredients and tools necessary for the rest of the day.

The PDA on the prep table beeped to remind Adriana of her upcoming appointments. She scooped it up, shut off the alarm, and glanced at the screen.

7:30 a.m.: Discuss daily specials with Juli and Consuelo
8:00 a.m.: Get update on hotel issues from Mami

"*Mi'ja, por favor.* Do you have to be so anal?" her mother asked with a playful tone and a mock scowl.

"What can I say, *Mami*? You taught me well."

Juliana's mother, Consuelo, jumped in, her tone less timid and more assured than it had been when she had first joined them. *"Niñas, vamos.* We need to get to work on today's specials."

Juli glanced at her watch. "And I have to meet Vince at ten."

Vince, Adriana thought with a smile. Who would have thought that Juli would go to class and come home with the professor? She hadn't had the courage to ask if Juli was sleeping with him, only she suspected Juli wasn't. It just wasn't her speed. At least not yet.

"So, let's get going," she urged and they quickly ran through the daily specials. Her mother, a regular whiz at management after her many years of working with her husband, provided a report on the status of the hotel. This week they had a newlywed celebrity couple who had barely made it out of their room during the first few days of their stay—maybe due to the special meals Juli whipped up especially for them, meals much like the one she had dreamed up for Tori's Night to Remember.

Tori.

She hadn't found the courage to call her or Sylvia no matter how much she missed both of them. No matter how much she wanted to tell them about all the changes in her life, from her relationship with Riley to the sudden introduction of the *mamis* into their work lives—changes that in large part came as a result of the fight they'd had what now seemed like ages ago. Although the changes were surprisingly welcome, the absence of her friends was not. But she still didn't know how to deal with either Tori or Sylvia. So she forced them from her mind and concentrated on the tasks at hand.

They were about finished with all the preparations for the day when her *mami* raised her hand to stop them as they were all ready to get up. "Just one more thing, *mi'ja.*"

With a huff because she itched to go back to her desk, finish a few things, and meet Riley, Adriana said, "What is it, *Mami?*"

Her mother opened up her planner and removed two envelopes. She put one before her and the other before Juli. "These were hand delivered this morning."

She glanced at Juli, who shot her a puzzled look. Reaching out, she grasped the envelope. No return address on the face of it. She turned it over, looking for one.

Gonzalez & Rodriguez, Attorneys at Law.

Tori and Gil? In practice together? It couldn't be, she thought, and ripped open the envelope to reveal the invitation, which only confirmed what the outside of the envelope had suggested.

Tori and Gil had opened an office together.

She wondered what had happened. Tori had been so excited at becoming a partner at her old firm. Pre-Gil, it had been Tori's number one goal to become a partner. She couldn't imagine what Tori was thinking now.

First there was her birthday night. Then the living together followed by the elopement.

And now this?

It was all too much for her to imagine happening, especially with normally predictable and reliable Tori. Although, given the last few months, those adjectives were probably no longer applicable to her friend.

"Adriana? Why would she do this?" Juli said as she, too, read the invitation.

Adriana shrugged, but before she could say anything, Carmen responded. "I ran into Tori's *mami* the other morning on my way to the hotel. She told me your *amiga's* old firm took advantage of a very old rule against married people working together."

"Those *hijos de puta*," Juli said with a scowl.

"So Tori and Gil gave in and left?" Adriana asked her *mami*, who grasped her hand.

"*Mi'ja*, I would call it payback. She and Gil decided to leave and from what I hear—"

"From who?" Adriana asked.

"I ran into Angelica in *la bodega* the other day," Consuelo said. "She had her *preciosa hijita* with her—"

"What a beautiful little baby," Carmen finished.

Adriana held the invitation up in the air, waved it back and forth to bring them back from the land of storks and diapers, a land she had no intention of visiting any time soon. "What else do you know about this?"

Carmen shrugged and held her hands up. "Tough for them at first. But then a lot of their old clients decided to change firms. So they've got a lot to celebrate."

Adriana stared down at the invitation, both glad that her friend had managed to make the best of a bad situation and sad that she hadn't been there to help out. "That's good to hear. Tori deserves it."

Consuelo asked, "Juliana. You're going, *verdad*?"

Juli glanced up from the invitation to face her *mami*. "It's on a Friday, *Mami*. That's a busy night for us." Turning to face her, Juli asked, "What do you think, Adriana?"

Fridays were always busy, but with the two mamis *there . . .*

"We can think about it, Juli, can't we? But if you feel uneasy . . ."

"*No se lo que siento*," Juli admitted, still nervously fingering the invitation in her hand.

"You can't keep avoiding each other forever. Not after so many years, *chicas*," Carmen urged, and gave Adriana a reassuring squeeze.

"*De verdad*," Consuelo chimed in. "It's been too many years to allow a little *lucha*—"

"It was a *big* fight," Juli corrected and put the invitation down on the prep table.

Adriana couldn't argue with Juli. But she missed Tori and maybe as her mother had said, the time had come to stop avoiding one another. "We can at least think about it. It's over a week away, and with the *mamis* here now—"

"*Sí*, of course we can handle it. It's not like we didn't handle *mil cosas* before this," Consuelo said confidently.

Adriana smiled, liking the new conviction in Consuelo's voice, which mirrored the self-assurance her partner had gradually developed over the last few weeks.

She turned to face her partner and met her anxious gaze. "Juli?"

"We can at least think about it," Juli confirmed.

Adriana breathed a sigh of relief, and suddenly a sense of lightness developed within her. She had no doubt that come next Friday, she would be at Tori's special gathering.

36
Sylvia

The *magazine hit the streets* barely two weeks after Carlos's late night visit, and despite her last-minute request to Harry that he delay the story for another month so that she could complete her remaining interviews without her sources deciding to clam up due to the possible exposure.

By the next day, two different television stations had called, wanting interviews. The growing trade in designer drugs in Miami's hot spots apparently ranked high enough to make the evening news.

The attention delighted Harry and despite Sylvia's repeated assertions that she worried whether the increased attention would create a chilling effect on the contacts she had yet to question, Harry demanded she take the interviews.

She did the best she could to answer the television reporters' questions while protecting her sources. She hoped not to screw up the meetings she had lined up to complete her report. In particular, Carlos. If he still had business to complete with the Reaper or others, he might decide to avoid her and her questions.

By Friday night, she had hit the street again, her photographer in tow. They visited the opening of a new club just doors down from the magazine's offices on Española Way. Bright searchlights rotated in the night sky while music blared from the club's speakers onto the street to appease the crowd waiting to get in. A long line wrapped around the corner.

They walked up to the bouncer and Sylvia flashed her invite and press pass. He allowed them to enter, but they didn't linger long, just enough to snap some pictures of the club's interior, which in keeping with the Mediterranean flavor of the street had been decorated in all dark woods and lush fabrics. Pale beige stucco walls, artfully graced with hand-painted tiles bearing more modern, geometric patterns, were indirectly and discreetly lit with wall sconces. The booths along the walls would make great spots for intimate activity, she thought.

Her photographer snapped off picture after picture while she walked around and chatted up the owner.

Once outside, she let the photographer go home and resumed her investigations—a short walk to one club on Lincoln Road, followed by visits to two other locations close by on Washington and then Ocean Drive.

By midnight she'd spoken to three people who others had hinted were involved in the new pharmaceuticals making their rounds in the clubs. Two seemed to be just flunkies responsible for small supplies of the drugs and dealing them. The information she got from them wasn't all that different from what she'd gotten from her contacts in law enforcement.

The third person—a young woman she'd seen in and around the clubs—seemed interesting, but also more troubling. The woman claimed to know the Reaper and explained in detail where he got his product and to whom he sold it. She even knew about the upcoming sale to Carlos and warned Sylvia to keep her nose out of the Reaper's business.

To emphasize her point, she picked up the hem of her shirt to display a series of ugly-looking burn marks along her ribs. "He used his cigar on me," she explained as Sylvia examined the marks. "Was pissed I'd looked at another guy," she tacked on.

"You and he were involved?" she asked as she furiously wrote down notes about her appearance and attitude for the article.

"I was his bitch," the young woman answered without hesitation.

She could imagine just what that entailed, but she wanted to confirm it to make sure it was right once she wrote about it. "Which means?" she asked, and gave a go-ahead motion of her hand.

"I slept with him and whoever else he wanted me to sleep with. Until he did this and then decided I was used goods," she replied and pulled her shirt back down to hide her scars.

Being used goods also meant she might have an axe to grind, only Sylvia's radar told her this girl was on the up-and-up. "So why are you talking to me now? Aren't you afraid of—"

"What the Reaper will do to me?" the young woman asked, and then gave a careless shrug. "I've changed my ways. Got a teaching degree, and I'm headed up north for a job in a few days. Figured I could do some good by telling my story."

"You can. And I promise, no names. Only, will he know—"

"That it's me?" the young woman interrupted. "Girl, I'm not the only one he's marked like this. He's a sadistic bastard, so you better watch your own tail. You're just the kind he likes."

With that, the interview concluded, leaving Sylvia to worry about what she had gotten herself into, what might happen to Carlos if he crossed the other man.

That worry urged her to keep a low profile around the parties and clubs over the start of the weekend, as did Carlos apparently. Again she didn't see him, although one night she thought she caught a glimpse of his vintage Corvette just a few blocks from where she'd seen the Reaper. Which didn't make her comfortable at all. Reaper didn't seem like the kind of man to be kept waiting.

Sundays were normally quiet, but that day there were a series of extreme sports events going on along the Beach, and after, a number of the clubs were holding special parties in honor of the participants. South Beach was hopping for a Sunday.

Throughout the day she attended the various sporting events. By midnight, she had visited two or three of the clubs before she told her photographer to quit for the day. A couple of hours later, she decided to call it a night herself and exited onto the sidewalk in front of the club, when she ran into—literally ran into—the Reaper and a couple of his "friends." They all wore dark suits, and sunglasses even though it was dark. Their size, number, and stern-faced demeanor created a ripple of fear within her.

"Sorry." She took a step back from them so she could walk away, but Reaper didn't let her pass. He grabbed hold of her arm again and yanked her close.

"Saw you on the news. Heard you been talking to people about me. Not nice to cause problems, Sylvia."

"Didn't mean to, Reaper. Just doing my job."

He got right into her face, his platinum tooth bright in his sneer of a smile. "Think you *did,* bitch. Plus your boy Carlos is still late with his shit. He was supposed to be here an hour ago." To punctuate his point, he jerked her arm roughly and tightened his grip.

She wouldn't let on that he was hurting her. He'd probably like that. Instead she calmly glanced around, hoping one of the bouncers would notice and phone the police. No one else was out on the street. The bouncer must have headed back into the club thanks to the late night lull.

Trying to not appear afraid, she picked up her head and said, "I relayed the message, Reaper. Don't know why Carlos isn't here."

"Maybe because of your story. Or maybe he needs a little encouragement." With that, he looked over his shoulder at his two beefy friends. "Think our little bitch here will help make Carlos show?"

She thought of the scars she had seen a few days ago and told herself not to panic or overreact. To keep her mind clear and free of fear, she started counting down.

Ten, nine, eight . . .

Someone was bound to see them taking her, she thought as Reaper yanked on her arm and dragged her up the block toward a tricked-out silver Escalade sitting at the curb.

Seven, six, five . . .

Jimmy the bartender and Carlos would both know this Reaper guy had a connection to her, she told herself as Reaper and his friends stopped in front of the large SUV. Of course, that little bit of information would only help the police figure out who'd either beat her or raped her or killed her.

Four, three, two, one . . .

Where the fuck was Carlos when you needed him? she thought as panic finally settled in.

As if in answer to her query, Carlos swung around

the corner of the block, a leather knapsack slung over one shoulder. He was dressed casually tonight, in jeans, a loose white guayabera, and a black leather jacket.

When Carlos noticed them, a surprised look came to his face, but he quickly schooled his features and calmly called out, "Hey, Reaper. What's the hurry?"

Despite his words and easy tone, he increased his pace until he stood right before them. He glanced at Sylvia with a little discomfort before turning his attention to Reaper and his friends. "Sorry I'm running late, but the heat's been on for the last few days. Got something you want here." He patted the strap of the knapsack.

Reaper shot her a sidelong glance and angrily jerked his head in her direction. "Your bitch here has been causing problems."

Carlos took hold of her other arm and urged her toward him. Reaper finally released her, although with a little shove. "Why don't you and I finish business? Then *I'll* take care of this problem," Carlos said.

Reaper gazed back and forth between them and, after, at his two friends, before holding his hand out for the knapsack. Sylvia assumed it contained the money Reaper had been so hot to get.

Reaper took hold of the bag, unzipped one of the pouches, and grinned, displaying his platinum tooth, which winked with the light from one of the neon signs on the club behind them. With a sniff, he said, "Love the smell of all those dead presidents."

"You have my shit, Reaper? I've got places to be," Carlos said, uneasily looking around. But even as he said that, he tugged on Sylvia's arm and prodded her to stand behind him.

She didn't hesitate, the tension in Carlos's body communicating itself to her through the way he gripped her arm, forcefully but gently.

Reaper met Carlos's gaze and, without looking, handed the knapsack back to one of his men, while the other one popped open the door of the Escalade and extracted a small leather satchel. Reaper snapped his fingers and his cohort handed him the satchel, which he held out to Carlos.

Carlos slowly sidled over just a little, placing his body completely between Sylvia and Reaper and his friends. Taking the bag, he opened it and with a nod said, "I think our business is concluded."

"I don't think so. You promised to take care of the bitch. I'd like to watch." Reaper smiled and smacked his lips with anticipation. He motioned with one finger to the building behind them.

Both she and Carlos turned in unison. A small alley nestled between the two buildings, but not so small that Carlos couldn't "take care" of her there.

Carlos, however, shook his head. "Too many eyes. Let me—"

He didn't get to finish as the Reaper and his friends slipped back their suit jackets to reveal the Uzis sitting in holsters beneath. *"Now,* Carlos. Unless you want to talk to my little friend." He tapped the body of the Uzi to stress his intent.

Carlos nodded and when he faced her, he mouthed, "Believe in me."

Believe in him?

She had wanted to think he didn't deal drugs, but tonight had just shown her otherwise. Now he was about to take her into an alleyway and do Lord knows what to her and he wanted her to believe in him? Not that she had much choice. She would take her chances with Carlos anyday over the Reaper.

Carlos placed his hand at the small of her back and gently walked her toward the alley, Reaper and his

friends just a few feet back. As they neared the entrance
to the gap between the two buildings, she noted the
Dumpster off to one side, as did Carlos apparently.

He quickened his pace, pushing her in its direction, as
beneath his breath he murmured, "We've hit an iceberg."

From behind him came the sudden screech of car
wheels, followed by the snap and lock of weapons being
readied.

With a shove, Carlos thrust her the rest of the way so
that the Dumpster shielded her body.

She experienced anger at his manhandling as she
stumbled and fell onto her butt. Anger quickly turned to
shock as Carlos pivoted on his heel and drew a weapon
from beneath his jacket.

A second later, a barrage of bullets erupted in the
alley and beyond. The force of the gunfire sent Carlos
reeling backward and he landed heavily on the floor of
the alley. He lay there, barely feet away, immobile while
the sounds of gunfire continued to pepper the air.

With each gunshot, her body jumped, but she
couldn't crouch there in safety, cowering while Carlos lay
there way too still, blossoms of deep crimson blooming
along his white shirt and jeans while bullets continued to
fly down the alley.

Bits of brick flew off the wall by her head and nicked
her face. The metal of the Dumpster pinged and groaned
as it was struck repeatedly. Her heart pounded in her
chest with each impact.

She covered her ears, trying to lessen the sound, and
took a deep breath, reminding herself she had to stay
calm.

Calm.

Safe.

Carlos.

She risked a glance beyond the edge of the Dumpster.

Carlos lay exposed to the ongoing gunfire.

Her stomach clenched at the sight of him. Vulnerable. Wounded because he had put her safety above his.

She couldn't leave him there.

Taking a deep breath, she crawled on her knees to the edge of the garbage bin. She flinched as another round of gunfire sounded in the alley and against the metal of the Dumpster. Forcing back her fear, her hands shaking, she reached out, took hold of Carlos's arm. With a heave powered by adrenaline, she pulled his large body into the protected space created by the large garbage bin.

She kneeled beside him and examined his wounds. He had been struck several times. Leg. Chest. Abdomen. So much blood.

Too much blood. The smell filled her nostrils, metallic and sharp. Her stomach turned and her heart clenched before she controlled herself.

She cradled him in her arms, rocked him against her for a moment, keening crazily with her fear of losing him. But then reason kicked in once more. She pressed one hand against the wound right near his heart, trying to staunch the flow of blood.

Leaning close to him, her breath ragged in her throat as tears slipped down her face, she whispered, "Carlos. Talk to me, Carlos."

She wasn't sure if he'd heard her, or if it was just an involuntary response. He opened his eyes but stared straight ahead, his pupils wide and unfocused. Beneath her hand the warmth of his blood seeped too easily between her fingers no matter how much pressure she applied.

With her free hand, she cradled his head until he looked at her. "Carlos, please. Hang on."

Suddenly the touch of a hand came on her shoulder. She jumped in surprise. Looking upward, she finally realized the gunfire had stopped. A police officer kneeled beside her, and beyond him a few more stood by the sidewalk. "Miss, we'll handle this now."

She shook her head and held Carlos close. "No. He needs help."

"Ambulance has been called. If you step away, we can take care of Detective Ramirez."

Another officer kneeled beside her and before she knew what was happening, she stood on the sidewalk as other officers went to work on Carlos. The one who had spoken to her had an arm around her shoulders and gently led her toward his squad car.

On the sidewalk sprawled the motionless bodies of Reaper and his two friends. Bullet holes marred the Escalade and other nearby cars.

She crossed her arms and rubbed at the chill deep inside her. Only her one hand was sticky. She glanced at it—blood.

Carlos's blood.

"Are they dead?" she asked the police officer while looking down at the bodies once again.

"Yes, ma'am, they are."

"Good."

At that moment, the ambulance arrived, but the officer continued to walk her toward his police cruiser.

"I can't go."

"We have some questions, ma'am," he said as the EMTs raced down the alley with a gurney.

She stood her ground, poking a finger into the officer's chest to make sure he got what she said. "The only place I'm going is the hospital to make sure Carlos is okay. You get that? I'm going wherever Carlos is going."

The officer considered her carefully, his eyes narrowing as he did so. "Were you and he . . ."

"Involved? Yes, Officer"—she peered at the name on

his badge—"Smith. Carlos and I are involved, so unless you're charging me with something, take me to the hospital."

As she said that, the EMTs came rushing by with Carlos on the gurney. He was still alive, she thought, thankful for the moment. She faced Officer Smith and he nodded grimly, held his hand out in the direction of his squad car.

"I'll take you to the hospital."

She didn't sit in the surgical waiting room, but in a special area set aside for police officers' families.

Police officers' families.

Carlos was an undercover cop. Still hard to take in, but it explained why he had kept on asking for her to believe in him.

She peered down at her hands, still bloodstained in spots. At her Alberta Ferretti dress, torn and ruined beyond repair.

She didn't care, and despite the very obvious proof visible, she still found it hard to comprehend just what had happened earlier that night. Someone entered the room, and the movement made her look up.

Adriana and Riley, holding hands. *Adriana and Riley holding hands and not in a friend kind of way. Finally.*

She rose to greet them and stood before her friend, slightly awkward that this should be the first time they saw each other again after their big fight. But that unease evaporated as they were suddenly hugging each other. Fear receded just a little, thanks to her friend's presence. After they broke apart, Sylvia asked, "How did you know I was here?"

Adriana seemed uncomfortable again. Riley glanced down at her, grasped her shoulder gently, and said, "I'll be back."

He hurried out, leaving the two women alone. They hadn't spoken in weeks, although a day hadn't gone by when Sylvia hadn't wanted to call Adriana or Tori. Even Juliana on occasion.

They stood there, looking at each other but having physically withdrawn after that first almost spontaneous hug. Finally Adriana said, "I didn't know you were here. Carlos is Riley's old partner."

The old partner who'd almost gotten killed at the same time Riley had been shot, she realized, and sat down heavily in her chair. That explained the older scars on Carlos's body, scars earned when Carlos had saved Riley's life several years earlier, just as he had risked his own life tonight to save hers.

Adriana wasn't there for her. She was there for Riley.

Her friend sat beside her and laid a hand on her arm. "We would have come sooner, only it took some time for the news to get to us," Adriana explained.

"I've been going crazy just sitting here by myself, wondering if Carlos is going to live or . . ."

Sylvia couldn't finish the thought, unable to think about losing Carlos when she hadn't really had a chance to get to know him. Burying her head in her hands, she battled back thoughts of all the might-have-beens and tried to find the courage to be optimistic.

It became a little easier as Adriana wrapped an arm around her shoulder and whispered in her ear, "He's going to be all right. You've got to believe that."

She nodded and dragged a hand through her disheveled hair. "You're right. He'll be fine."

She faced her friend and, once more, they hugged. Hard. Holding on as if they didn't want to let go for fear of losing each other again. But finally they moved apart.

Adriana brushed back a stray lock of Sylvia's hair and barely grazed the side of her face with her fingers, wincing as she noted the slight bruise and cut on her face. "You're hurt."

Sylvia shook her head. "Not really. Carlos made sure I was safe."

Adriana nodded, grabbed hold of her hand, and then the two friends sat back in their chairs to wait.

"How do you know Carlos?"

Sylvia raised her eyes to the ceiling and laughed harshly. "He was a Bad Boy who caught my eye a few months ago. He seemed to know lots about what was happening in the club scene. I tried to get info from him for my investigative report. Only he isn't a Bad Boy, is he?"

"Carlos is the best. Riley always says that about him," Adriana replied, and tightened her hold on her hand. "He's going to be okay, Sylvia."

"It's my fault. If he hadn't been trying to protect me, this wouldn't have happened." Tears rolled down her cheeks as she confessed to her friend what had transpired that night, how her story had caused problems.

"You were doing what you had to," Adriana said to comfort her, but it wasn't enough to allay her guilt.

"He asked me to believe in him, but I didn't. I shouldn't have given in to Harry and gone on the news shows." Dejection filled her voice at the realization that she had failed Carlos by allowing Harry to bully her in a way that had risked him.

Adriana remained silent for a moment before brushing back Sylvia's hair so that she could see her face once again. "You've mellowed," Adriana said with a hint of wonder.

Sylvia wiped the tears from her face with her free hand. "I'm in . . . trigued by him. And you? What's up with Riley?"

Adriana shook her head and a worried look sprung

onto her face. The words came out in a rush. "He's not marrying Becca, and we're sleeping together."

A little bit of Sylvia's old self returned, and she sensed just what her friend needed at that moment. "You go, girl."

Smiling at her encouraging words, Adriana said, "I knew you would say that. Whenever I doubted myself, I asked, What would Sylvia do?—and then I did it. I don't regret it for a moment. You shouldn't regret what happened tonight."

Adriana's words had a calming effect on Sylvia. Funny, really. Tori had always been the calming one in the group. "You've changed, too," Sylvia said.

With a shrug, her friend said, "Sometimes you're so involved in things, that even though you know something's not right—"

"You don't say anything until it's too late. Like with all of us. We were afraid to trust each other enough to be truthful."

Adriana met her gaze directly. "Tomorrow's Monday, *sabes?* Once Carlos is out of surgery and we all feel comfortable that he's going to be fine, maybe we can think about getting together again."

Sylvia smiled. "I think that sounds wonderful."

37

Las Amigas

Tori sat at the table, anxious and filled with trepidation.

Adriana had been the first to call, then Sylvia, and finally Juli.

She liked to think her invitations had somehow motivated the calls, but the tension in Adriana's and Sylvia's voices belied that belief. As for Juli, there had been an assertiveness there that had set Tori back a little.

When Juliana had said, "You'll be there tonight, won't you?" it hadn't really been a question, but a command.

Not that she wouldn't have gone. It was long past the time when they all should have given up foolish pride and spoken to one another.

Evidently Adriana and Juli already had, but she had expected as much. They had to work together and keep their business going. Hard to do if you weren't speaking.

The waiter came by once more and hovered as he asked yet again if she needed anything else. But then she saw her three friends arrive at the door of the restaurant.

They stood arm in arm, Adriana and Juli bracketing Sylvia, who seemed a little drawn and unsteady.

Juli . . . Tori almost did a double take as the change in her friend registered. She looked stylish and had thinned down a bit, no longer hiding her beauty beneath over-sized clothes.

Tori stood up and raced toward her *amigas,* but came to an abrupt and awkward stop right before them.

She saw now that besides looking pale, Sylvia displayed a small bruise and cut that marred her cheekbone, as if she'd been struck. Tori cradled her friend's cheek. "Tell me his name and I'll make sure he doesn't see the light of day for a good long time."

A second later, Sylvia was in her arms, hugging her hard. "It's okay, Tori. *I'm* okay," she whispered, although her voice faltered.

Tori tightened her hold on her friend and looked beyond her to where Adriana and Juli stood watching.

Was it her imagination, or were they a little misty-eyed?

When Sylvia released her and stepped to the side, first Juli and then Adriana embraced her.

She held on to Adriana for the longest, having missed all their early morning jogs and girl talk. "I'm sorry, Adriana. I should have told you about Gil and me."

"No, I'm sorry. I was a bitch."

"And I *was* being a coward," Juli piped in.

"And I think the manager wants us all to shift this to another locale," Sylvia added, which helped to alleviate the tone of what was otherwise becoming a maudlin reunion.

"You always know just what to do." Tori grinned at her friend and looped her arm through hers.

As they walked back toward the table, Sylvia shook her head and said, "No, *amiga.* Contrary to what I used to think, reality has taught me that I sadly don't."

Once they were seated and the hovering waiter had been placated with a drink order, Sylvia recounted the story of what had occurred with Carlos over the last several weeks, culminating with last night's shooting.

"Is he going to be all right?" Tori laid a hand on her friend's.

Sylvia twined her fingers with hers and nodded. "He is. I dropped by today. He was glad to see me." That made her sigh harshly. "I get the man shot and he's glad to see me."

Her voice shook, and clearly she was on the edge.

Adriana grasped Sylvia's shoulder. "Riley thinks Carlos really cares for you."

"I think I care for him," Sylvia admitted, her voice stronger now with her conviction. "Hard for me to acknowledge, since I was possibly attracted to him for all the wrong reasons. Just like Mama and Pablo."

"But Carlos isn't like your *papi,*" Juli said.

Sylvia smiled. "No. He isn't at all like my father. I suspect he's the kind who doesn't run away from a challenge, and neither do I. I plan on being there for him."

"I'm sure it was tough for Carlos not to get more involved with you. I'm sure he held back because of his investigation," Adriana said, obviously with the benefit of information from Carlos's ex-partner Riley.

Sylvia nodded. "He's an honorable man. They're few and far between. Speaking of which, care to tell us what's up with Riley?"

"Turns out he never asked Becca to marry him. In fact, he broke it off with her because he realized he couldn't give her all of himself," Adriana explained.

The quick-with-a-pun Sylvia of old rose up immediately. "Tell us, girl. *Is* he giving you *all* of him?"

"*Sucia,*" Juli broke in, "of course he is. *Chicas,* you should see how *nuestra amiga* is all smiles and cheer in the morning, but a little bowlegged." Juli mimicked Adriana's waddle from her seat.

Adriana playfully jabbed her partner. "Keep some of my secrets, *por favor.*"

Tori grinned at the unexpected freedom of Juli's and Adriana's responses with each other. Clearly their relationship had reached a newer and better plane. A more equal one.

"So is Riley the one?" Tori asked, and was a bit surprised by Adriana's answer.

"After twenty years you'd think I know, but I don't. I keep on asking myself why has it taken so long, but . . . I enjoy being with him this way."

"And *that* way and every way, *chicas,*" Juli teased, which made Adriana blush.

"Seems to me she's not the only one all smiley and cheery," Tori said, sensing something different that way about Juli.

Juli glanced around at each of them, a broad grin on her face. "I met someone. His name is Vince."

"He's a certified hottie," Adriana added and winked at her partner.

"Tell us more," Sylvia asked, genuine interest in her tone. In the past, Tori had always gotten the sense that Sylvia had little concern for what Juliana did or, for that matter, what any of them did. No longer.

Sylvia eagerly listened to Juliana explain about her class and meeting the professor, in addition to all that had happened afterward.

Well, almost everything, Tori thought as, after one of Sylvia's questions, Juli blushed. Tori expected Sylvia to press onward, careless of Juli's feelings, but instead Sylvia said, "It's always tough when it's a new thing, isn't it, Juli?"

Juli seemed a little taken aback for a moment by

Sylvia's understanding, but then she smiled and asked, "Was it as hard for you with Carlos?"

The waiter came by, dropped off their drinks, and took the requests for their meals, which they ordered without even looking at the menus since they had all been there so often.

After, Tori sat back in her seat to watch, amazed by the changed dynamics of the group. Pleased by it. Her *amigas* chatted on and on, not only about the men in their lives but about the other unexpected differences as well. Welcome differences.

Adriana and Juli had their *mamis* working with them. Amazing. After they first opened the restaurant, her friends' relationships with their mothers had worsened considerably. Those issues thankfully seemed to be on their way to being resolved.

Part one of Sylvia's investigative report had apparently drawn a good amount of attention from various sources, including that of some editors at the bigger local newspapers. Part two involved an interview with the undercover detective about his work, but without revealing his true identity. Her editor even thought that Sylvia might be better off as something besides the After Dark and Gossip reporter.

After she finished, Sylvia looked at Tori. "Care to tell us what's up with you?"

Which left everyone suddenly looking her way. "Me? My life's been boring compared to what all of you have been up to," Tori kidded, but then filled them in on the problem with the firm, the decision to go into business together, and of course, the very large and noisy reunion with her family.

Juli grasped her hand. "That sounds wonderful, Tori. Really, really wonderful."

"It does, but you know what?"

Her *amigas* looked from one to the other, but remained silent, waiting for her to finish.

Taking a breath and hoping it wouldn't come out totally inane, Tori said, "I always thought I was successful. Partner at a top law firm. Then I met the man of my dreams and everything came crashing down. I suddenly didn't have my job, or my family, or, worst of all, my best friends . . ."

She reached out and grasped Sylvia's hand on one side and Juli's on the other. In turn, they each reached over and took hold of Adriana's hands, forming a circle of friendship. "I have Gil. I know now that whatever may come, he will always be by my side. But I can't imagine not having all of you in my life. I need you all as well."

Her words threatened to release the flood of tears that had barely been held back all night long. Luckily the waiter came by at that moment with their third round of mojitos. As he laid a drink before each of them, Tori raised her glass and repeated the words she had uttered for years at almost every Monday gathering, birthday, or other special event: "To life, love, and always being friends."

As they brought their glasses together, Tori had no doubt that no matter how difficult being totally honest with one another had been, it had set them free to explore new challenges in their lives and set old wrongs right—but even more important, to know that their friendship was strong enough to survive for always.

Tori had gotten lucky.

She had the best friends any woman could ask for.

Up Close and Personal
With the Author

What inspired you to write this book?

I realized that my friends and I were all going through similar experiences, not just in our friendships, but in our relationships with other women. As we married, had kids, invested time in our careers, etc., our relationships with everyone around us changed. Sometimes the friendships disappeared, which was sad. I wanted to write about these universal issues and how a group of long-time friends dealt with the life changes that so many women experience. I also wanted the women in the book—Adriana, Juliana, Sylvia, and Tori—to reflect the kinds of women that I had connected with in my life—strong, driven women who were being pulled apart by the demands of family and career, and by their friends as well. And, of course, I wanted to send the message that it was possible to survive these kinds of changes and emerge stronger afterward.

Were any of the women in the book patterned after real life friends?

Not really, although I did name some of the characters after friends and family. However, with respect to the relationships of the four women with their mothers, I did use some of my own personal experiences to delve into certain issues: controlling mothers, mothers who want you to be successful, the fear of disappointing your mother, etc. While I dealt with some of these issues myself as I was growing up, I can say that overall I was blessed with a wonderful mom who was always supportive and inspired me. She was my mother, my mentor and, most importantly, my best friend. I hope that my own daughter feels the same way about me.

Which character do you identify with the most? Why?

I am most definitely Tori. From the moment I came out of the womb, it was instilled in me that I had to be the responsible one—the one everyone could count on—and I am just that. Inside of me, however, there is definitely a risk taker who likes to push the envelope. A lot of times, I do that through my writing.

You were born in Havana, Cuba, and now live in New York, and your novel takes place in Florida. Why did you decide to set your novel in Miami's South Beach?

I left Cuba when I was very young and have not had a chance to go back. My parents chose to live on Long Island to avoid the ongoing issues with politics in Cuba. My mother was a very political creature and it would have been difficult for her to stay uninvolved. Because her politics had caused problems for the family before, she chose to move us as far away from it as she could. But we did visit Miami regularly as children. Many years later, I fell in love with South Beach when my husband and I visited. I go to Miami instead of the Cuba I can't visit. It's where I get my fill of all things Cuban and because of that, I've set many novels in Miami and will hopefully do many, many more there.

This book is so different from your other books. Why the change?

I have written several contemporary romances and have an ongoing vampire series, but I always wanted to write a bigger book that would let me explore issues that women face in life. In fact, all my books, even the vampire ones, have dealt with "issues," since I think it's important to get across a message while entertaining people. With *Sex and the South Beach Chicas*, I decided to try and get that message across in a very sexy and humorous way, and I hope you will think that I succeeded.

So, what's next in your varied writing career?

I am very pleased to say that I am busy finishing up a story that revolves around Sylvia and Carlos. I loved these characters as well as Virginia, Sylvia's mom. I wanted to do a story just about them in order to more fully explore the baggage that Sylvia has been carrying around by virtue of her dysfunctional family life. Plus, I wanted to play with the concept of what would happen if you realized that your fortysomething mother was getting sexually involved again and with none other than the father you have never wanted to acknowledge! In addition, I will be writing two novellas for Pocket Books, and the fourth book in my vampire series will be part of the launch for Silhouette's new paranormal line, Nocturne.

Whether you're a Good Girl or a Naughty Girl, Downtown Press has the books you love!

Look for these Good Girls...

The Ex-Wife's Survival Guide
DEBBY HOLT
Essential items: 1. Alcohol.
2. A sense of humor.
3. A sexy new love interest.

Suburbanistas
PAMELA REDMOND SATRAN
From A-list to Volvo in sixty
seconds flat.

Un-Bridaled
EILEEN RENDAHL
She turned the walk down the
aisle into the hundred-meter
dash...in the other direction.

The Starter Wife
GIGI LEVANGIE GRAZER
She's done the
starter home and
starter job...but she
never thought she'd be a
starter wife.

The New York Times bestseller!

I Did (But I Wouldn't Now)
CARA LOCKWOOD
Hindsight is a girl's best friend.

Everyone Worth Knowing
LAUREN WEISBERGER
The devil wore Prada—
but the bouncer wears
Dolce.

The New York Times bestseller!

And don't miss these Naughty Girls...

The Manolo Matrix
JULIE KENNER
If you thought finding the perfect
pair of shoes was hard—try staying
alive in them.

Enslave Me Sweetly
An Alien Huntress Novel
GENA SHOWALTER
She has the body of a killer...
and the heart of a killer.

Great storytelling just got a new address.

DOWNTOWN PRESS
A Division of Simon & Schuster
A CBS COMPANY

Naughty Girls

Available wherever books are sold
or at www.downtownpress.com.

14185-1

There's nothing better than the perfect bag...

Unless it's the perfect book.

Good girls go to heaven...

Naughty Girls go Downtown.